Neil Flambé

and the
AZTEC ABDUCTION

Also by Kevin Sylvester

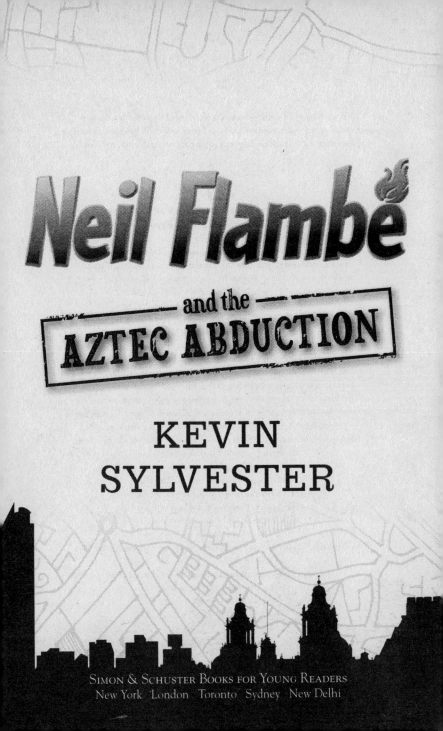

Neil Flambé

and the
AZTEC ABDUCTION

KEVIN
SYLVESTER

SIMON & SCHUSTER BOOKS FOR YOUNG READERS
New York London Toronto Sydney New Delhi

SIMON & SCHUSTER BOOKS FOR YOUNG READERS
An imprint of Simon & Schuster Children's Publishing Division
1230 Avenue of the Americas, New York, New York 10020
This book is a work of fiction. Any references to historical events, real people, or real places are used fictitiously. Other names, characters, places, and events are products of the author's imagination, and any resemblance to actual events or places or persons, living or dead, is entirely coincidental.
Text and illustrations copyright © 2010 by Kevin Sylvester
Originally published in Canada in 2010 by Key Porter Books Limited
First U.S. edition January 2012

For information about special discounts for bulk purchases, please contact Simon & Schuster Special Sales at 1-866-506-1949 or business@simonandschuster.com.
The Simon & Schuster Speakers Bureau can bring authors to your live event. For more information or to book an event, contact the Simon & Schuster Speakers Bureau at 1-866-248-3049 or visit our website at www.simonspeakers.com.
Also available in a Simon & Schuster Books for Young Readers hardcover edition
Cover illustrations © 2014 by Kevin Sylvester
Cover design by Laurent Linn
Interior design by Laurent Linn and Tom Daly
The text for this book is set in Goudy Old Style.
The illustrations for this book are rendered in pen and ink.
Manufactured in the United States of America
0914 OFF
First Simon & Schuster Books for Young Readers paperback edition October 2014
2 4 6 8 10 9 7 5 3 1
CIP data for this book is available from the Library of Congress.
ISBN 978-1-4424-4607-6 (hardcover)
ISBN 978-1-4424-4608-3 (pbk)
ISBN 978-1-4424-4609-0 (eBook)

For Lolo, Schmoo, and Tink

Neil Flambé

— and the —
AZTEC ABDUCTION

CHAPTER FOUR

HIGH ALTITUDE AND HAUTE CUISINE

Neil Flambé looked down at his spotless, gleaming workstation. It was perfect. Of course it was—he'd prepped it himself.

Neil's cooking knives spread out from the right side of his giant maple chopping block in an obsessively neat row. There were ten knives in all, each with a specific task: paring, fish deboning, delicate slicing, chopping through huge joints of meat. All had been handcrafted and weighted for his hands, and his hands alone.

In just a few moments he was going to be reaching for them, unconsciously and quickly—and he did not

1

want to be "feeling around" for the right razor-sharp blade. That's how former three-star chef Reiner Saumagen had earned the nickname "Stubby." Stubby was currently working as a busboy at a burger-and-chicken-wing joint in Buffalo. Neil shuddered. He would be more careful.

With the knives securely in place, Neil had time for one last check of the rest of his station. He looked to his left. The stove and oven, all gleaming stainless steel and seething blue flame, were sparkling clean, within an arm's reach and preheated to 350 degrees.

He looked back at the countertop. His seasonings— salt, pepper, and containers filled with fresh herbs and savory of every size and color—sat at attention along the top edge of the cutting board. He felt like a magician with the ingredients for a magic potion. In a way he was. At fourteen (almost fifteen), Neil was one of the greatest chefs in the world. His food was often described as magical—and not just by Neil.

Neil allowed himself a self-satisfied smile. Soon he would be well on his way to winning the biggest cooking competition of his life. This wasn't some seedy one-off contest like the underground duels he had won in the past. This was the *Azteca Cocina*, a culinary cook-off featuring North America's top chefs.

He had absolutely no idea what he was going to be asked to cook.

He would only have one hour to cook it.

He was thrilled.

The *Azteca Cocina* was being held in the thin air and amidst the gorgeous architecture of Mexico City. A chef-to-chef battle would take place every other day for nearly two weeks, with every moment shown on TV. The winners of each battle would advance until only two remained, ready to face each other in a final thrilling cook-off on the Zócalo—the stone plaza that sat at the historic center of the city. Rumor had it that the square would be jam-packed with more than one hundred thousand hungry, food-crazed fans. The winner would be the chef supremo of North American cooking, and would also claim the $250,000 top prize.

But first things first. Today was Round One and Neil's opponent was Pablo Pimento. Neil smirked as he looked over and spied Pablo nervously wiping beads of sweat off his forehead. "Even Stubby Saumagen could beat this hack," Neil thought, "with his one good hand tied behind his back."

Neil didn't waste any more time sizing up the so-called competition. Instead, he took a few seconds to examine the scene of the battle. He and Pablo were facing off in the atrium of the wonderfully ornate national opera house, the Palacio des Bellas Artes. Two kitchens had been set up in a semicircle on a stage in the middle of the marble atrium. Neil's kitchen was on one arc and Pablo's on the other. Bleachers filled the remaining space and the crowd was heady with anticipation. Neil smiled as he saw spectators taking their seats, pointing at him and whispering hushed comments.

He was used to being on display, used to attention,

but he knew he was still just a curiosity. Winning this competition was going to change that. He would be taken seriously not just as a boy chef, but as a *great* chef. And that would bring more customers—higher-paying customers—to Chez Flambé.

Even now, back in Vancouver, Chez Flambé was undergoing a transformation. Two weeks was a long time to close a restaurant, so Neil had decided to kill two birds with one stone (his personal preference? Free-range quail with a good pizza-oven brick). Chez Flambé was closed for renovations, expensive renovations. Amber and Zoë Soba, the twins who waitressed at the restaurant, were busy decorating and painting the dining room, and a brand-new fridge was scheduled for delivery any minute.

"Don't count your chickens before they're hatched," his mother had told him when he'd revealed his renovation plans and asked her to cosign for a temporary loan.

"I always count my chickens before they're hatched," Neil had told her. "They're called eggs. In fact, there are three unhatched chickens in each and every one of my world-famous omelettes."

Neil knew he'd be able to pay back the loan when (not if) he won the *Cocina*. "If" was not a word Neil used, or even thought, when it came to his cooking (unless "if" was included in sentences such as "Larry, if you don't dice those onions into smaller bits I'm going to dice you into smaller bits.").

Larry was Neil's older cousin and assistant—his sous-chef. Larry could cook pretty well, and he could follow orders—Neil loved to give orders—but Larry was also a bit of a flake.

Neil glanced over at his cousin, standing a few feet away at the far end of the steel counter. Larry met his gaze and smiled, the grin rustling the whiskers on his face. It was hard to tell, because Larry's perpetually disheveled hair was covering his eyes, but Neil thought he also gave him a wink.

"Larry, if you don't tuck that hair under your hat I'm going to personally give you a buzz cut"—Neil paused for effect—"with a rusty lemon zester!" Hair was not an ingredient Neil planned on including in any dish coming from his kitchen . . . especially not Larry's hair.

Larry didn't stop smiling for a second. He'd been working with Neil for a couple of years now and was used to the bluster. He carefully pulled a hair net out of his pocket, tucked his hair into it, and then slopped the whole mess up into his black sous-chef cap.

"Ready, spiffy and able to aid you, señor chef," he said with a salute. Neil looked Larry up and down. He worked hard to make Larry at least appear at home in the kitchen. Now that his hair was tucked up and away, he looked clean and ready. Except, Neil thought with a double take, for one thing.

"What is that?" Neil said irritably, pointing at Larry's stomach.

Larry looked down at the front of his chef's jacket. "What? I don't see any more stains."

"Look lower," Neil said. "What's that red thing tied around your waist?"

"You're right," Larry smiled. "It's a sash, not a belt! I have it on wrong. Hey, thanks for pointing that out, Neil."

As Neil stared incredulously, Larry untied the red fabric and lifted it up and over his head. One side came to rest on his left shoulder and the rest draped down across his torso. Now Neil could see that the sash had the words "Viva Zapata" stitched down the front, with a picture of the legendary Mexican revolutionary printed alongside.

"Viva Zapata?" Neil said.

"I looked for one that said 'Viva Frittata,' but they didn't have any."

"Ha ha," Neil said dryly. Larry had bought the sash at a tacky tourist stall the day before. Neil assumed it was a present for some girl back in Vancouver. Apparently, he had been wrong. "Why are you wearing that in my kitchen?"

"It's for good luck," Larry said, running his fingers down the soft red material. "Zapata was a big part of the revolution here—and don't you and I want to revolutionize the restaurant industry? Plus, I like his big mustache. I'm considering growing one just like it."

"Didn't Zapata die in an ambush?" Neil wasn't sure how he knew this, but Larry quickly reminded him.

"Hey! You've been paying attention to my guided tour!" Larry said happily.

"Sadly, yes. It's hard to avoid," Neil said, rubbing his temples. Larry had what Neil politely called an obsessive personality. He would throw himself into a subject with every fiber of his being—surfing the Net, reading every book he could—and then do his best to keep Neil in the loop, whether he wanted to be in that loop or not. Their trip to Mexico City had filled Larry with an incredible curiosity for all things Mexican, and he had given Neil a nonstop history lesson as they walked through the streets and markets.

They'd been in the city for two days. To Neil, it felt like a month.

"And besides, we're on high-def TV, and I look so good in a sash." Larry smiled.

"Do you have to wear it?" Neil asked, sensing he was not going to win this latest argument.

"Viva Zapata! Viva Team Flambé!" was Larry's response.

Neil was about to continue the argument when he heard the squeaking of wheels. The *Cocina* crew, dressed in white, was wheeling in huge carved wooden boxes. Inside were the ingredients for the opening

match, including the all-important secret ingredient upon which the entire meal would be based. Neil would have to live with the sash, for today.

"We'll discuss this later," Neil hissed.

"Aye, aye, *commandante!*" Larry saluted again.

There was one last thing Neil needed to do before he gave his full attention to his cooking. He looked at the crowd, scanning for one particular person. Their eyes locked. He smiled. She smiled. She was Isabella Tortellini, Neil's friend (quite possibly his maybe, sort of, he wasn't one hundred percent sure, girlfriend) and a world-famous perfume maker. Neil could faintly make out the smell of her latest lavender-scented concoction. She had taken a break from her own business—researching scents for a new line of Aztec-inspired perfumes—to show Neil some support. He appreciated the gesture, especially since it wasn't easy for her to be here. Her father had died in a head-to-head cooking duel with Neil's mentor Angel Jícama, but that had been an underground battle, not an organized and legal spectacle like the *Azteca Cocina.*

"*Buona fortuna,*" she yelled to Neil. Then, with a flash, the TV lights switched on, the house lights went off, and the kitchen set was bathed in bright light, leaving everything else in darkness. Neil was temporarily blinded.

A tall man in a shiny blue tuxedo stepped into a spotlight at the front of the makeshift kitchens and turned on his microphone. He was Rodrigo Hernandez, owner of the Cortez Corn Oil Company, the tournament's sponsor.

"Señors and señoras," Rodrigo spoke. "I want to thank you all for coming to this first battle of *Azteca Cocina.*"

Applause filled the room, but Neil paid no attention. He was concentrating on something else—the fresh bouquet of uncooked food.

"But what kind of battle WILL IT BE?" Rodrigo asked with a theatrical flourish. He gestured to the carved boxes, which were suddenly bathed in light.

Neil sniffed and waited for his secret weapon to kick in. Neil Flambé was blessed with a love for cooking, but also with an incredibly keen sense of smell. He used it to discern perfect blends of spices and ingredients, the exact mixture to make any dish perfect. Unbeknownst to any but his closest friends and family, he sometimes used his nose to help the Vancouver Police Force solve crimes. Now he was going to use it to get a head start on planning his menu. That head start, he thought, would be the difference between winning and winning easily. Neil caught a glimpse of Pablo in the lights of the cameras. He was still sweating.

"In just a moment, we will present these two great chefs with their secret ingredient! Will it be chicken thighs? Pinto beans? Rice?" Rodrigo was warming into his role, teasing the crowd and building suspense.

Neil smiled. He had caught the scent and the secret

ingredient wasn't chicken or pinto beans. Imperceptibly, he pushed his largest knife closer to the cutting board. The secret ingredient was lamb shanks.

"Psst, Larry," Neil whispered, covering his mouth with the back of his hand. He signaled for Larry to lean in closer. "We're going to make Oaxacan Mole sauce and lamb shanks."

"Whack-a-mole sauce?" Larry said. "On pancakes? I dunno. Sounds gross to me."

Neil tried to articulate the menu again, slowly, while still whispering, "I said 'whoa-hock-an mole-eh' sauce."

"Mohican bowling socks?"

"Never mind," Neil sighed, rubbing his temples so hard that he left an indentation. He gave up trying to whisper and turned to face Larry. "Look, as soon as we get the signal, just heat some oil and grate some chocolate as quickly as you can."

"You got it, Neil," Larry said. "You can count on me." He walked back to his place at the counter, still wondering what bowling Mohicans had to do with grated chocolate and cooking oil.

"The contestants do not know what ingredients are in these boxes." Rodrigo was now speaking dramatically in a low voice. The audience leaned in to catch his words. He practically scared them out of their seats when he yelled, "But now it is time to reveal all!"

The waiters pulled ornate metal keys out of their coat pockets and inserted them into the golden locks that held the lids on tight.

Neil was already running through the steps of the meal preparation in his head. The chocolate-and-chili-based mole sauce was pretty simple. But lamb shanks were packed with tough chewy meat, with a huge bone in the middle. Ideally, a chef would be able to stew the shank for more than three hours to get the meat really tender. Neil would have to speed up that process considerably. He pondered for a second before deciding on his plan. He would quick-fry the shanks to sear the flavor inside. Next, he would cut off the meat to make big stewing chunks. Then he'd throw it in the oven and leave it there until right before the final bell.

The bubbling mole sauce would do the job of slow-roasting the meat, and the resulting dish would be sublime. Poor Pablo, Neil thought. He was probably going to make a thin soup full of lamb meat chunks with the consistency and flavor of golf balls.

The men in white stepped aside and lifted the lids of their boxes.

"The secret ingredient is"—Rodrigo paused for full effect—"LAMB SHANKS." The crowd oohed and ahhed. Then the starting gun fired with a loud *boom*.

Neil rushed to grab his shank. He could see Larry starting the oil. Pablo was shaking from head to toe, and sweating so much he looked like he was marinating himself.

This was going to be a cinch.

Neil reached his box and looked inside. There, on top of the pink fatty joint of meat, was something Neil's super sense of smell hadn't detected: a handwritten note. A series of weird symbols had been drawn around the edges and in the middle, in a deep red, blood-like ink, were the words . . .

> *Neil Flambé,*
>
> *You have ignored our first warning.*
>
> *We are afraid that you are now going to lose this competition . . . on purpose, in the final. You may scoff, but consider this: We have your perfumed friend the flower bringer. If you win this competition, she will die. If you make losing too obvious, she will die. If you lose before the final, she will die. You must lose in the final. You will follow these instructions to the letter if you want to see her alive.*
>
> *Do not attempt to contact the police or we will know and she will die.*
>
> *We are watching.*
>
> XT

Neil glanced quickly over the open lid of the box. Isabella had been sitting in the third row from the back, right on the aisle. He squinted through the glare of the bright lights.

Her seat was empty.

Isabella was gone.

CHAPTER ONE

THREE CHAPTERS AND TWO WEEKS EARLIER THAN CHAPTER FOUR

I t's not a duel!" Neil Flambé yelled, rattling the pots and pans that hung over his head. People who heard Neil yell were often impressed by how well the fourteen-year-old chef could imitate a bullhorn.

Angel Jícama, however, was unfazed. He just crossed his arms tighter and narrowed his eyes.

"Neil's right, Angel," Larry said. "It's actually more like six duels, spread out over two weeks."

Neil glared at his cousin. "You're not helping!" he fumed. He turned back to Angel. "It's just a TV show!"

Neil, Larry and Angel were in the kitchen of Chez Flambé. Larry and Angel were sitting on stools, watching Neil pace up and down between the stainless-steel counters. Neil was hoping to convince Angel to come to Mexico City as part of his team for the *Azteca Cocina*.

"I'm just saying that Angel may have a point," Larry said. "You know what they say 'If it quacks like a duck, it's quite often a duck.'"

"If it quacks like

a duck and I get my hands on it," Neil blared, "then it's duck à l'orange!"

Larry crossed his legs and lifted his hands into some kind of yoga position. "If the words are not correct, then what is said is not what is meant; if what is said is not what is meant, then what must be done will not be done."

Neil stood in open-mouthed silence for a moment. "What the heck does that mean?" he eventually asked.

"It's Confucius saying if it quacks like a duck it's a duck, no matter what you say it is," Larry said with a sombre slow nod, uncrossing his legs.

"It's confus-*ing*," Neil shouted. Then it hit him. "Wait. Let me guess. You're dating a Confucius scholar?"

"She has a name, you know. It's Rosetta," Larry said. As far as Neil could tell, Larry always seemed to have a different girlfriend, with a different area of expertise, and he went to great lengths to impress them. Neil knew that it was one of the main reasons Larry's head contained so many obscure bits of information.

Neil gave up trying to figure out what this particular bit had to do with whether the *Cocina* was a duel or not. "I think you need a coffee," he said. "You're brain is starting to hiccup through your vocal chords."

"I always need a coffee," Larry smiled. "Maybe if you drank some, you'd be able to follow my brilliant train of thought."

"That train derailed a few stations back."

"Ouch." Larry smiled. "I've said it before and I'll say it again: Please leave the jokes to me. I'm a professional."

"A professional idiot!" Neil yelled even louder.

"Yelling! Now that's something you're good at."

Neil grabbed for a paring knife and waved it menacingly at Larry. "Remember what else I'm good at? Preparing and cooking things that quack like ducks."

"Quack," Larry said, and then he started to shake with laughter. "Are you seriously threatening me with a whisk?"

Neil looked at his hand. He was sure he'd grabbed the paring knife, but he was indeed holding a wire whisk. He'd have to be more careful, more in control. Why did Larry drive him nuts so easily? He threw the whisk across the room in disgust, and it crashed through the back window. The cats that hung out below meowed their disapproval. Usually Neil threw out food he was unhappy with, not kitchen utensils. The cats hovered in anticipation whenever they heard him raise his voice. They were quite fat.

"Great," Neil said. "There's another repair I can't afford."

Chez Flambé was not in the best part of town. It had been a rundown fish-'n'-chips shop, slated for demolition when Larry won it in a poker game. It had cost thousands to clean up the layers of grease and calcified fish batter, and there were still plenty of other repairs needed.

Neil shook his head in disbelief, then rubbed his temples and looked at Angel.

"It's fine if you don't want to come, but you're not going to talk me out of going," Neil said.

"Talk?" Larry said, waving his hand in front of Angel's scowling face. "I don't think Angel has said a word in ages, although I think I heard him growl a few minutes ago."

Angel said nothing.

"Maybe that was his stomach growling," Larry smiled. "Angel, would you like a snack?"

Angel said nothing, even louder.

Larry chuckled. "I'll take that as a no."

Neil stopped in the middle of the floor, his back turned to Larry and Angel. "Look, Angel, I've already hired contractors to come renovate the kitchen and the dining room. Amber and Zoë have bought fabric and paint and new chairs. If I close the restaurant for two weeks without making any money, I'll lose everything. Anyway, this isn't some grungy little cook-off. This is the big time, a made-for-TV event with real sponsors. I won't be in any danger and I won't be putting anybody else in danger."

Neil avoided Angel's face, but he could easily imagine the look of disapproval that was etched there.

Neil and Angel had had their first real fight over a duel. A little more than a year ago,

Neil had accepted an invitation from a mafia boss in Venice to a chef-versus-chef battle. Neil had asked Angel to be his sous-chef on that adventure, but his mentor had said no. Neil stormed off and took Larry instead. Neil won, but after having a gun waved in his face, he'd been forced to accept only half of the promised cash.

Angel had first-hand experience with the dangers of the seedy side of international cuisine. Years before, he'd taken part in a deadly duel that had left another chef dead—chef Tortellini, Isabella's father. Angel had immediately quit the high life of haute cuisine, losing himself in back alleys and country markets around the world. He was in search of the real meaning of food, not culinary glory, not anymore.

"I was hoping you might come along this time," Neil added in an almost whisper. "You know Mexican cuisine almost as well as I do."

"Almost?" Larry choked. Angel's family, on his father's side, was from Southern Mexico—at least according to legend—so Neil was being cockier than usual, if that were even possible.

Angel uncrossed his arms and let out a deep sigh. "Neil," he said softly. "This isn't about my past and it isn't about putting other people in danger. You've already shown your willingness to do that to yourself and to Larry." Neil's shoulders tensed at the rebuke. "This is about how you continue to waste your gifts on these ego-boosting adventures."

"What do you mean?" Neil asked.

"Yeah," Larry added. "Neil's ego doesn't need any

boosting. Trust me." He spread his arms wide. "It's huuuuuuuuuuge."

Angel waved him off. "I mean this, Neil: Is your cooking great because someone else says it is? Or because it is?"

"I already get plenty of praise. I need the money."

"There are other ways to get money," Angel continued.

"Oh, really? From you maybe? You give all yours away!"

This was true. When Angel had returned from his self-proclaimed exile, he hadn't opened a restaurant. He had a different plan. He now cooked just one dish a year. He practiced and practiced until he felt it was perfect, or as near to perfect as he could achieve. Then he invited a handful of wealthy guests to come to his home and dine with him. They paid handsomely, but Angel gave almost all the money away to the city's food banks.

"Have you tried hard work and patience?" Angel said.

"Have you tried keeping food fresh in a refrigerator that's held together by duct tape?"

As if on cue, the compressor on the ancient walk-in fridge spattered and coughed.

Larry walked over and kicked it, and it came back to life. "I did the duct tape," he said jovially. "Kind of adds a homey touch to the place."

"I already work hard," Neil said.

"But you hunger for glory—"

Neil cut him off, speaking quickly. "If I'm hungry, it's for what I deserve. Someday I'll be the most famous chef in the world." He seemed to be talking to himself as much as to Larry and Angel. "I won't just have one dumpy restaurant, but a whole chain of Michelin-starred Chez Flambés. I'll be cooking with the best ingredients and not worrying about how much it costs. I'll have the best of the best." He turned to face Angel. "I want it fast. I don't want to be stuck here the rest of my life watching Larry fix things with his feet."

Angel walked over to Neil and placed his hand on his shoulder. "I didn't say patience was easy. But in the end, it is more rewarding. Believe me. You need to look inside yourself to see what it is you want. Fame and riches are easy goals. Can you search for something deeper?"

"The only deep thing I care about is my deep fryer," Neil said, shaking off Angel's hand.

"No matter how successful and rich you become, you will not be happy," Angel said, walking toward the back door, "unless you have happiness and peace inside you."

"That's crazy," Neil said. "I'm already great, and unhappy. I'll be happy and peaceful enough when I'm great and rich and famous."

The sound of sudden drizzle and wet cats wafted in through the broken window. Angel stopped and put on his raincoat. As he began to unfurl his umbrella he said, "I have lived this life that you want so desperately and have lived it to the end. It leads to misery and death. It took one life, and almost took my soul. I do not want it to take yours."

He walked out the door and disappeared into the late-summer mist.

Neil stomped over and slammed the door shut. The fridge sputtered and coughed again. He was so frustrated he almost wanted to cry. He respected Angel. Angel had always been there for him, even more than his own parents. But what he was asking of Neil, what he was always asking, wasn't fair. He wanted Neil to be content with this dump, with making great food for small crowds, with squirreling away small change when he could be charging top dollar at a ritzy downtown location.

Just because Angel had screwed up his own life didn't mean Neil would. He was Neil Flambé, after all. He wouldn't make the same mistakes as Angel. He'd learn from them, but he wouldn't repeat them. He was great, and he was going to become even greater.

He stood up straight. "Larry, kick that fridge again and grab some scallions and garlic. Dinner service starts in four hours. Let's prep."

"You got it, Neil. Anything else I can do?"

"If you really want to be useful, why don't you start dating a chef who's an expert in Mexican cuisine?"

"Her name is Juanita. I'm meeting her for dinner next week."

CHAPTER TWO

MAKING SCENTS

This weather is horrible," Isabella Tortellini said to the gloom. She drew the hood of her cloak tightly around her face. August was often the most beautiful month in Vancouver, but it was her luck to arrive just before one of the rainiest and coolest on record. She had moved here from Northern Italy a few months before, and this was not the weather she'd hoped to find in her new home. Thank goodness she would be in Mexico City soon, enjoying the warm, dry weather and the wonderful fragrances of the surrounding countryside.

She had been invited to visit by the head of the Xochipilli Tallo flower farmer's collective—a fair-trade

organization that hired poor people from the city slums and took them to farms to grow organic flowers. It wasn't a profitable business, yet. But if the flowers and their scents were up to her exacting standards, Isabella was going to pay top dollar to secure them as a supplier.

"Don't count the cents when you make great scents," read the banner on her website. Isabella Tortellini had made a name for herself in the perfume industry by using only natural, fair-trade ingredients. Others might make bigger profits, but Isabella wasn't worried about that.

She had booked her tickets immediately. And Jones, her sort of bodyguard (he was more of a big, scary-looking family friend), had insisted that she book him a flight as well.

They had met this morning to go over the details.

"I called some contacts I have down there," Jones said. "The farm seems to check out."

"Xochipilli—what a strange name," Isabella said.

"Apparently Xochipilli is the name of the Aztec flower god."

"Flower god?" Isabella perked up immediately.

"Oh no," Jones said. "I've seen that look before."

Isabella ignored him and pulled out her phone. She typed in Xochipilli and searched the Net. Her eyes grew wider and wider as she read. "I never knew flowers were so important to the Aztecs." Isabella clicked from site to site. "They traded them as currency. Sometimes they even ripped out food crops to make room for more flowers."

She looked up at Jones with an enormous smile. "A culture that values flowers and perfumes more than gold!

This is fascinating. Perhaps I will develop a whole line of Aztec-inspired fragrances!"

Jones sipped his herbal tea. "I'm sure it will be a success. Most of your crazy ideas work out . . . eventually."

"Yes," she said, "you're right. This is a great plan."

"Um, that's not exactly what I said."

"I will need to spend extra time there." She'd started tapping her phone again, and before Jones realized what she was up to, she'd changed her flights.

"There," Isabella said with a sigh. "Two more weeks in Mexico."

Jones spat out his tea. "WHAT?!" He was not happy. To begin with, he wasn't a big fan of spontaneity, and Isabella consistently was. Then there was a problem with timing.

Isabella raced on. "I'll mostly stay in Mexico City, but now I have time for plenty of side trips to the country and the farms."

"But I'm supposed to be back in Canada before that flight home you just booked."

Isabella patted Jones' hand. "Don't worry so much," she said. "I didn't change your flights, just mine. You go to your little camp and have a good time playing with your friends."

Jones growled. "It's not a little camp, and we are not playing."

Jones had enrolled in an elite nature survival course in the Arctic. He and his guide would be dropped on top of a glacier with nothing but their clothes, a flashlight, a fingernail clipper and a pack of bubble gum. Cell phones were prohibited. He would be completely unreachable for at least a week. Three other pairs of thrill-seekers would be dropped miles away. The first pair to make it to Tuktoyaktuk got a trophy, bragging rights and first place in line to be treated for the inevitable frostbite.

"I'll drop out of the course," he said firmly.

"No, you will not," Isabella said, just as firmly. "You've been on the waiting list for two years."

"I don't like the smell of this."

"My perfume?" Isabella smiled.

Jones didn't. "I don't like the smell of you walking around a foreign country alone. You were only supposed to be there a few days, not two weeks."

"Don't worry so much," Isabella said. "Neil and Larry will be there to help protect me after you leave. Larry can even help me with my research."

Jones had scowled so fiercely Isabella worried he was going to break a tooth. "Those dolts couldn't protect themselves in a tank with a bazooka."

"I'll be fine," Isabella laughed. "I'm from a foreign country, you know. They're not so scary."

Jones did smile at this, sort of. It was more of a very slight tremor along his upper lip. "I guess I treat you as too much of a kid sometimes. I forget you are sixteen."

"Almost seventeen. And I promise I'll stay close to crowds. There are more than 20 million people in Mexico

City, so that should be easy."

"It also makes it easy to get lost," Jones said.

Isabella patted him on the back of the hand one more time and smiled.

What a wonderful coincidence that she would be in Mexico at the same time as Neil, although she still wasn't comfortable with his reasons for visiting. He'd told her "it's not a duel" a few too many times. What was it her mother had said about "people who protest too much"? Still, even she felt there was something special about this trip, something that could put Neil in the top echelon of chefs. She knew first-hand how hard it could be to make it in business when everyone around you saw only a child. Neil was a great chef. She would offer her support, and keep her worries to herself. Besides, if he won, he would never have to do this type of competition again, or so she hoped.

She was almost at Chez Flambé now. There were benefits to having a relationship with Neil Flambé, and a standing reservation at his restaurant was one of them. Of course, Neil didn't cut her any slack on the bill, which actually made her respect him more. The last thing a strong young woman wants is a fawning suitor.

The drizzle turned to rain. "This weather is perfect for *Pommes de Terre à la Flambé* and pan-seared salmon," she thought as the wind helped the damp chill find its way past the warm wool of her shawl.

She heard the crash of shattering glass and stopped. Was someone breaking into the restaurant? She hurried her pace and turned the corner just in time to see a large figure moving under the dim glow of the light over the back door of Chez Flambé. Even though it was early afternoon, it was as dark as night. She slipped into the shadows and held her breath. The alleyway in this part of town was not a place to be caught alone with a stranger.

The figure stopped a few steps away from her and turned to look back at the restaurant. The street light illuminated the profile of a middle-aged, bearded man.

It was Angel. Isabella slowly let out her breath. She still found herself fighting against the years of bitterness she had harbored for this man. But as she grew to know him, she found none of the evil she had expected to find; instead, she had seen only sadness and remorse.

"Angel," she said, stepping out of the shadow and touching him on the shoulder.

He gave a surprised shudder, but quickly recognized the voice of the young woman. He turned to face her with a kindly smile.

"Isabella! What are you doing out in this mess, especially with such a nice shawl?"

"It is a very warm shawl and can stand plenty of punishment—a gift from Jones."

"A man who knows about punishment," Angel chuckled.

"Let me guess what brings you out, with your rather shabby *impermeabile*." She looked askance at Angel's worn and frayed trench coat. It was missing at least three buttons and seemed to be absorbing as much rain as it shed. "You ought to at least keep enough money to dress yourself properly!" She tried in vain to prop up his collar around his neck, but each time it fell sloppily back.

She gave up. "So, Neil is trying to get you to go with him. Correct?"

"Yes."

"And you refused." It wasn't really a question.

"Yes."

"And you will not help him prepare for this competition, even though he stubbornly insists he will go no matter what."

"Yes." Angel couldn't help but smile. Isabella had a way of making an interrogation seems like a pleasant chat. "You know him very well, don't you?"

"Yes," she said, smiling. "And like you, I know that he has an ego the size of a *balenottera azzurra*."

"A blue whale," Angel translated.

"*Sí*. But he is a great chef, there's no doubt, and inside there is a nice, caring young man."

"I know. And I know that Neil is in danger."

Isabella started. "How do you mean? Has someone threatened him . . . again?"

"I mean he is in danger of ending up like me," Angel said with a frown. "Burning out and taking others down with him."

They let their history pass between them. Isabella spoke first.

"Angel, have you considered that he might need

your help, and not just your advice, to discover those truths himself?"

"I have tried. He does not want to listen. He only cares for what I can teach him about food."

Isabella paused for a second to think. "When I was a *bambina*, my mother would often tell me about the mistakes she had made when she was a businesswoman. She was a designer, you know."

"Yes. She made beautiful clothes. I remember her shows in Milan."

"But she did not have a *testa*, a 'head,' for numbers. She had to sell everything to her partner to stay out of *prigione*, 'prison.'"

"And she wanted you to avoid that life."

Isabella nodded. "But it wasn't until I started making mistakes myself that I learned anything useful. She stopped telling me what to do; instead, she started to help me understand what had happened to me. She would catch me when I fell, like a . . . how do you say . . . *saltimbanco?*"

"Acrobat."

"*Sí*. I fell from the high wire many times. She was always there to catch me, and she always sent me back up to try again." She looked at Angel. "Do you see what I am trying to say?"

Angel thought for a minute before responding. "It's too hard for me to go back to that life, to cook with him in anything resembling a duel or a competition. And, Isabella, it's not just about what happened. If truth be told, there is still a part inside me that I cannot stamp out; that still wants fame and glory. I must not fan that flame—in him or in me."

"You say it would be hard for you. Doesn't that often mean something is worth the effort?"

"Possibly."

"Come to Mexico City," she said.

"Why?"

An idea had suddenly occurred to Isabella. Jones was still threatening to cancel his trip. What if Angel agreed to be her chaperone? That would be perfect for everyone, she thought confidently. And once Isabella Tortellini had a thought, it usually became reality.

"Because Jones wants you to come."

"What? Why?"

"I need a chaperone, someone to keep an eye on me after he leaves. And you could also keep an eye on Neil. There would be no need to cook with him, but you would be there in case he falls from that high wire. Be there to help him go back up again."

Angel thought for a long moment. "I will consider it," he said at last. He gave Isabella a warm smile then turned to go. After a few steps he looked back. "Are you sure you're only sixteen?"

"My mother says I have an old soul," she laughed. "And usually a new shawl."

Angel smiled and walked away. Isabella watched him slowly make his way through the gathering storm, toward his apartment building. It would take him about fifteen minutes to walk there. Plenty of time, Isabella thought, for him to come around to her way of thinking.

She turned back to Chez Flambé, where she could make out Neil and Larry through a newly cracked window. They were busily chopping vegetables in anticipation of the evening rush. She watched Neil for a few minutes as his hand flashed through the air. Then she tapped on the kitchen door and walked inside.

CHAPTER THREE

A MISSED WARNING

Amber and Zoë Soba stared at the dining-room walls of Chez Flambé.

Neil and Larry had left a few hours earlier, and the twins now had the restaurant all to themselves. Amber held a giant sledgehammer in her hands.

Zoë was repeatedly passing an electric blue crowbar from one hand to the other.

They looked at each other and smiled.

"This is going to be . . ."

"A blast."

Amber slipped a Metric CD into an old metal boom box. She turned the volume to maximum.

Zoë pressed play.

They flipped their safety goggles into place.

"Time to demo CHEZ FLAMBÉ!" They rushed at the wall. Within seconds they had torn off the old wood moulding and begun to rip down the aging cracked plaster and bone-dry wooden slats that lay underneath. The music blared away in the background.

"This is performance art at its most vital!" Zoë yelled over the crash of hammer against wood mixed with thrashing guitars.

"If the gang at school could see us right now!" Amber replied.

The twins were students at the Emily Carr School of Art in downtown Vancouver, and they were definitely in the avant-garde of the student body. Sure, they could draw and paint extremely well, but occasionally they pursued other, more vigorous methods of artistic expression.

Once, the sisters had blown up the cafeteria's cappuccino machine in protest over the low quality of the coffee. They submitted footage of the explosion as their final project for Applied Arts 301, figuring the professor could either fail them and call the cops, or give them an A+. They explained that the explosion was caused by the coffee itself, a sure sign of its undrinkability. They hadn't done anything, really, but light the noxious gas that was leaking out of the filter. Professor Valdez had watched their grainy presentation with her mouth and eyes wide open. A coffee lover from Colombia, she had (to the twins' relief) come down firmly on the side of the A+.

Of course, there was a note on their transcripts telling them never to do anything like that again. So it had been a while since they'd had the chance to do some serious, authorized, demolition. They were having so much fun they missed the knock on the back door—at first. Within five minutes the interior walls of the dining room were stripped down to the studs. Finally, as they stepped back into the dust cloud to examine their work, they heard a loud *boom boom boom*.

"That's coming . . ."

"From the kitchen."

The delivery man, Fred Gedaire, was practically kicking in the back door by the time they found the keys and unlocked the deadbolt.

"Finally," Fred said, looking down at his clipboard. "I've got a new fridge in the truck. It's for some guy named Neil Frumpy."

The twins started laughing so hard they could barely speak.

"This, haha . . ."

"Is, haha . . ."

"The, haha . . ."

"Right, haha . . ."

"Place," they sputtered out between laughs. They were still giggling as Fred wheeled the giant cardboard box into the kitchen and eased it off the end of his dolly.

"Are either of you this Frumpy guy?" Fred asked. "Or maybe his girlfriend?"

That sent the twins into yet more spasms of laughter. He just stared at them like they were a couple of baboons on a sugar high. Fred was supposed to wait and make sure the fridge was undamaged, and get them to sign a waiver form saying everything had been delivered in good shape. But with the way the two were rolling on the floor, he figured he'd never be able to get them to sit still long enough to look. He had more deliveries to make. He'd just call later.

A few minutes after he pulled away, the twins sat on

the floor with their backs against the box, gasping for breath.

"There's only one way to direct such positive energy," Amber said finally.

"Get back to work knocking down Chez Flambé." Zoë answered.

"Don't you mean Chez Frumpy?"

The fridge sat in the box for three days before the twins opened it. That's when they saw the note. It was written on translucent paper, decorated with strange red symbols, and lay on a shelf inside the gleaming stainless-steel fridge.

It read:

If you come to Mexico we will have no choice but to declare war. The second you begin the Azteca Cocina, the celestial fates will be set in motion.

    There will be no turning back.

    It is the Flower Bringer we desire. You must not interfere. Submit to our will and you will enjoy the friendship and protection of the empire. Set foot in our empire, and you will have declared yourself an enemy.

This is the first warning. . . .

XT

The twins looked up from the note, mouths agape.

"Oh no," they said together. "That note arrived the day Neil and Larry left."

"I guess he was supposed to read it before heading to the airport."

"We'd better call Neil," Zoë said.

"Right away," Amber said.

"And who the heck is the Flower Bringer?"

Amber reached for her cell phone.

"Wait." Zoë looked at the clock that hung over the back window. "He won't answer."

Amber nodded. "His first match is today."

"He's competing right now."

"I guess the war has started."

CHAPTER FIVE

JUST SECONDS AFTER CHAPTER FOUR

Neil lurched forward, squinting into the glare of the lights. The faint smell of Isabella's perfume still hung in the air, but it was disappearing quickly. He moved from behind the counter to look for her then remembered what the note said. A chill went down his spine. "You must lose in the final. You will follow these instructions to the letter if you want to see her alive."

Neil's mind raced, trying to absorb all of this new information. Isabella couldn't have been gone for more than five minutes— maybe he could catch her and her abductors before they got away! But if not, he would certainly forfeit the match and Isabella would die.

36

He stood frozen to the spot.

"Neil. Neil! NEIL!"

Someone was calling his name. Neil looked over at Pablo Pimento, who was furiously rubbing his lamb with a mixture of chopped herbs and spices.

"NEILLLLLLLLLLLLL!"

Larry was now standing next to Neil, shaking his shoulder vigorously.

"The time for meditating has passed, *hombre*, it's time for marinating!"

Larry was right. Neil had to cook, and he had to cook well. He had no other choice.

Isabella was gone.

Neil's split-second advantage was gone.

He'd consider his options later. Right now, he had to win.

"Larry," Neil said, choking back a mixture of anger and fear, "heat a cast-iron skillet now." He pressed his eyes shut and ordered himself to concentrate.

Neil did his best to lose himself in the lamb and the delicate preparation of the mole sauce. He wasn't entirely successful. Isabella was on her way somewhere right now, getting farther away by the second. But Mexico City was huge—no, it was gigantic. He thought back to his first glimpse of the expanse. As his plane had banked to land it had dipped, giving him a view of the great metropolis. Neil had gasped. His entire field of vision was filled with houses and jam-packed streets. He'd never seen such a sprawling fusion of high-rises, shanty-towns and suburban-style subdivisions. The edges were obscured by the omnipresent smog that the teeming population added to daily, and that the surrounding mountains trapped and kept over the city like a perpetual shroud.

It was nothing like the images of Mexico he'd seen in movies. This city was modern and metropolitan, like New York or Paris, but on steroids. Isabella was now lost somewhere in that vastness, but where?

"AAAAAAAAAAAAAAAAAAAAAHHHH!"

Pablo Pimento's yell broke into Neil's thoughts. He'd elected to cut his lamb into small pieces and thread them onto skewers. But in his haste, he hadn't trimmed them properly, and there was too much fat. It was now burning, charring the meat so much that it looked like an overdone row of marshmallows.

Neil jerked back to reality, just in time to see his own lamb braising too darkly in the pan. He flipped it and continued to chop the chilies for his sauces. His nose told him that he would need to counterbalance them carefully. They were hot—spicy hot. He reviewed his planned menu from start to finish. Fried stuffed tortillas for a starter, like little Mexican spring rolls. He'd use the marrow from the lamb bones to make a silky, pâté-like filling. He'd follow with a salad of local greens and savory, then the lamb mole. It was a lot of spiciness to throw at the judges. He needed to make some calculations.

"Grab some vanilla beans," he called to Larry, "and some heavy cream. We're going to finish this whole feast with an ice cream and chocolate sundae." That would keep the judges from focusing too much on the burning sensation on their tongues—no matter how sensational the taste—and would send them back to their score cards with warm memories of sweet dessert and strong coffee.

"No-hay *problema, señor!*" Larry called back, as he quickly got the ingredients together.

Pimento let out another yell as more flames leaped up from his grill, setting fire to the wooden skewers. Bits of fat dripped into the flaming blue jets, sending the flames even higher. Neil picked up a faint smell of singed eyebrows mixed in with the carbonized meat.

Neil quickly cut his lamb into chunks, covered them with the mole sauce that had been simmering on the burner, and placed the mixture in the oven on low heat. Now he could turn his attention to the side dishes. Once the buzzer went, Pimento would be serving four plates of charcoal briquettes. Neil would be setting out three plates of magnificent, spicy yet perfectly balanced lamb-based dishes and a heavenly, light dessert. He would win, easily.

Forty-five minutes later the judges confirmed Neil's not-so-humble opinion. Pimento extended a sweaty hand to Neil, who shook it firmly and bowed to the crowd. Then Neil turned and bolted out the front door as fast as he could. It was windy and smoggy outside the opera house. He stuck his nose in the air, in vain. If Isabella had come this way, her trail had run cold. Neil hesitated, unsure of what to do next.

Larry came up beside him. "Why the rush, champ? They want you back inside to tape some interviews."

Neil ignored Larry and continued to scan the crowd. There were hundreds of people hanging around the piazza in front of the opera house, grabbing shade under the many trees of the nearby park and going up and down the stairs to Bella Artes subway station.

"The subway!" Neil yelled, and he was off like a shot. The wind might have blown away Isabella's perfume outside, but traces might still be lingering in the mustier air of the underground—if they had gone that way. Would kidnappers take a hostage on the subway? It was a long shot, but that was all he had.

Larry stared after Neil, dumbfounded by his cousin's odd behavior. He had just started to follow him when he felt a yank on his shoulder. "If your cocky boss is too important to talk, then you will have to do," said a producer with a headset and an angry scowl.

"Viva Zapata! Viva Team Flambé!" Larry yelled after Neil before disappearing through the gilded doors and into the glaring TV lights of the atrium.

Neil almost slipped down the subway stairs he was running so fast. He stopped as soon as he reached the ticket kiosk. Air currents were moving back and forth along with the tumult of people, but it was nothing like the steady wind aboveground. He closed his eyes and took a big sniff. It was there! He was sure of it—the faintest scent of lavender mixed in with the odors of oil and dirt and humanity. "Isabella's perfume smells different on her than on anyone else," Neil had once explained to Larry. "It's like the way the same spices can smell different on different cuts of beef."

"Boy, Neil," Larry had said with unmistakable sarcasm, "you are an incurable romantic."

But now, the unmistakable scent of Isabella and lavender was coming from inside the station. Neil pushed his way to the front of the line, ignoring the shouts of the patrons.

He threw in his fare and rushed through the turnstile.

Neil was like a bloodhound. He walked down the entire length of the platform, shoving people back and forth as he attempted to locate the spot with the strongest smell. There might have been a fight if the train hadn't arrived. The busy patrons forgot about Neil and climbed aboard.

Neil sniffed and sniffed. He realized that the reason he could pick up the perfume at all was that the particles weren't just suspended in the air: there were droplets all over the marble floor. "Isabella, you are a genius," Neil said to himself. He got down on his knees and inhaled.

He could only smell perfume on about half of the platform, from the entrance to the middle, and it was strongest right in the middle. Somehow, standing in this spot, Isabella must have managed to spill her perfume as a clue. But what had happened next? Had she been ushered onto the train?

A train pulled into the station. Neil stood up and watched the doors slide open right in front of him. It was heading north—toward the far reaches of the city. Neil took a step forward to climb aboard. He would look for more clues, more traces of perfume, or perhaps Isabella herself. Then he spied the map of the subway system that hung over the opposite door.

To a first-time visitor, Mexico City's subway system is a sprawling, winding mess. There are more than 160 stops on nine different lines. Even locals could get lost

underground and end up miles from home or work. To Neil, the map resembled a coiled nest of snakes. Neil stepped out of the train and back onto the platform. The doors closed and the train pulled away.

He stared down the tunnel as the train noisily rounded a bend and disappeared. Anger and frustration rolled over him and he shouted as loud as he could, "XT, if you hurt one hair on Isabella's head I'll chop you to into tiny, digestible bits!"

Completely drained, he walked slowly back to the opera house and arrived just in time to see Larry smiling at the TV cameras and saying, "Winning was easy, especially with my expert chocolate grating. I think it put us over the edge."

What Neil yelled after that was edited out of the on-air broadcast.

CHAPTER SIX

HELL'S SMELLS

Isabella couldn't see a thing. Wherever she was, it was pitch black. Or perhaps her eyes had stopped functioning. That was a definite possibility. Her eyes hurt—the pupils and everything around them. It took a real effort just to lift her eyelids. In fact, every part of her body ached. To say she felt groggy would have been an understatement. Her mother often complained of migraine attacks. A small change in air pressure could exile her to a warm bathtub in a darkened room for hours, sometimes days, on end. Isabella had never had a migraine herself, but she was pretty sure that this was how one felt. She had a new and profound sympathy for her mother. She also had a burning desire to make somebody pay.

"Where am I?" she said, and heard her words echo. No one answered.

So she couldn't see, but her hearing seemed to work. That was a mixed blessing. In addition

to the sound of her own voice, Isabella could hear rats scurrying somewhere in the darkness. With an effort—her ankles were tied together—she drew her knees closer to her chest. She could hear dirt and small stones on the floor scrape as she slid her shoes over them. She was sitting with her back against a wall of some kind. It was very hot, and only her cashmere sweater was keeping the heat from singeing her back. Her wrists were bound, with her arms in front of her. At least she could move them.

As Isabella continued to wake up, she became more aware of her surroundings, including the smell—garbage and rotting food. It made her gag. She leaned forward and tried desperately to avoid throwing up. She failed. Unfortunately, it didn't make her feel much better, and it certainly didn't make the place, whatever it was, smell any better.

"How did I get here?" she said out loud. There was no answer aside from the scurrying feet.

Isabella remembered very little of the last few hours . . . or was it days? She ignored the pain in her temples and concentrated on remembering. She had been watching Neil prepare for the first battle in the *Cocina*. She and Neil had exchanged glances, and she'd shouted words of encouragement. Then the lights over the audience had gone out.

And that was when she had received the note. A hand had reached through the darkness with a piece of paper and an incredibly fragrant flower. Isabella had tried to see who had handed her the message, but her eyes had not yet adjusted to the gloom. By the time they did, the aisle was empty.

The note was from Lily, the woman who ran the flower collective. Isabella and Jones had already made one visit to the farm. Lily had shown her fields of flowers, but said that they were not quite at their peak. They had looked wonderful, but Isabella didn't make money creating perfume from pretty flowers. They had to smell wonderful too. Isabella was scheduled to visit the collective again later that week, but perhaps Lily had come into town. She unfolded the delicate paper.

> *Dearest patron Isabella,*
>
> *I am sending this letter to you as an urgent request to meet me outside. I have the most wonderful collection of flowers here that I am about to take to market. I dare not leave it alone, but I knew you would want to see a typical harvest. It will take only a few seconds of your time.*
>
> *Lily*

Isabella took a deep sniff of the flower. It was glorious! Lily's plants must have ripened quickly under the hot Mexican sun. If there was indeed a cartful of these wonders just outside the Bella Artes, she could certainly sneak out for five minutes to see. If the harvest was as good as Lily suggested, perhaps they could agree to a deal on the spot. She slipped out of her seat and went outside.

As she passed through the doors, a breeze had come up and blown the flower from her hand. Isabella watched it skip away across the courtyard, and, as she did, she scanned the crowd. She didn't see Lily anywhere, and there was no cart of flowers.

Something was wrong.

Isabella started to turn around, but a sharp jab in her lower back ended that idea. It wasn't the first time she had felt a gun against her body. She was tempted to yell out, but another nudge from the barrel and a stern "shhhhh" told her that silence was the only option. She tried to turn her head to catch a glimpse of her attacker's face, but a large gloved hand came up to her cheek and pointed her face forward. Then the hand rested firmly on her shoulder.

"Move," said a deep voice. The words were accompanied by another harsh jab in the back. Isabella slowly started to walk forward, the steel barrel and the iron grip directing her toward the subway.

"What an *idiota* I am," Isabella thought. Jones had been right. She had fallen for a trap. Still, a kidnapping? In broad daylight? Jones had told her that Mexico City had one of the highest kidnapping rates in the world, but she had assumed that local aristocrats were the most likely victims, along with tourists who took misguided strolls down dark alleyways at night. Jones had left for Canada the night before and was no doubt well on his way to the far north. Angel had been delayed. She, on the other hand, was being propelled toward who knew where.

The entrance to the subway was crowded with men in worn jeans and checkered shirts. They wore hand-drawn cardboard signs around their collars, advertising their expertise in trades such as electrical work, plumbing and carpentry. Isabella had seen these groups at almost every public plaza in the city. Perhaps one of the men would see that she needed help.

"Help me," she mouthed, and her heart leaped as several of the men started walking toward her. But instead of attacking the man with the gun, they surrounded Isabella. Anyone watching from outside would have been unable to see her in the instant crowd.

They made their way down the stairs and into the station. One of the men must have flashed a group pass because they entered through a large metal entrance gate, all the while the gun barrel jabbing her in the spine, and the entourage hiding her from everyone else. It was then that she remembered the bottle of perfume in her purse. She slowly reached her fingers inside and slipped it out. Carefully, she tilted the bottle so that a small droplet fell to her feet. It was an imperceptible clue for most people, but not, Isabella was sure, for Neil Flambé. She was certain he would come looking for her. She would make sure he had a trail to follow.

They made their way halfway down the platform. A train arrived and the gloved hand slipped a damp handkerchief across her mouth. She dropped the bottle, spilling the remaining liquid. Her eyes were wide with panic and she screamed, but the noise was drowned out by the loud *whoosh* of the approaching train. Isabella felt her

energy drain away. She went limp. The train doors opened and then everything went black.

"As black as this reeking hellhole I'm stuck in now," she said. A shaft of light broke through Isabella's thoughts. Someone had opened a large metal door and its rusty hinges protested the movement with a piercing whine. Bright light bathed the scene in front of her, sending another shock of pain to her head. She shaded her eyes with her bound hands, but couldn't make out further details about her surroundings or the man who was now leaning his face close to hers.

"*Señorita*, I am sorry for these squalid conditions," said an accented voice. Was it the same man who had kidnapped her from the opera house? She couldn't tell. The man continued, "Soon, though, all of this will end. You will be crowned with flowers and you will become a goddess!"

Isabella's eyes were starting to adjust to the light, but before she could see anything, the shadow in front of her tied a thick cloth over her eyes.

"I am fine being what I am," Isabella said, and she spat in the direction of the man's face.

The man chuckled. "You will honor the heavens with your fire. Come, we must move." He untied her hands.

"*Bruta!*" Isabella tried to reach her hands up to grab the blindfold or punch at the man. She failed. In an instant, he had gathered her slender wrists in his large hands, and repositioned her arms behind her back. A second later she was bound again, and a gag inserted into her mouth.

"Before we depart," the man said, turning calmly back to Isabella, "I need to make a small cut."

Isabella tensed. Cut? Her face? Her arms? She heard the click of some kind of blade and tried to scream through the gag. The man yanked her hair. She heard a snip and then she was released.

"See, *señorita*? That wasn't so bad." The man put a firm hand on her shoulder and urged her forward. "And now to your new life." The sun was bright enough to bleed through her blindfold and Isabella knew she was now outside. But the fresh air vanished quickly as she felt herself being lifted and then tossed onto a large pile of what felt like plastic bags. A wooden door slammed behind her. She was packed in too tightly to move, almost too tightly to breath.

Isabella heard a donkey braying, a loud shout, and then everything lurched forward. She was in the back of some kind of donkey cart! This was better? And what the heck did the man want with a lock of her hair?

CHAPTER SEVEN

ON THE EDGE

Neil sat on the edge of his hotel bed, exhausted. He'd been too tired to throttle Larry in front of the cameras, but he'd been so angry that he had dragged him back here without stopping along the way for dinner. He hadn't even bothered to take off his chef's clothes, and the smell of mole sauce and lamb still clung to the fabric. He had used his last bit of energy to tell Larry about Isabella's disappearance and his brief investigation.

"Don't beat yourself up," Larry said, more gently than usual. "Getting on the subway would have been like walking into a maze blindfolded. Or maybe, in your case, nose-folded." Larry was sitting cross-legged on the floor, looking at a huge map of the city. "And I would like to add that if you don't change that outfit soon I'm going to eat it."

Neil just shrugged. Larry frowned. Neil tried to hide it, and did a good job most of the time, but he was still a fourteen-year-old. For Isabella's sake and for his own, he needed to keep it together. Larry knew it was going to take a pinch of helpful advice, a dash of research and a healthy portion of good humor to keep Neil from sinking under the pressure.

Larry examined the map closely. "Let's see if we can figure out where she could be."

Neil looked over at the map, but that just depressed him even more. It was like looking out the window of his plane all over again. Half the subway line lay north of the Bella Artes stop, with plenty of opportunities to transfer back south, or east, or west—or in circles forever. It was as complicated as his recipe for Stuffed and Roasted Tête du Sanglier avec Crème Anglaise, Asperge, Citron, Poivres, Clam Geoduck et Saucisson D'agneau Moderne, which Neil had developed and written down over a three-week period during his grade four history class. Mr. Waiters hadn't been impressed. Neil was supposed to be preparing a project on great canoe-makers of the nineteenth century. Only a last-second gift of an apple torte had salvaged a passing grade.

"So who is this XT jerk?" Larry asked, looking at the note Neil had dropped onto the map.

"I have absolutely no idea. But if I find him . . ." Neil let the words trail off. He wasn't sure what he would or could do. He clenched his fists.

Larry tapped his fingers on the map as he thought out loud. "Well, X is pretty common in Mexican names. So is T. Of course, you can see that with a quick scan of the phonebook—doesn't take a genius."

"Then you should be perfect for the job."

"OH! Slam! Depressed, cooked out and pooped,

but still willing to attack his favorite cousin."

"Only cousin."

Larry smiled. This was a good sign. A combative Neil was a Neil who could cook and think.

"XT, hmm," Larry ran through some XT words he knew. "Tlaxcala, Xaltocan, Teixeira."

"And those are?"

"The first two are towns in ancient Mexico. The last one is a baseball player."

"From Mexico?"

"No, Maryland. But he helped me win my fantasy baseball pool last summer."

"Could you please focus?" Neil yelled. He said this to Larry so often that Amber and Zoë had made him a sign he could just point at during dinner prep. It hung over the sink. Neil was kicking himself for leaving it at home.

"Xipe Totec is an XT," Larry said at last. "Could be Xipe Totec."

"Shippy? That starts with an X?"

"Mexican Xs are pronounced like Ss . . . or sometimes 'sh,' and sometimes J . . . depends a bit on which academic you're reading."

"Or dating?"

Larry smiled dreamily. "Nahuatl—language of the Aztecs—and Jennifer Veracruz. The Spanish had a hard time translating a lot of Nahuatl words, so they inserted Xs to approximate the sounds. Not very close, really."

"Skip the history for once."

"How about more details on Jennifer? She had this cool tattoo of the Mexican flag right over her—"

"FOCUS!" Neil cut him off. "Is this Xipe guy someone we can trace?"

"Well, Xipe's not a person, *per se*. The symbols on the note look Aztec. Xipe Totec was the Aztec god of agriculture."

"A food connection—I should have seen that coming."

"Well, doesn't take a genius," Larry joked.

"What else do you know about Xipe?"

"He's one of those gods of everything. Goldsmiths too, I think, and animals. Maybe even ice cream."

"What?"

"Just kidding on that last one. I'll do some more research."

Neil put his head in his hands. He needed to think. He had the scent of Isabella's perfume on the platform of a northbound train, the initials of an ancient food god, and a lot of assumptions. That plus fifty pesos would get him a cup of—

"Coffee. I need a coffee," Larry said, jumping to his feet. "Did you know that coffee is a major crop in Mexico, but it wasn't from here originally? It was only brought here in the 1700s!"

"Fascinating," Neil said, utterly unfascinated.

"I know," Larry said, making his way to the door. "But then again, on the flip side, a lot of what we think of as European started off here and was brought to Europe by Columbus and those guys."

"Like what?" Neil said, lifting his head a bit.

"Oh, potatoes, tomatoes, sunflowers."

"I need to call the police," Neil said, suddenly.

"Um, not sure what that has to do with tomatoes, but doesn't the note say not to call the police?"

"So? Xipe doesn't need to know I've called."

"You don't even know who Xipe is."

"You think he could be a police officer?"

"Remember how Zapata was killed in an ambush?" Larry pointed to the sash he continued to wear over his chest.

"Um, yeah. So?"

"He was ambushed by the police."

Neil fell back onto the bed with a low moan. "That was seventy years ago!"

"Look, how about this. I'm off to get a coffee. At least wait until I get back and then we can talk about calling the police, or Interpol, or the RCMP."

Neil raised himself up on his elbows and nodded. "Fine, but make it quick."

"I move even faster when I've had caffeine." Larry smiled and walked out the door. Before closing it, he turned back toward the room. "Neil," he said softly, "we're going to find her, okay?" He shut the door with a click.

Neil looked at the old rotary phone that sat on the table next to his bed. Even if he was convinced that the police were trust-worthy, there was a good chance that thing was either bugged or filled with ancient wires that overlapped with every other phone in the hotel.

He pulled out his cell. Neil was usually married to his phone, but the rules of the

Cocina didn't allow outside electrical devices into the kitchens, so he'd turned it off before lunch. It was also extremely expensive to call home from Mexico City, and he wanted all of his money to go into Chez Flambé, not long-distance bills. But now he had to place a call—to Inspector Sean Nakamura.

He pushed the power button. A blue screen welcomed him to international roaming. Neil watched as a small hourglass started turning around and around. It was hypnotic. He lay back on the bed and waited for the phone to connect to the network. Within seconds, he was fast asleep.

The phone connected.

A small envelope flashed silently over the words, "You have twenty-five new messages."

CHAPTER EIGHT

BUTTING HEADS

Angel Jícama and Sean Nakamura stared silently across the tattered mat that guarded the entrance of Angel's apartment. The word "welcome" was stitched with black thread into the fading cloth in more than twenty languages. Angel reached down and flipped it over. "Go Away" was written in bold English, with red fabric paint.

Nakamura looked down at the insult and scowled. "I didn't come here for a pleasant cup of tea, you know. And I am not going away." With a fluid motion he flipped the mat back over with his foot. Now it looked like Angel was the one asking for entry.

"You must have been quite a soccer player before you got grumpy and out of shape," Angel said.

"Look who's talking." Naka-mura pointed at Angel's Buddha-like belly. "Maybe you're eating too much goat cheese?" He raised an eyebrow and cocked his head at Angel.

"So that's why you're here," Angel said through pursed lips. "My goats."

Nakamura relaxed his shoulders and let out a big sigh. "Look, Angel, Chief Strong is starting to give me grief. I can't look the other way anymore."

"She always gives you grief."

"Yeah, but she's been in a really bad mood lately, ever since I messed up that Kopi Luwak sting." Nakamura winced at the memory. It had been a costly failure.

Kopi Luwak is the most expensive coffee in the world. It's harvested in only a few countries in Asia, and how this is done makes it unique, and incredibly expensive. Barely ripened coffee berries are favorite treats for the rare palm civet, a kind of forest cat. They digest the fruit that surrounds the bean, but poop out the rest onto the forest floor. Locals gather the beans, clean them and then roast them. Kopi Luwak can sell for hundreds of dollars a pound. Normal coffee sells for about ten.

A man named Felix Crema was selling his own Kopi Luwak brand from his home in Surrey, a suburb of Vancouver, and was raking in the dough. Larry had tried a cup, and tipped off the police that something wasn't right. One sniff from Neil had confirmed that Crema was really feeding beans to common house cats. The "Kitty-LuWhacked" coffee scam, as Larry called it, had to be stopped. But after breaking down the door to Crema's warehouse, the cops had been swarmed and attacked by hundreds of caffeine-crazed felines.

The resulting paid sick days had added up to thousands of dollars, and Crema had escaped in the commotion.

Angel crossed his arms. "And now you're here to take it out on me?"

"Look, Jícama," Nakamura said, pulling a pad of paper from his coat pocket, "rules are rules. You can't run a farm on a busy downtown street."

"Why not?" Angel said angrily. "Human beings have been growing their own food for centuries. It's better for you and better for the planet."

"Tell it to the judge," Nakamura said, writing Angel's address on the ticket.

"My cheese tastes better than the mass-produced wallpaper paste they sell in the supermarkets. Those rules you love so much are written by big business to keep food production in the hands of big business." He jabbed a finger in Nakamura's chest for emphasis.

Nakamura scowled. "If you'd like, I can double the fine so you can feel twice as morally superior."

"My goats—"

"And chickens."

"And chickens—"

"And cows."

"I don't have a cow!"

"You're having one now!" Nakamura chuck-led.

Angel ignored the latest of Nakamura's notoriously bad puns. "Urban farming is cleaner than factory farming, my friend, and better for the animals than being crammed into giant food factories."

"Tell that to the judge too."

This was a battle that Nakamura and Angel had on a fairly regular basis. It usually ended with a couple of extra blocks of herbed goat's cheese, offered in exchange for another stern verbal warning from the Vancouver Police Department. This time, though, Nakamura seemed determined to actually write the fine. But just then, his cell phone started ringing. Angel's phone rang at the same instant.

They answered, but neither had a chance to even say hello.

"Inspector Nakamura, it's Amber."

"Angel, it's Zoë."

"Neil . . ."

"Is in big . . ."

"Trouble!"

The twins told the two men about the note in the fridge, and the messages they'd left on Neil's phone—messages that had gone unanswered even though the first battle of the *Azteca Cocina* must have ended. By the time the twins hung up, Angel and Nakamura had forgotten all about the great goat-cheese confrontation.

"Angel, I'm heading back to the office. I've got a contact with the Mexican police. A guy named Enrique. He was just up here for a conference, actually, but he should be home by now. I'll call him and then call you as soon as I know anything."

"That will be difficult. I will be in transit and I don't own a cell phone, I'm afraid."

"In transit?"

Angel pulled an airline ticket from his shirt pocket. "I'm leaving for Mexico City in an hour. I should have

gone down yesterday, but it was a . . . difficult decision."
A pained look crossed Angel's face. Nakamura knew a
little of Angel's past—enough to not push for an explanation. "Well, I'll keep trying Neil's phone as well. You
pack and get down there as fast as you can."

Angel nodded. "Good luck."

"If I find anything out, I'll try to contact you."

"How?" Angel called back. "I said I don't have a cell
phone."

"Don't worry. I'll think of something."

Angel watched Nakamura hurry down the hallway.
He looked unhappily at his bags. If only he had been less
hesitant, he might have been there already. He had told
Isabella he would be there to chaperone, but he hadn't
told Neil. By the time he had resolved to go, he couldn't
book the flight he wanted. Jones had not been happy,
but what could he do? Isabella had told them that
nothing would happen if she were left alone for just one
day, and Jones had reluctantly agreed to let her stay.

Angel dialed her cell phone now. Maybe she would
know what was going on. No answer. He grabbed his
bags, walked down the stairs and hailed a cab. He wished
he had a better idea of what awaited him in Mexico City.
What was going on? And if something really was wrong,
what could he do alone? It was too bad Nakamura
couldn't come along as well, but Angel knew that cops
weren't always welcome in other cops' jurisdictions.

All of this and more ran through Angel's mind as he
made his way to the airport. So he was surprised, a few
hours later, when he took his seat on the flight to Mexico
City and found Nakamura sitting next to him.

CHAPTER NINE

CORTEZ, CODEX, AND COOKING

Larry sighed contentedly as he approached the door to the hotel room. It was a large room. Neil had one king-sized bed, and Larry slept on the couch. Neil had been hoping for nicer digs, Larry knew, befitting the crown prince of cuisine. But Larry argued that the money they saved would be better spent on the renovations to Chez Flambé.

Larry didn't tell Neil that the big selling point for the hotel in his *Caffeinated Planet* travel guide hadn't been its cheapness, but its proximity to the best café in the city. Larry had been making his own pilgrimage at every opportunity. Karimba, the barista at Our Lady of Guada-Latte, was both beautiful and a fan of disheveled hair.

The CP guide did warn that the hotel was right behind the enormous national cathedral, but didn't specify why this was important. Larry and Neil found out on their first

night. The cathedral's enormous bells rang until midnight, and re-commenced the following morning at 5 a.m. Between that and Neil's snoring, Larry wasn't getting a lot of quality sleep. He compensated with more coffee.

Neil hadn't been getting much sleep either, and a kidnapped girlfriend wasn't likely to help, Larry thought. So he was a little surprised to find Neil snoring away when he opened the door.

"Sleep tight, cousin," Larry said, carefully laying a blanket over Neil. "There's nothing we can do right now." Neil responded with an ear-splitting snore.

Larry winced. There was no way he was going to sleep through that. He carefully tip-toed over to his couch, flopped down as quietly as he could, flicked on his reading light and opened his copy of the *Codex Mendoza*.

"The codex is an amazing document," Larry had told Neil, repeatedly. Neil was only interested in the passages about food, of which there were many. "It's a book, and what a book!" The codex was a first-hand account of the Spanish conquistadors' encounter with the "new" world's very old Aztec culture. It was written just twenty years after their arrival, when most of the Aztecs had been wiped out by battle or had died from strange new diseases the European explorers had brought with them.

Antonio de Mendoza had been one of the first governors of the newly conquered Spanish colony, and he'd asked some of the remaining Aztec scribes to write the history of their people. They did this through colorful and often strange pictures of gods, human sacrifice and wars. The Spaniards then added their own notations to explain the images. There were other codices, but this was Larry's favorite.

Neil snored away in his king-sized comfort as Larry read of the great city that the Spanish leader Cortez had discovered in the Mexican mountains. It had been a bustling metropolis, filled with great artists, commercial tradesmen, busy markets and a vast army. If the Emperor Montezuma had told Cortez to turn around and go home, rather than inviting him inside the walls of the city as a guest . . . well, Larry thought, history would have been a whole lot different. In no time, Cortez had taken control of the city and the country and had shipped as much Aztec gold and jewels as he could jam into his ships back to Spain.

Larry was taking it slow with the codex, drinking in the amazing, detailed drawings of flowers, lakes, gardens, volcanoes, clothing and Aztec deities. It was a frozen moment in time, captured in pen-and-ink just before disappearing forever. But something was nagging him. It wasn't the book: it was the uncomfortable way Neil was lying on the bed. One of Neil's arms was dangling over the side of the mattress. The last thing Neil needed in the kitchen was a stiff arm. As Larry tiptoed over to move him into a more comfortable position, he noticed a faint blue, blinking light coming from under the bed. He got down on his hands and knees. It was Neil's cell phone. He grabbed it and looked at the screen.

"Twenty-five missed calls!" Larry thought. "Neil, I hope you didn't call the police. Honestly, Boy Wonder, you may know your way around a kitchen, but when it comes to street smarts I've seen brainier fire hydrants!"

Larry debated waking Neil, but the last time Larry had woken Neil up after a big duel he'd had to get corrective surgery on his eardrum. "Some people sleep walk. Neil sleep yells," Larry had explained to the audiologist.

Anyway, Larry knew the PIN to Neil's voicemail, so he typed it in with his thumbs and listened. The first message made him jump. It was Isabella. She had called just before the big battle. Larry listened all the way through, but the message contained only some encouraging words and a very audible smooch. Isabella ended by asking if Neil would like to visit some flower farm tomorrow. Larry made a note to ask Neil what flower farm she was talking about, then pressed the save button and moved on to the next message.

It was Amber, or maybe Zoë . . . or maybe both. "Neil, um, you got a note . . . that is, we got a note . . . that is, there's a note. It came three days ago, but we didn't see it until today, but it says something about flowers and, well, war . . . and Neil, we know you're in the duel right now, but call us as soon as you can. We'll call Nakamura, and Angel and, well, anyway, good luck today and all. Oh, and say hi to Larry!"

What? No smooch? Larry thought with a sigh. He pressed save again. The next twenty-three messages were all from one person, Inspector Sean Nakamura, and they were all exactly the same.

"Neil, it's Nakamura. Give me a call. It's urgent."

Typical cop, Larry thought—no tip about why he wanted to talk. There was a hint in the tone of the messages, though. Each went up in urgency and pitch so that as Larry played them back-to-back he got the distinct impression that he was listening to some weird avant-garde choral concerto. Larry dialed Nakamura.

"NEIL!" Nakamura said, recognizing his signature Neil ring-tone, the Swedish Chef song from *The Muppet Show*.

"Larry, actually. Sorry for the disappointment."

"No time for jokes," Nakamura said. "Is Neil there?"

"Let's just say I'm Sleeping Beauty's personal assistant right now."

"I guess that makes you Waking Ugly?"

"I thought you said this was no time for jokes. That was a joke, right?"

"Listen, comedian, here's the deal: The twins got a note in a fridge delivery."

"I know. They called and left a message. But they didn't tell me what it said."

"Okay. I'll read it for you. It says, 'If you come to Mexico we will have no choice but to declare war. The second you begin the *Azteca Cocina*, the celestial fates will be set in motion. There will be no turning back. It is the Flower Bringer we desire. You must not interfere. Submit to our will and you will enjoy the friendship and protection of the empire. Set foot in our empire, and you will have declared yourself an enemy. This is the first warning. . . .' And then it's signed—"

"XT," Larry said.

"Um, yeah. How did you know that?"

"Someone must have gotten a deal at the Aztec stationery store," Larry said. "We got an XT note as well, just after Isabella disappeared."

"Isabella WHAT!?!"

"Well, here's what our day has been like," Larry said. "First of all, we won the first duel, I mean battle . . . thanks in large part to my expert chocolate shredding."

"And . . ."

"Oh, and my expert chili chopping."

"I meant, and what else happened!"

"Well, turns out Isabella was kidnapped during the duel . . . I mean, competition."

"WHHHHHHHHHAAAAAAAAAAAAAAAAA-AAAAAAT?"

"Ah. I see we are now into the second movement of the Nakamura Suite in G-Minor!"

Nakamura didn't say anything. Being used to Larry's oddness and dealing with it were two different things. He took a deep breath . . .

"Nakamura, you still there?"

. . . and counted to ten. "Larry, who kidnapped her? Do you have any leads?"

"Well, Neil followed her trail to the subway near the opera house, and that's where it ends. He wanted to call the police. I said it probably wasn't a great idea until we have a better idea of who this XT person is."

Nakamura considered this. "I hesitate to agree, but that was probably a good idea."

"A compliment! My goodness, let me mark the day on my calendar!"

"That's why I hesitated to agree," Nakamura said with a note of weariness.

Larry continued. "Listen, jokes aside, this is pretty serious. All the XT guy said in his note to us was that if Neil wins the competition, he'd kill Isabella. If he loses before the final he'll kill her. And if Neil calls the police, he'll kill her, so he probably has someone inside the force to tell him if Neil calls. We have a day off tomorrow and we're going to start our own investigation."

Nakamura took all this in. Finally he said, "Look, the department has a mobile forensic kit. Let me sign it out and I'll head down there. You get some sleep and tomorrow we'll get to work."

"You got it. Oh, and Nakamura . . ."

"What?"

"Bring some cash as well. I've blown most of our budget on coffee."

"Cute barista?"

"You know it."

"I know you. Fine. I'll contribute to the coffee fund, but you owe me."

Nakamura hung up. Larry smiled. He loved getting Nakamura's goat, so to speak. This was a serious situation.

Larry knew that. But he also knew that humor was a necessary way to deal with stress. He liked laughter.

He looked over at Neil, who was still sleeping soundly. Neil was going to need as many laughs as he could get over the next few days. He was sure Neil would disagree, but that was the way things always were between them. Larry began to flip the cell phone shut. It started ringing. He stared at the screen—*número no cotizable*—"unlisted."

"Hello?" he said quietly.

A muffled and accented voice spoke. "This is your third warning. In the subway, you said to not harm a hair on her head. If you need proof of our resolve, please look to your door. Adios."

There was a beep. Larry stared at the phone, horrified. Was this XT? How had he gotten Neil's number? And what did he mean about the subway? Neil hadn't said anything about talking to anyone. Larry flipped the phone shut. He looked with a sense of dread toward the thin sliver of light that crept under the door. An envelope was lying there, with a slight bulge in the middle. He hadn't heard footsteps or the sound of it sliding under the door. Who had placed it there?

Larry made his way to the door and opened it slowly, making sure not to step on the envelope. The hallway was empty. He slid the door shut and locked it. Larry knelt and carefully picked up the envelope. He held the paper up to his bedside light. There was a clump of something inside. It was . . . hair?

"Oh, man," Larry thought, looking at the dark curls, "That's Isabella's for sure. Or at least, I'm ninety percent sure." Nakamura and his handy-dandy forensic kit were at least a day away. There was only one surefire way to confirm the hair's origin right now. Eardrum pain or not, Larry was going to have to risk waking up Neil. He wrapped a pillow around his head and began tapping Neil with his foot.

CHAPTER TEN

BELLS AND WHISTLES

ong.
Bong.

Bong. Bong. Bong. Bong.

The cathedral bells rang on the hour.

Neil squinted as the early morning sun streamed into the room.

Bong! Bong bing. Bang. Bong bing bing. Bong. Bong bang. Bong bing.

Bong. Bong. Bong.

Soon, every bell in every bell tower was ringing, celebrating in unison the awakening of another day in Mexico City.

"Mexican bell torture," Neil mumbled, staring at the dimly lit ceiling. He threw off the sheets and swung his legs over the side of the bed. Larry was still sleeping across the room, or at least he was stubbornly refusing to open his eyes.

"Next time, we hire a travel agent," Neil said grumpily as he rubbed his eyes. He hadn't slept a wink after Larry had woken him the night before. The people three doors down on either side probably hadn't either.

The bells continued to ring as Neil walked over and poked Larry in the head.

"Wake up."

"Is that the bells or are my ears still ringing from when I woke you up?" Larry said, refusing to move his head off his pillow or open his eyes. Neil grabbed Larry's sheets and yanked them, along with Larry, onto the floor. Larry lay face down against the rug in an awkward jumble of arms, legs and hair.

"Ouch," he said in a muffled voice.

"Move it," Neil said.

"You shower," Larry mumbled into the rug. "I'll look for clues here in the rug. Aha! Dust mites! I'll ask them if they've seen anything suspicious."

Neil just growled, stepped over Larry and walked into the bathroom.

Larry had woken Neil for a good reason, of course: a bona fide clue—an envelope with a lock of Isabella's hair. After he'd finished his yelling fit, Neil had confirmed with just one whiff that the hair had definitely come from her head. Neil's super sense of smell was also able to pick up something the kidnappers hadn't likely intended him to know: Isabella had been in or near some really horrible, putrid garbage.

"It's almost like she was resting her head on a pillow of decomposed cabbage," Neil had said as quietly as he could, taking careful sniffs. "I can also make out stale pop, rotting chicken and even some cornmeal. She's been held, or is being held, in a garbage dump."

Larry had taken a whiff. He could make out a slight tinge of garbage. "How do you know the aroma isn't coming from the envelope?" Larry asked, looking over at Neil, who was gently rubbing the hair back and forth under his nose.

Neil narrowed his eyes and clenched his teeth. "I can smell the aloe vera hand soap your friend the barista uses on the coffee cup you have sitting on your bedside table."

Larry looked across the room at the paper cup he had tipped over hours ago, lying next to his copy of the codex. "You really creep me out sometimes, you know?"

"Tell her she needs to do a better job of rinsing."

"Okay, you creep me out all the time."

"Now let's get some sleep," Neil had said. "It's late."

"Early."

"Whatever. We aren't going anywhere tonight. Tomorrow, we investigate. First of all, we find out who Isabella was supposed to meet today and then we look for a—"

"Don't say a garbage dump."

"Okay, I won't say it. Now get some sleep. I'll set the alarm for seven."

The bells had had other ideas.

Bong. Bong. Booooooooooooooooooooooooooooong.

Neil showered quickly and walked back into the

room. Larry was snoring quietly into the rug. Neil snapped him in the butt with his towel.

"Ouch," Larry mumbled, still not moving.

"Let's go get a coffee," Neil said. "And bring the map."

Larry was up like a shot. "Coffee? I was just dreaming about some."

Larry quickly showered and then they left the room, scanning the hallways for any sign of somebody following them. There was no one. Neil and Larry made their way through the hotel's polished chrome doors and down the stairs. At the bottom, Larry started to turn right, heading like a zombie for the Guade-Latte. Neil grabbed him by the shoulder and shook his head.

"We can't go there," Neil said. "If the kidnappers have been watching us, they might know where you go. And we need to chat someplace out of the way, secluded." He turned Larry around and started walking.

Larry looked back over his shoulder with a tinge of sadness. Guade-Latte was the closest caffeine fix to the hotel. If he knew Neil, there was going to be a lot of walking before he found a place that was far enough away to feel safe. Larry was right. They doubled back twice, went in circles, stopped in two doorways, got on the subway for three stops, doubled-back one stop . . . and finally found a tiny café tucked into an alleyway.

By this time, Larry looked like a hiker who'd been lost in the desert for a month. He practically crawled to the counter and ordered the largest coffee he could. Then he ordered three more and carried them like a treasure over to the corner table Neil had selected. Neil was taking in the whole place with a suspicious gaze. A few patrons lined up, ordered and left. Only a handful of other people were sitting down, and they seemed lost in their copies of *La Reforma* newspaper. Larry slurped back his first cup of coffee and sat back with a deep, satisfied sigh.

"This coffee is amazing!" he said with a low whistle.

"I'll take your word for it," Neil said as he sipped his herbal tea. Larry was sometimes amazed at how little sleep Neil got, and how hard he worked, without ever drinking anything stronger than tea. Then again, Neil was so high-strung that coffee might make him explode.

"So far, all we know is that Isabella is being held in a garbage dump," Neil said.

"Or was," Larry suggested.

"And XT could be Xipe Totec."

"Or not. And Isabella wanted you to visit some farmer's collective with her today."

"Flower collective," Neil said. "But she hadn't told me the name of the place. Jones might know, but he's on that retreat up north."

"I'm not volunteering to call him," Larry said with a shiver. "That guy could beat me up through the phone."

"It doesn't matter. Isabella said he was unreachable."

"And Jones let her stay here without him?"

Neil scowled. "She said she had arranged another chaperone. She told me it was a surprise."

"Maybe she was lying so Jones would let her stay."

Neil cringed. If that were true he'd failed her even more deeply than he'd thought. Why couldn't he have seen it coming? If only the twins had opened that fridge earlier! He pushed those thoughts out of his head and tried to concentrate.

"So where are the city's garbage dumps?" Neil asked.

"I was afraid you were going to ask that."

"It's probably not the sort of thing that's listed in the guidebooks, even yours—unless there's a café nearby."

Larry pulled out his mini foldout map. There were hundreds of cafés and hotels listed all over the city, but no garbage dumps. Larry let his eyes wander over the area just outside the enormous downtown, with its never-ending maze of streets and buildings. "Wait a minute." Larry rested his finger on a vast grey space at the very edge of the map. The word Nezahualcóyotl was written across in red ink. "What's this?"

Neil looked at where Larry's finger had stopped. "I don't know. Maybe a park or a nature reserve?"

Larry took the map and walked over to the young woman behind counter. "Excuse me señorita," he said in his best Spanish, "but what is this place?"

"Nezahualcóyotl is a suburb of sorts, but this big grey area is a *vertedero*, a 'dump' for the *basura* . . . the 'garbage.'"

"All of this?" Larry asked incredulously. "It's huge."

"*Sí*, It is very, very large. It has been the dump for many years. It was once a giant lake, but it was drained many years ago. Now there is just garbage."

Larry let out a low whistle. "Wow, and *gracias*. Oh, and one more coffee, *por favor*."

Neil was as dumbfounded as Larry at the discovery.

"I can't believe you couldn't smell the dump from our hotel," Larry said.

"It's not exactly close," Neil replied. He paused, and went on sheepishly. "And I have to admit that the smog here has been somewhat dampening my senses." It seemed to pain Neil to admit anything like an Achilles' heel—or nose.

"Mucus and particulate matter is clogging your nose pipe?"

"Not completely, but thanks for the lovely image."

"No prob."

"Let's just say the thin mountain air and smog aren't helping, especially when we're outside. Anyway, is this nessa-co-at-all landfill on the subway?"

Larry looked at the map again. "The Canal de San Juan stop isn't far. But maybe we should wait for Naka-mura. If he caught a flight last night he should be here soon. I can't imagine the city dump is in a great part of town . . . and maybe he can find some local security goons to go along with us."

"Sure, and then maybe he can help us find a trail that's even colder than it is already. Don't forget that we have another match tomorrow. I can't lose that or they'll be sending us more than her hair in an envelope . . ." Neil stopped. He wanted to stay cool, to act tough, but this last remark made him feel strange. He was angry with himself for even thinking it, and a little sick to his stomach that he'd said it out loud. "I just mean that we need to follow our leads when we get them," he continued in a softer voice.

"All right, stubborn boy, your brain is clearly fixated on trash. Let's go sift through some."

CHAPTER ELEVEN

IN-FLIGHT ENTERTAINMENT

Somewhere over Colorado a loud crash woke Sean Nakamura from his sleep. He'd been having a dream about being a matador in an enormous bull ring. But instead of bulls, Nakamura was being attacked by goats. Goat after goat ran at him, horns first. He attempted to lure them away with his red cape, but the goats kept snapping at the cloth, tearing it to shreds. Eventually they butted him to the dirt and began to pound him with their hooves. Just as their bleating turned to laughter the crash came and Nakamura woke up.

The crash turned out to be his own food tray, which he must have knocked over with his wild swinging and kicking.

Angel Jícama was awake next to him, chuckling. "The flight attendant delivered that while you were sleeping. It looks like you aren't getting any lunch."

Nakamura looked down at his trench coat. Luckily he'd been too tired to take it off. It was now covered with something that might have been chicken in an earlier life, covered with a red sauce that resembled poster paint.

Angel grabbed a piece of the chicken off Nakamura's coat and popped it in his mouth. He gave a swallow and grimaced. "Disgusting. I always wondered what this stuff tasted like."

"You've never tried airline food?" Nakamura couldn't believe a globetrotter like Angel had never eaten on a plane.

"I've smelled it, but I've just never actually swallowed it before. And I've certainly never risked the so-called chicken cacciatore you're wearing."

"So how does it taste, super-chef?"

"Like cardboard. Wait, no, cardboard has more texture."

"Hm. Well, maybe it's better on me than in me."

"That's certainly true. Most of this food is salt, anyway."

Nakamura brushed the rest of the food onto his tray. "You didn't smuggle in anything better, did you?"

"Homemade goat cheese. Want some?"

"Um, no, thanks. Goats are off my list at the moment." Nakamura changed the subject. "Explain why you didn't book a direct flight from Vancouver."

"By the time I decided to come, all the direct

flights were booked. Besides, I get more opportunities to try chicken cacciatore this way."

"Ha ha," Nakamura said dryly. "Two transfers? I could have driven to Mexico City faster than this."

"At least you have more quiet time to do research."

"You always look on the bright side, don't you?"

Angel smiled.

Nakamura looked down at the Mexican guidebook that he'd bought at the airport. He'd been reading a section on sports before he'd drifted off. Mexico's first bullfight had been held in 1529, just a few years after the Spanish Conquest of the Aztecs. Angel looked at the image of the matador stabbing a bloodied bull.

"Interesting, isn't it, that the conquistadors called the Aztecs barbarians, and then introduced sports such as this."

"Not a fan of bullfighting?"

"Not a fan of people being critical of others without being critical of themselves at the same time."

"The Aztecs performed human sacrifices, you know."

"And the Spanish ended that unthinkable practice by killing an awful lot of Aztecs. Ironic, don't you think?"

"You're from southern Mexico, aren't you? Oaxaca?" Nakamura asked, sensing that Angel's criticism might have a personal edge to it.

"So now this is an interrogation," Angel sighed. "Let's just say that I have travelled there many times."

"Lots of Aztecs lived in that area?"

"It's not so simple. There are many tribes and indigenous people. They have always attempted to keep their traditional ways, no matter who claims to rule over them." Angel stared out the window. "I haven't been back there in more than twenty years."

"Sounds like a hotbed for radicals, if you ask me. The sorts of radicals who try to do crazy things—like raise goats in the middle of cities."

Angel changed the subject. "Do you have any theories on Isabella's kidnapping?" Nakamura had told Angel about Isabella as they'd taxied down the runway before takeoff.

"Well, gambling is probably involved. Maybe someone has made a big bet on Neil to lose in the final and Isabella is their collateral."

"Then why send Neil a note here warning him not to come?"

"Don't know. Once we get there, I'll do some digging."

"And the XT of the notes?"

"Larry thought it could be almost any Mexican word, but maybe Xipe Totec?"

Angel nodded. "An Aztec god, and not a particularly nice one."

"That doesn't sound cheering."

"It isn't." Angel stood up to stretch his legs. "Remember that bullfighting picture, with all the blood and violence?"

"Yes." Nakamura said, picking up his tray and moving into the aisle.

"Well, that's right up Xipe's alley."

CHAPTER TWELVE

TRASH TALK AND TAMALES

Neil and Larry stepped out of the Canal de San Juan subway station. The street, like every street in Mexico City, was packed with bumper-to-bumper traffic. On one side of the street a series of buses stood idling.

"Should we grab a bus?" Larry asked.

Neil stuck his nose straight in the air. A breeze carried the distinct smell of rotting garbage and methane gas, a by-product of decaying trash.

"No. We're not far. We can walk. Follow me."

As they walked down the street Larry noticed the buildings getting more and more run down. Soon the houses were replaced by shelters made from metal or plastic sheets, supported by sticks and salvaged bits of lumber. People stared at them from makeshift windows and door-ways, wondering what could possibly have brought these two young men to this part of town. Graffiti covered every available space of wall.

Larry suddenly felt very happy that they hadn't waited to visit the dump. Daylight was clearly their friend. He'd lived in some pretty run down parts of Vancouver, but this was something else entirely.

"Neil, let's make this visit fast."

Neil didn't say anything. He concentrated on the increasingly pungent odor. He was trying to separate the various smells that were assaulting his nose, the same way he could sit before a plate of another chef's pasta and mentally disassemble the sauce into its component parts. It was an ability that allowed him to recreate more than a few "secret recipes" in the privacy of his own kitchen.

Isabella's hair had had a distinct odor of rotting chicken. That smell should still be hanging around. This was not a search he was going to enjoy. Neil stopped in the middle of the street and took a big sniff. "Over there," he said, pointing down a wide, filthy boulevard. A gigantic dump truck rumbled past.

Larry watched the truck travel down the dirt street toward a giant metal gate, covered with barbed wire. To the side, a queue of donkey carts waited their turn to enter.

"This is cheerful," Larry said with a gulp.

Neil walked up to the metal gate. Another dump truck rumbled past and made its way in, waved on by a guard who sat in a hut just inside the entrance. Peering past him, Larry and Neil got their first look at the dump. It was like a vision of hell. A vast, flat expanse of garbage stretched as far as the eye could see, a sea of plastic, metal, wood, rotting food, bones. Wind swept up paper and plastic bags, forming tiny tornados that spun and disappeared constantly. Methane gas poured out of metal pipes that stuck up in regular intervals over the landscape.

They watched as one donkey cart, laden with hundreds of plastic bottles, came toward them. The driver gave a polite smile and wave to the Flambés as she exited the dump. As soon as she turned the corner an empty cart made its way inside. The driver stopped and got into an animated conversation with the guard. The conversation ended with the driver angrily throwing a few loose bills at the guard, who angrily waved him into the dump.

"What was that about?" Neil asked.

"Recycling."

"Seriously?"

"Seriously. The man on the donkey cart wants to go inside and look for recyclable stuff that's been thrown out with the trash. Then he can sell the stuff at a recycling depot."

"But the guard wanted a little payoff?"

"You got it, amigo."

Neil pulled out a few bills and handed them to Larry. "You haggle. I'm going in to look around." Neil walked right past the guard, who began to yell and gesture at him.

"That attitude is going to cost us more, you know!" Larry yelled after him. Larry waved half the bills at the guard, who stopped yelling but rubbed his fingers together in the universal sign for "it's going to take more than that."

Inside the dump, Neil fought the urge to throw up. The smells were overwhelming. The odor of a giant dump of chicken carcasses was still present, but where was it coming from? The swirling winds confused him a

bit. He looked to his left. About a hundred feet away was an abandoned transport truck. As Neil walked over, the smell grew stronger and stronger. On the side of the truck was a cartoon chicken with its eyes rolling together and the words Pollo Polo.

The truck stank. Neil pinched his nostrils together and opened the metal doors. The inside was dusty and dirty. It was also empty. Neil stepped inside to take a closer look. He could make out shoeprints in the dust and a clear track that suggested something, or someone, had been dragged across the floor. Neil got down on his knees. Mixed in with the smell of rotting chicken was just the faintest trace of Isabella's lavender perfume. She had been here! Neil sniffed around the rest of the container. There was an area near the wall where the dirt had been brushed aside. Isabella must have been sitting in this spot before being dragged to the door. He looked for signs of blood, and thankfully found none.

Neil walked slowly back to the doors, which swung menacingly in the rising wind. He stopped. There was another smell, right by the door. Neil sniffed. It smelled like some kind of oil, maybe corn oil. He sniffed again. Was it fresh, or leftover from some other shipment? He sniffed some more. Definitely corn oil. But why?

The clang of one of the doors slamming shut shook him from his thoughts. The last thing Neil wanted was to be trapped inside. He had no idea if Larry had even seen him enter the container. He ran at full speed and hurled himself through the opening just as the wind slammed the second door shut. He spilled out onto the ground and rolled, somehow ending up with an old plastic tarp wrapped around his body. He lay completely immobile for a good five minutes until Larry eventually walked up with an enormous smile.

"You look like a giant trash enchilada!" he laughed.

"If you don't get me out of this, I'll make you look like a boiled tamale!"

"Not gonna happen if you can't move your arms, cousin." Larry crossed his arms and grinned.

Neil stopped struggling. "Just get me out . . . please."

Larry unfurled Neil.

"She was here," Neil said as they made their way back to the entrance.

"Any clue where she is now?"

"Not really. I know she was pulled or dragged out of the container." He looked at the series of donkey carts and trucks that flowed in and out of the dump. "Maybe we could ask the guard."

"I already asked him if he'd seen a beautiful young woman around here, or anything else suspicious."

"What did he say?"

"That there was nothing beautiful here, and everything was suspicious."

"Very helpful."

"I asked the donkey drivers as well. They said they hadn't seen anything. Maybe you could sniff a couple of the donkeys and see if they're wearing any perfume?"

Neil did sniff the carts as closely as he could as their drivers raced past. He didn't smell anything but donkey and sweat. He and Larry headed back to the subway. Then a smell did hit Neil, and he actually staggered in his tracks. It was a smell he'd never expected in a place like this.

"Amazing!" he said in an awed whisper.

"What?" Larry said, but Neil was off like a shot.

"Hey, wait up!" Larry called as he ran after him. "You've got to stop running away from me like that!"

Neil turned down a side street. The smell was coming from a terra-cotta house at the very end. The front of the house had a giant open window with no glass and a doorway with no door. The smell coming through those openings was a mixture of cream, nuts and herbs, but he could also make out chilies, apples, pears . . . and they were blending together perfectly.

Neil peered inside. Five women were sitting around a table, cutting chilies, fruits, chicken, chocolate, tomatoes, onions and garlic. Another woman was standing in front of a small stove, stirring a brilliant white sauce in a banged up metal pan. The smell drew Neil into the kitchen like a fish on a hook.

"What is that?" he said, when he snapped out of his trance and realized he was standing right next to the woman at the stove.

The woman responded in perfect English. "It's *chiles en nogada*. Chilies cooked in a walnut sauce. It's a traditional dish, and very good."

Neil could tell from the smell that she was telling the truth. "Is that a poblano chili?"

"*Sí*, it is very mild but very tasty. We stuff it with a *picadillo*, a sauce with meat, and some spices and fruits. My cousins are making the ingredients right now in the dining room. Here, have a taste." She broke off a bit of one chili, and lifted a spoonful to Neil's lips. He closed his eyes and let the delicate combination rest on his tongue. Then he took a bite and the full power of the chili broke through the cream.

Neil's nose and his mouth were in perfect agreement. This was wonderful! But gourmet food in this place? "Why aren't you running a restaurant downtown?" Neil asked.

The woman gave a calm smile that instantly reminded Neil of Angel. "We are just people who cook the foods of our mothers and fathers and their mothers and fathers, and we are needed here."

"But you're making enough to feed an army."

"Lunch. We sell meals at lunchtime to the workers at the dump. There's also a recycling factory near here. We make very good money."

"And spend it on what? Clearly not new cooking pans." Neil looked askance at the dented and dinged pots and cooking utensils. This was worse than Chez Flambé.

The woman didn't take offense. "We spend it on programs for the poor. They come and eat after the lunch service, and they eat for free. Food is a human right. The poor should know that food can be delicious. Also, we run a school near here where the children can learn about computers and, maybe learn some English. That also costs money."

Neil nodded. He felt like a bit of an idiot. "I have a

friend you should meet someday. I think you'd hit it off. By the way, my name is Neil Flambé."

"Margarita Fresa," she said, shaking Neil's hand.

Larry came running into the restaurant, panting. "There you are!" he said to Neil. Then he stopped and smelled the aroma. "Wow. I'm famished. That smells good, whatever it is. Makes you forget about the rotting stuff down the street." Larry sat down at the table next to the women and instantly drummed up a conversation about the food. Within seconds, he was helping to chop the vegetables and was given a cup of strong coffee and some sweet empanadas.

Larry looked over at Neil, his mouth stuffed with the pastries, and gave a grin and a thumbs-up sign. Not for the first time, Neil was amazed at Larry's facility with people. Neil had been here for five minutes and had barely acknowledged the other women. He'd only spoken to Margarita because he wanted to know what she was cooking.

"That's my cousin, Larry," he explained to her. "He helps me cook in my kitchen back home. I'm a chef as well."

"I assumed as much by the way you appreciated my sauce."

"The ingredients are simple. The taste when they come together is definitely complex."

"*Gracias*. Would you like to have a seat?"

Neil took a closer look at the dining room. The tables were set beautifully, with hand stitched tablecloths and fragrant flower arrangements. The walls were covered in pretty painted tiles of deep blues and golden yellows.

"The cloths are hand-stitched by mothers who send their children to the schools," Margarita said, following Neil's gaze. "The children make the tiles. They are so proud of them when they sit down to eat."

"I didn't see any flowers in the area," Neil said, inhaling the fragrant dahlias, zinnias and lilies.

"No. Not much grows in this area, I'm afraid. But the flowers come from a flower collective just south of the city."

Neil's ears perked up. "Did you say flower collective?"

"Yes," she said. "The Xochipilli Tallo collective. They give jobs to many of the families here, and teach them how to grow flowers and food."

XT, Neil thought with a jolt. Larry glanced at him as well.

"Show-chipilli tie-oh? What does that mean?" Neil asked.

"Xochipilli was a flower god. *Tallo* is the stalk or stem of a plant," Larry translated.

"Yes," Margarita nodded. "It has a double meaning, as well. The collective grows flowers, but also wants the young people who work there to grow straight and strong. *Tallo*, you see? We also wish to do this through the money our *taberna* raises for the children."

"*Taberna?*"

"*Sí*, tavern or cantina. A small restaurant of sorts."

"What's the name of your *taberna?*"

"The Xochipilli Taberna."

"The same name?"

"Of course. The flower collective is run by my sister Lily."

CHAPTER THIRTEEN

PERFUMED PRISONER

Isabella awoke with a smile as the scent of flowers overwhelmed her. She took a deep breath and opened her eyes, eager to see the blooms that smelled so delicious. Nothing but blackness met her gaze. She was blindfolded. Her smile vanished. So, she was still a prisoner. Her hands were tied behind her back, and she could feel that she was lying on a rough stone floor. It was much cooler here than anywhere else she'd been in Mexico . . . assuming she was still in Mexico. An occasional drip of water echoed off in the distance.

But what a glorious aroma! It was as far away from the back of the donkey cart as she could get. The rolling and rocking of the cart must have lulled her into a deep sleep. She didn't remember arriving at wherever she was now.

"Hello," Isabella yelled and the sound echoed off the walls. Her gag had fallen off, or been taken off, although her jaw still ached as if it were there. "HELP ME!" she yelled.

She heard the creaking hinges of a metal door and then footsteps. The footsteps came across a stone floor and stopped right next to her. A man's voice spoke.

"I see you are awake. Did I not tell you that you would be headed for a better life? This is it—a life of flowers and feasts." The voice belonged to the same man who had cut her hair in the hot metal box.

"How can I know what my new life looks like with this stupid cloth on my face?"

To her surprise, the blindfold was immediately removed. Isabella looked into the smiling face of a man she had never seen before. He was quite thin and short, and possibly young, with tanned leathery skin, dark hair, a mustache and wrinkled eyes. He was also well groomed, and wearing a silk suit. He could have fit in among the tradesman begging for odd jobs, or the coffee drinking lawyers and businessmen at the downtown cafés.

"Thank you," she said. The man bowed.

She took a quick look at the room. It was a cave of some kind, with walls and ceiling fashioned from huge slabs of stone. The room was filled with the most amazing and fragrant assortment of flowers. It smelled like a florist's shop just before Valentine's Day. A *florist's shop with bars*, Isabella thought angrily.

She turned on the man. "Who are you? Why have you brought me here?"

"I am merely a servant—here to ensure you are treated like royalty."

"Whom do you serve? What are you talking about? I am not royalty."

"You must be hungry," the man said, ignoring her questions. "We have prepared a feast. Since you were asleep I took the liberty of choosing some wonderful food for you. Soon we will bring a proper chef here to serve you and then you can have any food you wish."

"I wish to be set free."

"That wish will come true beyond your wildest dreams." The man began to walk back toward the door.

"I wish to be set free now."

Isabella stood up to lunge at the man and noticed for the first time that her ankle was held by an iron chain. The chain was anchored to a giant round stone in the middle of the room. The stone had some words and images carved into it, but the language wasn't one Isabella recognized.

"You are free to eat and to walk about this place, within limits," the man said, standing just out of her reach. She sank to the floor, dejected and still fuming.

The man clapped and two young women dressed in white robes walked through the door, carrying trays of fruits, heaps of corn cakes, honey-sweetened corn porridge, vanilla-scented mugs of warm cocoa, and some kind of roasted chilies in a cream sauce.

Isabella had not eaten in days, or longer—it was difficult for her to reconstruct the time since her kidnapping.

The women lay the food down on the stone slab. It smelled amazing. Still, she hesitated. Seeing her caution, the man grabbed a chili and took a large bite. Then he took a long swig from a mug of cocoa. "It is all perfectly safe and, I can assure you, delicious."

He held up a corn cake and Isabella grabbed it. She ate it greedily. It was fabulous. Raw corn would have tasted good to her right now, but whoever had made this was a very good chef. She washed down the cake with a drink of the warm cocoa. It wasn't as sweet as the hot chocolate she had grown up with in Italy, but it was very rich and thick and the warmth spread through her body all the way to her toes.

The man smiled again. "After you have dined, these women will draw you a bath. We have new clothes to replace your filthy rags."

One of the young women held a brilliant white robe up to Isabella. The sleeves and hem of the skirt were a deep red. It was the perfect size. The woman placed a gorgeous turquoise necklace around the collar and two bright red sandals at the fringe. The women didn't speak. Isabella was about to address them when the man clapped his hands again. They bowed and left, and as Isabella watched them go, she wondered if they'd been drugged. They seemed so calm and dazed.

"I will leave you to finish your meal." The man's voice interrupted her thoughts. "When you are ready for your bath just call and the women will return to aid you." He turned to walk away then stopped. "There is one more thing I must do before I leave you." He walked behind Isabella, placing his hand on her shoulder to prevent her from moving. He pulled her long hair with his free hand and then must have clutched the end in his mouth. She heard the snip of scissors and felt the weight of her hair against her back.

"Gracias, señorita," the man said with a bow and, clutching the lock of her hair, he walked out.

Isabella watched him with gritted teeth. Any gratitude he'd gained through his politeness or the food was lost with this indignity. She threw a corn cake at him, just missing his head. It splattered against the wall.

The door closed and she heard a key turn in the lock. She threw another corn cake, which also splattered against the wall. Her energy spent, she felt her body calm down and she took a deep breath. She was alone. She was also well-fed and would soon, if she wanted, be clean again. She looked at the chain on her feet. She was also still a prisoner. What was going on? She was darned if she was going to dress in their clothes and eat their food! She kicked a tray of food and it flew in the air, strewing cocoa and cornmeal all over the room and her clothes.

How could she get out of this place? She knew Neil would be looking for her. Maybe he had even contacted the police, Jones, Nakamura, her mother. If only there was a way she could get word to them! But what would she say? "I'm in a cave . . ." But where? And why had the man let her see him? Where were they that he felt so secure? The only thing she knew was that the man called her royalty, and that he kept cutting her hair.

Her beautiful hair . . . why would they want it? Was it some kind of sick souvenir? She didn't think so. The man treated it like part of his job. Wait a minute, she thought. This was tweaking something in her memory.

There had been a famous kidnapping in Italy when she was a child—a politician's son. To prove that he was alive, the kidnappers had sent ransom notes to the family, each containing a small part of the boy's ear. She shuddered. Perhaps they didn't want to harm her, but maybe they were sending the hair along with ransom notes as a kind of proof they were holding her.

Isabella stared at the scattered food. A second later she was on her knees rubbing handfuls of the mixture into her hair.

CHAPTER FOURTEEN

XTREME

OUCH!" Neil yelled. His head banged on the roof of the tiny Volkswagen Beetle before he fell back onto the seat with a thump.

"Sorry," Margarita called from the driver's seat. "The roads outside the city, they are very bumpy."

"No kidding," Neil said, rubbing the lump that was forming on his forehead. The dusty, decrepit car had apparently been built before the age of seat belts, but Neil didn't have time to be choosy. It had taken forever to set out for the farm located an hour outside the city.

"There's another bump up ahead," Margarita called back. "Get ready!"

Neil gripped the side of the seat. He wasn't one hundred percent sure that Xochipilli Tallo was the right flower collective, but it was a coincidence he couldn't ignore. XT seemed to be popping up all over the place. Margarita's sister didn't have a phone, so they had to visit in person. She'd agreed to drive them, but only after lunch had been served.

The *taberna* had been packed with hungry customers, many in patched and re-patched jeans and T-shirts that were as thin as tissue paper. They all seemed to mix and mingle together with smiles and healthy appetites.

Neil and Larry had pitched in, prepping, cooking and serving. Apart from one disagreement, when Neil accused Margarita of using too much pomegranate, things had gone very well. They reserved enough of the food to serve the children who came after, with even more threadbare clothes and voracious appetites.

Margarita had received a huge last-minute order for corn cakes, chilies and hot cocoa. It had taken ages. Who needed so much food so fast? Finally, someone had arrived at the back door just as they were about to set off to pick it up. Neil had caught only a glimpse of the man, who was enormous. For a second he wondered if Jones had come back. Neil had peered in for a closer look but the man just grabbed the food and ran off.

Neil was pondering the *taberna*'s clientele as he and Larry sat in the back of the car. Isabella and Angel often criticized Neil for focusing on the high-end customer. "You focus too much on big recipes for big spenders, judging your success by the size of the tips rather than the look in their eyes. Happiness is found elsewhere."

Thinking about the satisfied expressions on the faces of Margarita's lunch customers, Neil wondered if they might have a point. Then he remembered the few pesos Margarita had left over after the meal service. He shuddered. Margarita was one blown gas burner or cracked water pipe away from scrounging for food herself. Neil would be better off sticking with his plans for glory, making his millions and sending Margarita a check.

He wished Isabella were here to talk to, to discuss these things.

Suddenly, his butt started to vibrate. At first he thought it might be bruising from the various potholes, but then he made out the theme from the old *Batman* TV show. Neil swiftly grabbed his cell phone and flipped it open.

"Nakamura! Took you long enough to get here," Neil said. "Did you fly the plane yourself?"

"Nice to talk to you, too. Where are you?"

"Heading to a flower farm. We think it's the one Isabella was planning to visit. How about you?"

"We just arrived at our hotel. Larry recommended the same one you're staying in."

"You won't need an alarm clock."

"What? Why?"

"You'll see. Did you say 'we'?"

"An old friend of yours came along as well. Chubby guy, likes to cook."

"Angel!" Neil said with a smile that surprised him. Two thoughts hit him at the same time. Angel was, like Neil, a lot smarter than Nakamura, and Neil hoped he could help find Isabella quickly. And, he wondered, was

Angel willing to cook? He looked over at Larry, who was taking a catnap and snoring away. Larry worked hard, but he was no Angel. "Nakamura, I'm running late. I need you to do me a favor. Isabella was staying at the Hotel Flor Hermoso. Can you take a look around there? Larry and I won't have time today."

"We'll head there right away. Any new leads on your front?"

"Maybe. I'll let you know after we visit the farm. Let's meet tonight at the hotel and compare notes."

"Deal. And Nose?"

"Yeah?"

"Be careful." Nakamura hung up.

Neil flipped his phone shut. Margarita had just driven past a row of gigantic agave cactus plants and through a wooden gate with Xochipilli Tallo painted overhead. She slammed on the breaks and crossed herself hurriedly.

Neil rolled down his window. Hot air rushed in, carrying with it the acrid smell of smoke. Neil looked ahead. A black cloud was billowing over the hollowed shells of a row of burned out greenhouses.

CHAPTER FIFTEEN

NOTES

Neil slumped in his chair and stared across the glass table at Sean Nakamura and Angel Jícama. He was exhausted and still stank of smoke. He and Larry had worked their hardest to help Margarita put out the fire, but everything at the farm—flowers and buildings—had gone up in flames. There were, thank goodness, no bodies in the ashes.

Everyone must have escaped, either voluntarily or by force, before the farm was torched. Why? Neil wondered. Was the fire meant to destroy evidence? Had Isabella been taken there after leaving the dump? Hundreds of questions swirled in his head.

He knew one thing for sure: the fire had been no accident. Neil could smell that the entire place had been drenched with corn oil and gasoline. It was like a grease fire in a kitchen—water would only make it worse. Margarita ended up collapsing on the ground, in tears. Larry had gently lifted her into the back seat of the car.

When the police had arrived to take

statements, Neil had been tempted to tell them why they were there, and what they were looking for, but he didn't. Larry's warnings scared him off that plan. They'd driven Margarita back to her restaurant, and then taken the subway back to the hotel.

"Not telling the cops was probably a good idea," Nakamura admitted reluctantly as they sat together in the hotel restaurant. "It's best not to talk to anyone else until we have some idea of who XT is."

Neil nodded, and coughed.

Nakamura leafed through the pages of his notebook. "We didn't really find anything in Isabella's room that would give us any clues. It hadn't been disturbed or ransacked."

"No fingerprints or physical evidence?" Neil asked.

Nakamura nodded. "Isabella's passport and some jewellery were still locked in the safe."

"So no robbery, apparently—just a kidnapping," Angel said.

"But why no ransom demands?" Neil asked. "Last time I checked, a kidnapping is designed to extort money. Has Isabella's mom heard anything?"

"I haven't been able to reach her. She still lives in Italy, and my calls kept getting bounced to her message service. Isabella left a datebook behind in her room: Jones is in the Arctic, it says, and her mother is at some weird New Age spiritual retreat in the Alps. I have the Italian police trying to track her down."

"So, as far as we know, I'm the only one who's received a note?"

"As far as we know. My working theory is that the

kidnappers are using her as leverage to make sure that you lose in the final. They'll lay a big bet against you and win. But while there are lots of bets on you to win and lots on you to lose—"

Neil looked annoyed.

"It could happen you know," Angel said.

"I know nothing of the kind," Neil said.

Nakamura continued. "While those bets do exist, there's not a large single bet that could lead us to a particular gambler."

"Of course," Angel chimed in, "it could also be that the gambler is going to hold off betting until right before the final. You make it, then he or she bets a large chunk of change on you to lose. That kind of bet wouldn't look out of the ordinary."

"But I need to win," Neil said sulkily. He pushed his water across the glass tabletop, watching as it left a trail of condensation. The water had been on the table when they sat down, but it was just one more thing in this city that Neil couldn't trust. He had been told not to drink anything but bottled water. All the seismic activity in Mexico City repeatedly cracked the water lines and underground pipes, making it next to impossible for city officials to guarantee a water supply that wasn't contaminated by dirty ground water or even sewage.

Larry had gone in search of a waiter, and returned munching on a tray of complimentary peanuts and nacho chips. "The kitchen opens in half an hour, but Manuel says he'll be here with some chips and

peanuts for you guys, too. These are good!"

"I'll take your word for it," Nakamura said as he reached, too late, for the last chip.

"I guess you'll have to." Larry smiled as he tossed the chip into his mouth. Then he grabbed Neil's glass of water and chugged. "They are salty, I'll grant you that."

"You're not supposed to drink the tap water!" Neil said.

"Whatever," Larry shrugged. "I swallowed enough water fighting that fire today to drown a fish, so one more glass isn't going to do any harm."

Neil just shook his head. "You're the one who told me about Montezuma's revenge!"

"Revenge?" Nakamura asked.

Larry nodded. "Montezuma was the last Aztec emperor. At first he welcomed the Spanish conquistadors. They thanked him by massacring his troops, raiding his treasuries and forcing him and his people to convert to their religion and political structure."

Neil looked at the empty glass. "Foreigners who come to Mexico and drink the water end up with horrible stomach cramps, nausea and diarrhea. The revenge is really bacteria in the city's untreated water."

"Yech." Nakamura pushed away his glass of water.

Larry shrugged.

"So where do we all head tomorrow?" Neil asked.

"You worry about your duel," Nakamura said.

"Competi . . . oh, never mind," Neil said with frustration.

"Quack," Larry added, tossing a handful of peanuts into his mouth and chewing happily.

"I'll take a look at that hair specimen with my lab stuff and see if there are any other clues there. Angel, how about you?"

"I'll ride the subway. Perhaps the kidnappers will return there."

Neil felt a pang. He was hoping Angel would at least come to watch the competition. But finding Isabella was more important . . . wasn't it?

"Does anyone have any idea who I'm facing tomorrow?" Neil asked.

Nakamura and Angel took a sideways glance at each other, but neither answered. The contestants for the first round of the *Azteca* had been a closely guarded secret. There had been rumors galore, of course, but it wasn't until the first round was underway that all the chefs' identities were revealed. There had been a few announced ahead of time for PR reasons, and Neil had been one of those. "Come see the freak show as the Boy Wonderbread takes off his diaper long enough to barbeque a salmon!" Larry had said, when the first ads hit the Food Network.

"Don't forget his sidekick, Superham," Neil had tossed back.

But the other chefs—the "challengers" as the organizers dubbed them—had remained anonymous. Neil had been running around Mexico City and the surrounding area ever since his first-round win, so he was completely out of the loop.

"I said, does anyone know my opponent tomorrow?"

Angel coughed. The TV broadcast of the first-round had aired earlier that afternoon. Nakamura and Angel had watched in the hotel to see if the cameras had caught any sign of Isabella's departure. They hadn't, but the show had revealed some significant news.

"Do you want to tell him," Nakamura whispered to Angel, "or should I?"

"Tell me what?" Neil said, sitting forward in his chair.

Angel strummed his fingers on the table. He spoke calmly as he could. "Tomorrow, Neil, you're facing . . . how shall I put this? You're facing someone who knows a thing or two about teaching Neil Flambé a cooking lesson."

Neil stood up so fast his chair slid back and crashed against another table, toppling the vase and spilling water all over the floor. "You don't mean?"

"Yes, I'm afraid I do. Tomorrow you're facing Giselle Calabaza."

CHAPTER SIXTEEN

NANNY NIGHTMARE

Giselle Calabaza was dressed all in black as she strutted menacingly to the center of the Plaza de Santo Domingo. Two identical work stations had been set up in the middle of the historic square. The cameras stood at the ready. Her rapid footsteps echoed off the stuccoed colonnades of the buildings that lined the square. She looked just like a gunfighter from an old western movie. And in a way, she was. Giselle hated Neil Flambé with a heat that could ignite a gas oven. That hardly made her a member of an endangered species, but the difference between Giselle and Neil's other enemies was that she had been Neil's nanny.

"Ah, sweet little Neil Flambé," she said with a scowl, grabbing a large knife and honing it rapidly on a metal

110

rod. "I see you put your baby bottle down long enough to beat that amateur Pimento."

Neil glared back with an equally intense loathing. "And I'm looking forward to making it two amateurs in a row. Any original ideas on how I should do that?"

"Why don't you run back to mummy and daddy and cry into their aprons, you freak." She walked to her station and stabbed the knife into her cutting board with a loud thunk.

Giselle had been the nanny from hell, as far as Neil was concerned. It had seemed like such a good idea at the time, at least to Neil's parents. Margaret and Eric Flambé were aficionados of burger joints and microwave dinners, and never quite understood their son's obsession with weird foods like mango, artichoke and purple Japanese shiso leaf (whatever the heck that was!). They also worked long hours—Margaret was a lawyer, Eric an ad executive—and didn't like the idea of their little boy sautéing bean sprouts and onion over an open flame after school with no supervision.

So they advertised for a nanny, preferably someone who was also a trained chef and could be a kind of tutor. Giselle had answered the call, fresh off a job as executive chef at a big downtown hotel. She'd moved to Vancouver from her home in Latin America to make it big in the continent's most interesting culinary scene. The hotel had gone bankrupt, so she needed work.

At first, things had gone well. Giselle was a pretty good chef, and Neil picked up all sorts of tricks from her, including a quick way to fillet salmon and where to buy the best fresh herbs in the middle of winter. It sure beat

the crayons and finger paints his previous babysitters had tried in vain to keep him entertained. Giselle and Neil spent hours after school each day experimenting in the kitchen. It didn't take long, however, for Neil to realize that Giselle was no Angel Jícama. Pretty soon, he was giving her unsolicited advice—and plenty of it.

"You're not much of an expert with charcuterie, are you?" or "I'm afraido your alfredo is a bit buttery . . . again." He took Giselle's stony silence for agreement.

More stony silences followed more criticism until one day Giselle threatened to quit. Margaret upped her salary, reluctantly, and Giselle agreed to stay.

It all fell apart a week later. Gabby Gruyere, the food editor from the local paper, dropped by to do a brief human interest story on the celebrated boy chef.

Giselle saw opportunity knocking and showed up early to help Neil get ready.

"You go get cleaned up and dressed, dearie," she'd said. "I'll whip up a little snack for Gabby."

While Neil showered, Giselle prepared a complete four-course meal. It was all ready to go the second an opportunity presented itself.

Neil walked out of his room and sniffed the air. "You used too much pepper again. And is that supposed to be pheasant? It smells like leftover dog food."

Giselle clenched her fists, but stayed in the kitchen, waiting.

Gabby arrived a few minutes later and spent some time asking Neil questions about his life, food, and his family. Then she'd asked to take some pictures in the kitchen.

Giselle smoothed her outfit and took a deep breath. She was ready.

"Is that your teacher?" Gabby said, noticing the woman in the chef's outfit peeking through the crack in the kitchen door.

"No, that's just my babysitter," Neil said. He pushed open the door and looked askance at the array of pots and pans and dinner plates Giselle had prepped. "As you can tell, she's not much of a cook. But if you want, I can whip up something really good in about five minutes."

Before Giselle knew what hit her, Neil had dumped all of her food in the trash. Then he'd made a fast sweet-and-sour stir fry while Gabby happily shot pictures.

Giselle stood against the wall fuming, clutching a sharp knife in her white knuckles. Neil, oblivious, cooked away. Giselle leaned forward, raising the knife to the level of Neil's shoulder blades. She stopped. No, she thought, there's a better way—a way that wouldn't end with her in jail.

When Neil finally turned back from the stove, expertly and artistically plating the stir fry, Giselle smiled sweetly at him. "Anything I can do for you, Neil?"

"You still here?" Neil said. "Can you do the dishes while I explain the spices I used to this newspaper lady?"

Neil didn't notice the twitch in Giselle's left eye as she kept smiling. "Of course," she said, and made her way to the sink.

The next day, Neil observed some strange behavior from his caregiver. Not surprisingly, it was his nose that noticed first. Neil had just created an amazing mushroom risotto with pecorino cheese for their after-school snack.

He'd plated the dish and gone back into the kitchen to grab some fresh crusty bread, just warm from the oven. When he returned, Giselle had already cleared her plate. "That was so delicious, I just couldn't wait!" she'd said. "Although, sweetie, I would have added slightly less pecorino and a hint more saffron."

Neil bristled at the suggestion. Was she crazy? The dish had been perfect.

Later, even after she cleaned the dishes, Neil could still smell the risotto, almost as if he had just made it. He followed the scent. Giselle was sitting in the living room, watching Gordon Ramsay abuse some poor line-order cook on TV. Neil sniffed the air. The smell was coming from the front hallway. He walked across the carpet, right up to Giselle's backpack, which was propped against the wall.

He carefully undid the zipper. Inside was a thermos. The smell of his risotto clung to the surface. Just as he was about to open it, his mother came home. Neil slid the thermos back inside just as Giselle grabbed the backpack and left.

The next day, Neil had his recipe book propped open on the counter, prepping some pan-roasted garlic potatoes and steak Diane, when he saw a flash. At first he was worried that he had ignited the sauce too early, but the pan wasn't on fire. There was another flash from behind him. He swung around.

Giselle was standing at the door with her hands behind her back. "That smells wonderful, dearie," she said. "Please continue." Neil turned back. A few seconds later there was another flash. He swung around again but Giselle was gone.

There were more flashes and more missing meals, and plenty of other bits of unsolicited advice from Neil, until, a week later, Giselle didn't show up for work. Neil called his mother.

"Whatever could have happened to her?" Margaret Flambé wondered. "Neil, you stay there. I have another court date but I'll be home later."

Neil went into the kitchen to begin prepping his dinner. He was planning on making a tourtière, a traditional meat pie. He kept a jar of his own special spice mixture in the walk-in pantry his parents had had built for his seventh birthday. He examined the shelves filled with glass jars of pickles, pastas, beans and spices. His special mixtures were kept on the top shelf. He stopped cold. They were all missing. Neil put turmeric and turmeric together and got fourmeric.

"Giselle is a thief!"

She took his risotto, his spices, and she must have been taking pictures of his recipe book over his shoulder! That book was as precious to him as any secret diary. Neil marched to the living room. He was going to call Sean Nakamura, rat out his nanny, and get his spices back. He reached for the phone, but before he could dial it started ringing. Neil looked at the caller I.D. screen. The call was coming from New York City. He clicked talk.

"I'd like to speak to Neil Flambé," said the voice. "Or his parents, if they are home."

"Whom can I say is calling?" Neil said. He was so angry that he spoke through clenched teeth, sounding much older than ten.

"It's Charlie Bloom, from the TV news show *Pepper Mill*."

Neil wasn't surprised that a TV reporter was trying to reach him. Still, *Pepper Mill* was a different kind of show, "ferreting out food fraud" was its motto. Neil had once seen an episode where Bloom had surprised a street vendor in the act of doctoring his stale mustard with yellow food coloring.

"I'm his, um, butler. What do you want to talk to him about?" Neil asked, making his voice sound as grown-up as possible.

"We've got a tip that this Flambé kid has been pulling the wool over everyone's eyes. He's been going on talk shows and catering dinners, claiming he does the cooking himself. But really, he has someone else do the cooking for him!"

Neil made a fist, almost cracking the phone in his hand. "That tip wouldn't have come from someone named Giselle Calabaza, would it?"

"That's the one! She's already parlayed the story into a tell-all book deal and a new job as head chef at Bistro Bologna. Her mushroom risotto is the headline dish, and apparently, her tourtière is sublime."

"Her what!?!" Neil began to hyperventilate.

"She says she was hired as the kid's tutor to make it all look legit."

Tutor? Traitor is more like it, Neil thought.

Charlie continued. "She taught him everything he knows, and covered for his mistakes. We're planning on running the story this Friday night. Did you want to make a comment?"

Neil debated spilling the goods right then and there, telling Bloom about the stolen spices, the stolen risotto and recipes, but who was going to believe a ten-year-old? Then a more creative idea came to him. Giselle had a head-start on telling the story she wanted, but he still had a chance to head her off at the pass.

"Listen," he said to Bloom. "I'll give you a real scoop. Show up at the Flambés' apartment tomorrow afternoon with a camera crew and I'll give you an exclusive that will knock your socks off."

"An old-fashioned 'gotcha' video?" Bloom seemed intrigued.

"You got it," Neil said. "Be here at 1:30 sharp."

The next day, Neil faked a fever, cleverly hiding a prewarmed oven mitt under his pillow, and stayed home from school to prep. "I'll call every hour," his mother said, and promptly didn't. As soon as the door closed with a click, Neil was up like a shot.

By one o'clock everything was ready. Neil heard a knock on the door. "Early," he said. "Perfect." Neil put on the best "deer-in-the-headlights" look he could muster, and answered the door.

The bright lights of a camera hit him in the face.

Charlie Bloom stuck out a microphone and started asking questions, "Neil Flambé, do you really know how to cook? How much of a debt do you owe Giselle Calabaza?"

Neil shook with make-believe nerves. "I was just making a peanut butter sandwich, but my nanny isn't here so I don't know what to do next!" Neil was even able to whip up some fake tears. He looked as close to a scared child as he could manage. He ran back into the kitchen with Bloom and the camera crew in hot pursuit.

The kitchen was a disaster. Peanut butter and bread were strewn all over the counter. Jelly and bits of banana were splattered on almost every surface. It looked exactly like a kitchen that a normal ten-year-old child had destroyed. Bloom lapped it up, filming everything. Then he turned the camera back onto a quivering Neil. "Is there anything you'd like to say to your fans and to Giselle?"

Neil stopped shaking and stood up straight. "Why, yes. Yes, there is something I'd like to say . . . this!" Neil reached over to his magnetic knife rack and took down a large chef's knife. He grabbed a bowl of vegetables that he had hidden under the table. As quick as lightning he chopped the onion, carrot, potato, zucchini and mushrooms into a series of odd shapes.

Neil's fingers flew as he slid the pieces onto metal skewers, fired up his own indoor grill, slathered the veggies with a mixture of olive oil, fresh rosemary sprigs and a little salt and pepper.

Bloom and the cameraman stood with their mouths

agape as flames licked the vegetables, heating the oil and sending succulent aromas into the air. Neil turned the skewers with his right hand as he opened the oven with his left, pulling out a tray of thinly sliced chicken on skewers resting in a ginger and garlic marinade. In a flash those were on the grill as well, and the marinade was bubbling away in a separate saucepan.

Neil flipped the skewers one last time, grabbed two plates from the warming tray of the oven, and in a flash, he plated the veggies and the chicken, drizzling the dishes with a combination of the marinade reduction and olive oil. A quick burst of salt, pepper and rosemary garnish later, the plates sat on the table in front of the cameras. Neil crossed his arms with an attitude of intense satisfaction.

Charlie Bloom looked at his plate. Not only had Neil definitely made this all himself, on camera, he had also cut the veggies and chicken into letters. There, carefully and delectably laid out on the plate, was the name "Neil Flambé."

The episode never aired. Bloom made a quick call to the publisher, and Giselle's book deal evaporated into thin air. The publisher phoned Bistro Bologna, and the executive chef job vanished as well. The last time Neil had seen Giselle she was standing outside his house, throwing jars of spices through the front window. She'd disappeared before the police arrived and was soon on a plane home. She had since become a personal chef to Hernan Tirano, her country's "*El Presidente*" for life. He was apparently won over by her tourtière and mushroom risotto, and had bankrolled her career ever since. She was his hand-picked representative for the *Cocina*, and she was expected to bring glory to Tirano and the country, in that order.

Now Neil and Giselle were face to face again, and about to do battle.

"Maybe you'd like to raid my spice rack before we get started?" Neil called from his side of the plaza. "Or perhaps you'd like some skewered veggies? I have a nice selection all prepped."

"I don't need to rely on some stupid 'kid's meal' to win this battle. And as for the skewers, I've a good suggestion where you can stick those."

"I'll just pull out the ones you stuck in my back," Neil yelled. He kept his gaze locked on Giselle as he walked over to preheat his oven for the battle, but something stopped him in his tracks—the unmistakable smell of corn oil, coming straight for him.

CHAPTER SEVENTEEN

MONTEZUMA'S REVENGE

Rodrigo Hernandez marched up to Neil with an angry scowl. His clothes were saturated with the smell of oil—corn oil. Neil was certain that it was the same brand he had smelled the day before—in the empty shell of a poultry truck and at the site of a terrible fire. He stood, rooted to the spot.

Neil had never met Rodrigo face to face. He emceed the *Cocina*, but someone else handled the post-match interviews. The smell of the makeup powder and corn oil was overpowering as Rodrigo pointed a finger into Neil's chest. "I have something to say to you, Señor Neil. It is an *advertencia*, a 'warning.'"

Neil had had plenty of warnings lately. Was Rodrigo tipping his hand? Was he, perhaps, coming out in the open as the mysterious XT? Neil reached for a knife.

"Don't you ever leave my crew hanging like that again," Rodrigo spat out the words.

"What?" Neil said, dumbfounded. He let go of the knife. "What are you talking about?"

"If you don't stick around for the interviews at the end of the battle, I will personally see to it that you are handed your *culo* on a platter!" With that he turned on his heels and stormed away, leaving a trail of corn oil aroma floating in the air. Neil was shaken from his stupor by the distinct sound of a guffaw from Giselle.

"You still have the same winning way with people," she laughed. "Too bad for Rodrigo that I'll be the one serving your butt on a platter."

Larry came up behind Neil. "Don't let them intimidate you, cousin. I'm here for you." Larry followed this with a rolling belch.

"What took you so long?" Neil said. He'd left Larry in their room at least two hours before, and had been expecting him at the Plaza ages ago. He was about to hurl more abuse when he noticed that Larry's face was completely drained of color. That wasn't precisely true: Neil could see a slight tinge of green around his cousin's eyes. Neil had a sinking feeling in his belly.

"Where have you been?" he asked slowly.

"Um, in the bathroom, mostly," Larry said. "Let's just say my plumbing is not working any better than Mexico City's."

"I told you not to drink that water!" Neil yelled. "We have a duel starting in five minutes!"

"I'll be ready," Larry said. "I've been drinking a lot of that pink stomach stuff. . . . Wait, I gotta go again." Larry took off toward the bathrooms, calling back over his shoulder, "It should kick in any minute now."

"Five minutes until we start," Rodrigo yelled through the microphone.

Neil stood there all alone. The waiters wheeled the wooden boxes into place. Rodrigo adjusted his tie and allowed the makeup artist to add a last-minute bit of powder to his forehead. The crowd surrounding the work stations buzzed with anticipation.

Neil sniffed. The secret ingredient was going to be turkey. Of course it was. Turkey was a staple of the Aztec diet—a bird that had been domesticated here thousands of years before anyone from Europe had even heard of it. It was also an ingredient, Neil knew, Giselle was talented at preparing. This was not going to be a slam dunk.

Rodrigo stepped up to the microphone. The studio lights hummed to life. Neil glanced toward the bathrooms. Larry was nowhere to be seen. It looked like he was going to have to fight this battle alone. The cameras started recording and Rodrigo began his spiel, working the crowd and signaling for the waiters to unlock the treasure chests. Neil stood there, a wave of anxiety and anger rolling up and down his spine. If he failed, he was going to be broke, and Isabella was quite possibly going to be killed. Neil didn't want to think about that. He was going to have to suck it up and work like crazy. He was Neil Flambé, after all.

Rodrigo ended his speech in full voice, "Today's secret ingredient is *guajolote*, 'wild turkey'!"

The waiters turned their keys and the locks fell away.

"Revenge will be mine," Giselle cackled as she ran back to her cutting board clutching a plump pink turkey.

Neil ran over and reached inside his box. There was no envelope this time, just vegetables and an enormous pink bird. Cooking it whole would take more than an hour. Chopping it up would take so long he wouldn't have time to properly prepare anything else. Neil's heart fell. He just stood there, too afraid and overwhelmed to figure out what to do next. Just then he heard a voice behind him say, "Neil, I think we should get to work."

Neil turned around to see Angel Jícama wearing Larry's chef jacket. It was way too small and Angel hadn't even attempted to do up the buttons, but he was wearing a smile and holding a large meat cleaver. Neil was too shocked to even speak. He had cooked so often with Angel in the past, and had dreamed of working with him in the heat of battle.

"Larry seemed a little under the weather at the café

this morning," Angel explained. "I figured it made sense to come here just in case."

Neil nodded dumbly.

"I am only here to help you cook, not to guarantee a victory. I still do not approve of these silly displays. But we are losing time. So, chef, what do you have in mind for our traditional turkey?"

Traditional. That was exactly the word that had popped into Neil's head. He looked straight at Angel and said one word, "tamales."

Angel smiled approvingly. "I will prepare the masa dough. I have an old family recipe that will work just fine." Neil had used masa many times and loved its grainy texture and slightly sweet flavor. It's a special kind of flour made from corn kernels that have been soaked in limewater. The lime changes the corn's molecular structure, making it one of the most nutritious flours in the world. Neil knew Angel would be able to extract every bit of flavor.

"Hand me that cleaver, sous-chef Jícama. I'm going to get that turkey ready for some seriously mind-blowing filling."

Tamales are the simplest and one of the most common foods in Mexico. They are basically a combination of meat and dough, wrapped in damp corn husks and steamed until the filling becomes firm. There was no time to waste if they were going to be done before the final buzzer.

Neil started hacking the turkey into a jumble of legs, thighs, breasts, skin and bone. He was practically whistling as he threw the parts into a preheated pressure cooker along with some onions, spices, fresh chilies and garlic. He covered it all with water, closed the lid and set the timer for fifteen minutes. As soon as it went off he'd rip the meat off the bones, preparing it for the filling. Then he'd spread the masa dough on the corn husk, place some of the turkey in the middle, fold it all together, tie it tight and quick-steam the tamales in the leftover turkey broth.

It was a funny thing. Having Angel by his side made Neil completely forget that he was in a competition. He would steal sideways glances, watching in awe as Angel masterfully slipped the seeds from fresh arbol chilies and diced the flesh into minuscule bits. He added them to the dough. They would dissolve in the intense cooking process for the tamales, spreading their potent spicy heat through the entire filling, but not burning the judges' tongues.

"I've got the corn husks soaking in a pot so they won't dry out," Neil called to Angel, who nodded. "We can start prepping the side dishes." Neil began chopping vegetables, more chilies, herbs, onions and tomatoes as he spoke. In a flash he had prepared three salsa dips— red, green and white—and arranged them on a platter in the pattern of the Mexican flag.

"Very artistic," Angel said.

"Thanks," Neil said, with a broad grin. "A fresh corn soup would be a good starter."

"We can add the extra bits of turkey to that for a bit of complexity."

Neil nodded. "And we could make a nice hot drink for the side. What's that corn-based one you used to make?"

"You mean *champurrado*," Angel smiled. "A corn

base with chocolate, with just a hint of sugar and vanilla. Tasty and simple."

Simple. That was always Angel's mantra. Neil couldn't believe he was actually making the type of uncomplicated food Angel was always pushing him to cook. Neil stole a glance at Giselle, who was making a five-layered turkey and Cotija cheese quesadilla. She was mounding the layers incredibly high on a tiny plate. Neil also noticed that she was using alternating layers of green chilies and red peppers to mimic the look of the Mexican flag!

Neil looked at his plate of dips. He'd stupidly left it to the side of his counter, in plain view of Giselle. He ground his teeth. "You thief!" he exclaimed.

Giselle glared at him. "I'm serving first, so guess who the judges will think is a thief?" She waved her hand over her quesadilla, sending its aroma Neil's way.

Neil suppressed a smile. Yes, the judges were going to find some flash in Giselle's presentation, but Neil could also tell that she had undercooked the peppers. That was throwing the flavors in her dish out of balance. An idea occurred to him. If Giselle was still pinching more than salt, perhaps he could get her to pinch something else. Hmmm.

He was interrupted by the timer announcing that the turkey was ready. Neil deftly pulled the bird from the broth and began tearing the meat into tiny bits. He and Angel rolled tamale after tamale. Within minutes, they had made at least sixty, and they threw these back in the pressure cooker and closed the lid. Each was subtly different in spice. Served together they would be an edible symphony.

"Perfect timing," Neil said. "They'll be ready to put on the plate and will still be piping hot for the judges."

Neil and Angel prepped more side dishes: fried beans and a crisp turkey and fresh herb salad.

Neil looked at Giselle, who was panicking a bit as she attempted to keep her quesadilla towers from collapsing and rushed to plate her incredibly convoluted mint-vanilla-prickly-pear and guava sorbet. She yelled at her assistant, "Can't you even fry a proper sweet potato, you insect?"

Neil flipped some fried chilies and tamales onto a paper towel to soak up the tiny amount of extra grease. Angel mounded the fresh herbs and turkey onto the plates. Neil artfully laid the fried chilies and tortilla strips on top. They grabbed the tamales, put a dozen on each plate and stood back to admire their work.

"Finished," Angel smiled. "And good work, Neil."

"Five more minutes!" Rodrigo called out.

"Actually, time for one more special dish," Neil said. He took the few extra bits of the toppings and grabbed a lump of leftover masa dough. He carefully placed crisp tortillas and chilies around the mounded lumps, and within a second he had a dish that looked almost exactly like a chihuahua. He slid the plate to the side of his counter.

Sure enough, Giselle caught sight of the last-second attention-grabber and rushed to make one of her own. The final buzzer went just as she set two fried Mexican pastries, or churros, onto the plate in the shape of a bone. Then she smiled an evil smile and refused to shake Neil's hand.

"Now let your babysitter teach you a lesson," she sneered.

Rodrigo stepped back into the spotlight. "Chef Calabaza will present first!"

The judges praised the effort she had put into the arrangement of so many turkey-inspired combinations. But they also criticized the sometimes muddled taste sensations, and her over complicated approach to the quesadillas, at least one of which was leaning like a Mexico City office tower after an earthquake. But she had done well. Neil was hoping his last-second gambit would give him the edge he needed to turn a close call into a rout.

Giselle brought out her dessert, and with a grand smile, announced "Chihuahua and Churros Calabaza!" The announcement was met with silence. One of the judges was a well-known history professor named Pablo Perro. He had been praising Giselle's use of local ingredients and knowledge of things Mexican, such as the flag, but he looked at the dish with horror. "Is this supposed to be a joke?" he said. He dropped his spoon and pushed his plate as far away as he could. The other judges did the same.

Giselle's face fell. She swung her head around to

look at Neil, who was leaning against his workstation wearing a broad smile. Thanks to Larry's constant lectures, Neil knew that one of the features of the ancient Aztec diet was a small hairless dog. For the modern Mexican it had become a cultural cliché that didn't always go over so well, especially when paired with food. "Serving dog would be a major fur paw. Get it? *Fur* paw!" Larry had said.

Neil's puppy dish had long since disappeared, dumped into the trash just before the final buzzer. Giselle picked up a plate of her wasted dessert and threw it as hard as she could. Neil ducked as the dish flew over his head and shattered against the paving stones. Giselle stormed off as Neil presented his dishes, by now a mere formality in confirming the victory.

Neil accepted the congratulations of the judges and then turned to face Angel, who was, to Neil's surprise, frowning. "You didn't even have the confidence in your skills to let the judges decide?"

"Confidence is not something I lack," Neil said matter-of-factly. "But we won, and it served her right, the thief. So spare me the lecture, please."

Angel shook his head, as he had a thousand times since first encountering Neil. He was about to launch into a short lecture on the importance of humility when Larry returned from his sojourn to the land of the porta-potties.

"You don't look so hot," Neil said. "I guess you and Montezuma are still locked in battle?"

"No," Larry said. "The pink stuff finally kicked in. But someone slipped this under the door. I was a little too preoccupied praying at the porcelain altar, shall we say, to notice until a minute ago."

He handed Neil an envelope, made of the same translucent paper as the other notes they'd received. Inside were another note and another lock of Isabella's hair. The paper smelled distinctly of corn oil. Neil looked hurriedly around the square. Rodrigo was nowhere to be seen.

CHAPTER EIGHTEEN

CHICKEN BONES AND CORN OIL

The note just says, 'You have now been warned a fourth time. Signed, XT,'" Neil said with frustration as he, Angel and Larry sat down at a patio café in the plaza. "Okay, I get that, but warnings of what exactly? I already know what I have to do—don't go to the cops and lose in the final. So why keep warning me?"

"Maybe it's just a friendly reminder?" Larry suggested.

"Well, they can save their precious paper," Neil said, crushing the brief note in his fist, and slamming his fist on the table. "I don't plan to go to the cops, or lose."

"Neil, do you want to find Isabella so you can save her or so you don't have to throw the final?" Larry asked as he sipped his coffee. His stomach was bouncing back in fine form: he'd already devoured Neil's leftover tamales and was hard at work on the churros and ice cream Giselle had abandoned in her kitchen.

"What kind of stupid question is that?" Neil asked.

"That's not an answer," Larry said. "Are you going to save her, or win so you can save the restaurant?"

"I'm going to do both, so it doesn't matter," Neil said.

"But what if we don't find her before the final?"

"Shut up."

"Also not an answer." Larry said, popping the tail of Giselle's abandoned chihuahua into his mouth. "This is pretty good. I've never had dog before—that I know of."

Angel sighed. "Let's please focus on the note and the hair. Do you notice anything else besides the corn oil?"

Neil had been rubbing the hair gently between his fingers ever since Larry had handed him the envelope, hoping to warm whatever aromatic molecules might be sticking to the delicate curls. "There's still the lavender of her perfume," Neil said. He didn't like to show it, but he was also holding onto the hair as long as he could to stay close to Isabella. He had to admit Larry's question wasn't totally stupid. Neil wasn't completely certain what he would do if Isabella was still missing a week from now.

They'd called Nakamura as soon as Neil had wrapped up his post-match interviews, and he was on his way over now with his portable forensic kit. Soon he'd be exposing the hair to all sorts of chemical analyses and tests, which might yield some new evidence, but would also destroy the unmediated connection of this hair in Neil's hand to Isabella, wherever she was.

"The corn oil is only on the enve-lope," Neil said. "As for the hair, there's also a faint scent of flowers, lilies for one. Possibly she was

being held at the flower collective before they set it on fire."

"Possibly," Angel said. "But now it's a smoldering mess."

"The hair doesn't smell like smoke, so if she was there, she was gone before the fire started burning."

"Or it was sent to you before the fire started."

"Either way, it doesn't tell us where she is now. There's also a faint smell of cocoa, and"—Neil sniffed again—"one other very faint smell. It's a little like cooked . . . bugs."

"What? Are you kidding?" Larry said.

Neil took another sniff. "No."

"Ugh. Please don't upset my stomach again," Larry said quietly. "I can barely hold down the last three tamales."

"I hope that's not what they're feeding her," Neil said.

"Please stop." Larry suppressed a gag.

"Why not feed her that?" Angel said. "Bugs are used as a great source of food protein all over the world."

"Remind me never to try your raisin cookies," Larry said, getting up. "I need to go stand by the bathrooms for a little bit, just in case." He ran off.

"I've smelled cooked bugs," Neil said, "but this isn't quite the same. Those are usually fried or baked, but these smell boiled. Not an ordinary way of getting the most flavor from them."

In the distance Larry slammed the door of a porta-potty.

Sean Nakamura walked up to the table.

"Something bugging Larry?" he asked.

Neil groaned. Even when Nakamura made an unintentional joke, he wasn't funny. "He'll be fine. What did you find out?"

"I've got some good news and some bad news. I've been doing some digging since you called. My friend on the force wants to remain anonymous, but Larry's suspicions about the *policía* Mexicana aren't unfounded." It always hurt Nakamura to admit that there were corrupt cops in the world, but he continued. "I've also done some digging into Rodrigo. His Cortez Corn Oil company isn't just sponsoring this event, it also owns the Pollo Polo poultry farm."

"Where the container at the dump was from."

Nakamura nodded. "Cortez just took over Pollo Polo a couple of weeks ago. In fact, Cortez has been buying up all sorts of food distribution companies lately."

"Interesting," Angel said.

"Maybe. Maybe not. Cortez is a multinational company. That's what they do. None of that gives them a reason to kidnap anybody."

"Anything else, like maybe something useful?" Neil asked.

"Well, once Angel told me he was going to help you cook, I decided to check out that flower collective myself. I found some empty corn oil containers in the bushes."

"Cortez Corn Oil?"

"It looks that way, though they were pretty mangled and blackened by the explosions."

"So no prints?"

"No. Now, all of this could be just a coincidence— the company is a huge supplier both here and around the world."

"Well, why don't we track down Rodrigo and ask him?" Neil said.

"That's the bad news. Rodrigo was last seen a half an hour ago."

"He's left the country?"

"In a manner of speaking," Nakamura said. "He was in a big car crash. His SUV exploded after colliding with a dump truck. He's in a coma."

As soon as news of Rodrigo's accident became public, the organizers of the *Cocina* held an emergency meeting at the head offices of the Cortez Corn Oil company. The fate of their host called the continuation of the competition into question. In the end, they decided that Jose Aciete, the vice-president of the company, would take over as both president and emcee. Aciete gave a moving speech about how important the tournament had been to Rodrigo and how much it would mean to him to go on.

Neil, Larry and Nakamura retreated to a restaurant near the hotel to wait for news of the meeting, and to see whom Neil would face in the next fight. Angel had stayed behind at the Plaza to see if he could glean any information from the TV crew about the strange envelopes or Rodrigo's involvement in any extortion scheme. "I promise to be discreet," was all he had said.

Neil was worried about asking anyone anything. He was obviously being watched. Someone seemed to even know what bathroom Larry was in at the Plaza. Neil was feeling a little creeped out.

"Why was Rodrigo rushing away from the competition at all?" Neil wondered. "He warns me not to leave early, and then takes off before the judges' verdict?"

"Maybe he was on his way to another battle," Larry said. "The traffic in this city is unbelievable. Maybe he wanted to get a head start."

"Or maybe he was heading back to the office," Nakamura offered. "Who knows? My friend on the force says the dump-truck driver seemed totally stunned. By all accounts it was an accident, pure and simple."

"That could make things worse," Neil said.

"How do you mean?"

"Let's assume Rodrigo was the mastermind behind the kidnapping. If this was an accident, then it could mean that nobody else knows where he kept Isabella." Neil felt a chill at the thought of Isabella all alone. "Maybe Rodrigo was on his way to check on her, and now no one will ever find her." His eyes began to mist and he gave an involuntary sniffle.

"Hold onto your imagination there, Nose," Nakamura said, placing a hand on Neil's shoulder. "The notes all say 'we.' It could be that Rodrigo's buddies will release her now that their leader is on life-support."

"Or Rodrigo could be completely innocent," Larry said.

"That is certainly possible," Nakamura had to admit.

"Does anyone know where Giselle has disappeared to?" Neil asked. "She seemed pretty ticked off."

"I told my contact to keep an eye out for her, but we

don't have any other way of tracking her down, I'm afraid."

"Maybe she's behind all this. She sure hates me enough," Neil said.

"You know, Neil, you should really consider trying to make more friends," Larry said. "Or maybe start wearing a bulletproof chef jacket."

"If you don't feel safe, maybe Angel could fill in for the rest of the competition."

"Sorry, Neil," Angel said, walking slowly to the table and sitting down. "I was an emergency replacement. Larry, judging by his appetite, seems ready to return." Angel nodded at the four empty nacho chip baskets in front of Larry.

"Quick, Larry, have another drink of tap water," Neil said.

Larry shook his head.

"I'll be more useful elsewhere," Angel said, "looking for Isabella while you two try to stay alive in the Cocina."

"Did you find out anything from the TV crew?" Larry asked.

"Rodrigo was the only one with access to the chests. Delivery people would drop off the food, but he placed the secret ingredients inside. Then he personally locked the chests."

"So I guess Rodrigo is back as our number-one suspect," Larry said.

Just then a waiter approached the table. "Is one of you the chef, Neil Flambé?" he asked. Neil raised his hand. "I have a message for you, señor." He handed Neil a translucent envelope with Neil's name written in red ink on the outside. Neil opened it immediately. The note said simply: "Two victories. Keep winning. XT." Neil's hands began to shake. Inside was one more lock of Isabella's hair.

"We'd better find her soon or she's going to go bald," Larry said.

"Who gave this to you?" Neil demanded, standing up and grabbing the waiter by the lapel.

"It was left at the front desk, señor. We didn't see anyone drop it off."

Neil let go of the waiter's shirt. "Sorry, um, *gracias*." He handed the man a 100-peso note. The waiter pocketed the bill and smoothed his shirt before walking away.

Neil sat down and looked at the lock of hair. "Maybe Rodrigo dropped this off before the accident." But he didn't believe it.

"Maybe," Larry said. "But the note says 'two victories.' You said you looked for him after the match, but didn't see him. How did he know you'd beaten Giselle?"

Neil took a big sniff of the curls. His eyes opened wide. "Oh, my goodness." He took another, deeper sniff to be sure. "Isabella rubbed food in her hair and mushed it in as much as possible."

"Gross," Larry said.

"No, brilliant," Neil said. "This was no accident—there's too much food."

"I repeat, gross."

Neil ignored him and concentrated on the smell. "This food is wonderful—a glorious, gourmet Mexican buffet. And I know exactly where that buffet was cooked."

CHAPTER NINETEEN

ON THE MOVE

Isabella felt a forceful shake of her shoulder. She opened her eyes slowly. "*No baño*," she said. "I don't want a bath." For two days, her two mute companions had been urging her to let them wash her in a large heated tub, but Isabella had refused to wash off the smells she had so carefully accumulated. The shaking continued and grew more insistent.

"Wake up! We must move." It was the well-dressed bricklayer, as she had come to think of him. "Hurry, we must move. Our safety depends upon it."

Isabella gave a hollow laugh. "Your safety, you mean," she said. She saw no reason to cooperate. "What's the matter?" she said acerbically. "Are the police on their way? Has your boss screwed up?"

The man knelt beside her and whispered urgently.

"You do not understand. We are in great danger if we stay here. There is a *tormenta*, a 'storm,' coming." He seemed genuinely frightened, but that didn't mean he wasn't lying. Isabella refused to budge.

"You might as well leave me here. I am not afraid of a little rain."

The man shook his head. "I cannot leave you here. You will die." He looked at the ceiling. "And then the stars and heavens will not be pleased." This struck Isabella as the strangest thing she had heard since she was abducted four days ago, and she'd heard plenty of strange things.

"What are you talking about?" she demanded. "What stars? Why are you so frightened? I can offer you more money, I am sure, than your boss. I have very rich clients who will gladly pay if you help me escape."

The bricklayer didn't say a thing. He fumbled for a set of ancient-looking keys and unlocked the iron chain that bound her to the stone slab. Isabella seized the opportunity. With one quick motion she lifted her leg and kicked him square in the groin. He doubled over and she kneed him on the chin. He fell backward, unconscious, and lay motionless on the floor. An ominous rumbling came from the ceiling. It rolled across the floors and walls, filling the room with noise. The bricklayer was right: something was happening and it wasn't going to be good.

Isabella ran across the floor through the open door. She began to push it shut. Then she hesitated.

The stairs to the outside were right behind her. A tiny sliver of daylight was coming from far away above her head. She could close the door, locking the man inside, and escape. But he had said that she would die if she stayed behind. Perhaps he wasn't lying. If so, could she leave him to the same fate? No. Isabella sighed. He was unconscious. Perhaps she could drag him here quickly, close the door and then escape.

She ran back. A hissing sound filled the room as water began pouring out from in between the stones of the ceiling. Isabella rushed back inside.

The man was heavier than she expected. Her hands were still tied, but she grasped him by the collar of his jacket and dragged with all her might. He slid a little on the wet floor. She stopped, took another breath and pulled again. The water was now starting to pour in like the ceiling was full of sprinklers. She pulled the man again and again and managed to drag him another few feet. There was no way she could get him to the door before they were both covered in water. She knelt down and slapped the man to try to wake him. He gave a groggy moan, but didn't move.

The water was now up to her ankles and rising fast. The ceiling stones groaned and creaked as if they were being pressed on by some giant beast. Isabella glanced up. It was only a matter of time before something gave way. She looked down at the man again. The water seemed to be rousing him.

"Tlaloc," he whispered, without opening his eyes. "Tlaloc is coming." He tried to stand, but reached for his forehead and fell back to the ground. Isabella had done enough research into the Aztecs to know that Tlaloc was the god of rain and storms. The man was having a delusional fit.

Isabella grabbed his arm and did her best to lift him up. He shook as he tried to support his weight on his own legs. She flung one of his arms around her shoulder before he could collapse again. "Come on, move!" she said. The water was up to their knees. The flowers and food began to swirl and float on the surface.

The man kept muttering "Tlaloc," over and over, but together they shuffled quickly toward the doorway. They passed through and the man fell forward and lay on the ground.

Isabella turned around to shut the door. The water was pouring through and she had to lean with all her might to fight against the weight of the churning pool. Finally, with a loud click, the door closed. She slammed down a large iron reinforcing bar as streams of water shot out from the cracks around the doorway. The door creaked and groaned under the tremendous pressure, but it held. Isabella let out a loud sigh and began to cry. She shook her head. She had to get a hold of herself and escape. She took a deep breath and turned toward the stairs. An enormous man was now blocking the way. He must have come down the stairs as she'd been fighting to close the door. The sunlight shone down on top of his head, distorting his features into a ghostly mask of muscle and menace. The bricklayer was standing next to him, leaning on his huge arm for balance.

"I told you Tlaloc was coming."

CHAPTER TWENTY

OIL AND WATER

Neil Flambé knew exactly where to find Margarita's Xochipilli Taberna. And as they approached, he knew, with a tight knot in his stomach, that the plume of thick black smoke they saw rising over the city was coming from that street.

"Please tell me you got the address wrong," Nakamura said.

"I'm afraid not," Neil said.

"Maybe it's some other building on fire," Larry said, unconvinced. Neil shook his head: he could smell the now all-too-familiar scent of burning corn oil and wood.

They rushed around the corner. A huge crowd had gathered in front of the burning ruins of the Xochipilli Taberna. A few of the local firefighters, or *bomberos*, stood helplessly by as the flames consumed the restaurant. They yelled to the crowd to get back.

"Why are they just standing there?"

Neil asked. Larry walked up and had a quick conversation with the closest firefighter.

"They say there's no water pressure so they can't fight the fire."

"How could that happen?" Neil was stunned. Mexico City was more modern than he had expected, and the idea of a fire department without the ability to fight a fire seemed bizarre. "Don't they have fire hydrants?"

"Yes, but they're not working right now."

"What! Why?"

"It's complicated," Larry said. "But basically, it's gravity."

"Gravity?"

"Mexico City is built on lakes and rivers and stuff, and it's sinking. They've built huge pumps to move the water uphill, but sometimes they fail and then the water rushes down again. The same thing for the sewage, I'm afraid. Kinda gross when you think about it."

"How do you know all this?" Nakamura asked.

"Let's just say that I've recently developed a keen interest in the water system." Larry belched.

"So the pumps have failed, and there's no water pressure for the firefighters?" Neil asked.

Larry nodded. "They've sent tanker trucks out to find any water they can."

Boom!

Bits of metal grate flew in the air and crashed onto the neighboring roofs. The crowd moved back a few steps, then stopped, transfixed by the spectacle of flames and smoke.

"Margarita's gas stove," Neil said, remembering how recently he'd enjoyed cooking on the old stove's burners. He hoped Margarita and her friends weren't inside. "Larry, ask them if everyone got out okay."

Larry walked over to a young boy near the back of the crowd and asked him what happened. He walked back with a concerned look on his face. "No one knows what happened. The restaurant had just served lunch and was closed."

"And Margarita and the others?"

"He says they won't know until they can get inside, and that will be a while yet."

Neil ran his fingers through his hair in frustration. He knew the food Isabella had mussed into her hair had come from the Xochipilli Taberna—he was sure of it. It was the combination of poblano chili and Margarita's own blend of spices and herbs. Leads and clues were coming at him from everywhere, but they were all going up in flames. Were Margarita and Lily somehow involved in Isabella's kidnapping? He couldn't ask them if he couldn't find them. Were Rodrigo's partners burning evidence that could lead back to him? And how could they possibly find anything in a city the size of Mexico! It was like looking for a needle in a haystack as big as Mount Everest.

"I'll go see if I can find out anything," Nakamura said. He disappeared into the crowd.

Smoke continued to pour out of the building. Finally, a few tanker trucks arrived with water and began using it to douse the roofs of the surrounding houses, lean-tos and shacks. "They're trying to contain the fire," Larry said, listening to the firefighters yell to each other over the roaring blaze. It wasn't working. "We should leave; maybe meet Angel back at the hotel." Angel had volunteered to ride the subway some more, looking for clues.

Instead of walking, Neil sat down on the side of the road and put his head in his hands. He needed a miracle, a sign, something. There were no useful leads. The police couldn't be trusted. Isabella was sending clues via her hair, but they weren't really giving Neil a heads up. He'd even tried to phone his parents. He'd left messages, but neither had called back. He looked up at the sky. "Just give me something to go on, anything," he said. Then he sank his head back into his hands and tried not to cry.

The tankers sped off, returning just minutes later, filled again. As they sprayed the houses, the intense heat turned the water quickly into steam. Soon the steam enveloped the entire block and a fine mist settled on Neil's shoulders and head.

Neil sniffed. Then he sniffed again. He lifted his head and sniffed once more, just to be sure he wasn't hallucinating. "That water, it smells like flowers— lilies . . . really fragrant lilies." He stood up and pushed his way through the crowd. The smell grew stronger the closer he got to the tankers. "Larry!" he called back. "I thought you said the water wasn't working."

"It's isn't." Larry spoke quickly with one of the firefighters. "There's a canal not far from here where they are going to fill the tankers."

"Where?"

Larry talked to the firefighter again.

"It's a long canal on the other side of the dump—an overflow for when the pumps fail or the rainy season hits."

"C'mon, Larry. We're going for a walk." Neil grabbed Larry by the arm.

"What about Nakamura?"

Neil looked around but didn't see the inspector anywhere. "We don't have time to wait for him. We need to find those flowers."

Neil looked over the giant canal. As he'd expected, or maybe just hoped, large quantities of sweet-smelling flowers were floating in the lazy currents and mini-whirlpools.

Larry sat down by the water's edge, and pulled out his map.

"The canal looks like it runs from the edge of the city and takes the water away to the northeast."

Neil thought for a second. "If we head the other way, southwest, we should see where the water and the flowers are coming from."

"That's a very good theory, but this canal runs for miles."

Neil fished a floating lily from the surface. He looked at the angular slash on the bottom of the stem. "These are cut flowers, and they're still pretty fresh. We won't have to go that far. The source is much closer. C'mon, let's get moving."

The countryside started off flat, but soon mounds of grassy earth rose up next to the canal. All the while more flowers drifted by lazily.

They walked for close to an hour before Neil finally stopped. The sun beat down. Larry was more than a hundred feet behind him, desperately craving a coffee and some shade. "Look," Neil called out. He was crouching down, looking at a spot near the side of the canal where the water formed swirls and eddies. A flower rose up from the gloom and floated to the surface with a *bloop*.

"Great," Larry said, catching up. "Are you diving in first, or do you want me to take the plunge? You are always telling me to wash my hair."

"I always tell you to soak your head—not the same thing. But if there's something big down there, a room filled with flowers for example, we should be able to find another way in." Neil jumped down from the concrete and started to search the tall grass that grew next to the canal. The swaying tops were the only indication of his whereabouts.

"Found it," Neil called from somewhere in the overgrown field.

"Great," Larry yelled back.

"I know I am," Neil said.

Larry chuckled. He had to admit the boy chef was finally getting quicker, well . . . a little quicker. *Must be my incomparable wit rubbing off on him*, Larry thought happily, as he walked toward Neil's voice.

Larry found Neil standing over a huge iron door that was set flat in the ground.

"Looks like some kind of Mexican hobbit hole," Larry said.

"Just help me get inside." The door wasn't locked, but it was heavy. Neil could only raise it a few inches before the weight pulled it back. Larry stood next to him and together they pulled. The door slowly rose, and they strained to heave it all the way open. It crashed down on the other side, ripping the hinges off.

"That's going to be one angry hobbit," Larry said.

A set of stairs led down to a paved stone floor. The floor seemed to be wet, but not completely covered in water. Neil rushed down the stairs, Larry right behind.

At the bottom they stopped and listened for any sign of life. There was nothing. Neil crouched and scanned the floor. "I can't make out anything but rancid water." He ran his fingers over the stone, hoping for some kind of clue, but there was nothing but loose bits of wood, plastic and sewage. He stood up and walked over to another door.

He lifted the large iron bar that was bracing the door in place. It flung open, knocking Neil back onto the floor, and a rush of filthy water soaked him. Neil cursed, then stood up and shook himself off.

"Thanks for the bath," said Larry, looking at his soaked shoes and pants.

"Now I need a shower," Neil said. "This is not going to make it easy for me to smell."

"No, you smell, trust me."

They stared through the doorway, blinking as their eyes adjusted to the gloom. It looked like a cave. Larry took out his keys.

"Your keys? What's that for?" Neil asked.

"A gift from my mum. The keychain has a small light at the end to help you see the lock on your door late at night."

"Or really early in the morning, more like it? Stops you from fumbling with your keys?"

"Yeah. It was probably more of a gift for my neighbors."

Larry pushed a tiny button and a small stream of light shot out into the dark. He shone the beam around the room. "The walls and ceiling are made from blocks of stone," he said.

"Surprisingly powerful light," Neil said.

"Eats batteries like crazy, though," Larry said, peering into the semi-dark space.

Flowers floated on the wet floor and a few clung to the walls and ceiling. There were bits of corn husks and bread scattered as well.

Neil walked over and grabbed a husk, giving it a sniff. "Despite the sewage, these smell a lot like Margarita's tamales. It's still pretty fresh. It's also the same corn mixture Isabella mushed into her hair." He stood up. "She was here."

"Was," Larry said. "We're two-for-two on finding out where Isabella has been, the dump and this place, but we don't seem at all close to figuring out where she is."

Neil nodded. "Hand me the light." He walked around the room and examined the walls.

"There's a drain to the canal." He pointed to an opening about a quarter of the way up the wall. "When the pumps failed the water flowed into the canal. It overflowed and then the water must have spilled into the room from there. The flowers floated to the top, and drained back out through the same spot."

"Where'd the rest of the water go?"

"Some soaked us when I opened the door, and the rest has been draining down through the cracks in the floor."

"The flood must have been a while ago for all that to happen."

"I guess so, a few hours at least." Neil ran his fingers over the stone. "Strange. This room isn't part of any modern canal system. It's not concrete."

"Wait a minute," Larry said. Something was knocking at his brain. "Shower, shower, shower . . . you said you needed a shower."

"So?"

Larry ran over to the carved stone in the middle of the room and ran his fingers along the carved symbols. "I don't believe it! If I'm right, then this is really COOL."

"What's cool?"

"I bet this in an ancient Aztec bathhouse."

"Bathhouse?"

"The Aztecs believed in cleanliness, much like we do today," Larry said.

Neil looked at Larry, and his disheveled hair. "If the Aztecs believed in cleanliness like you do, then they must have died off from irony."

"I'm clean," Larry replied indignantly. "I'm just not tidy."

Neil snorted.

Larry ignored him. "They bathed every day . . . and that's what this is: a bathhouse! Somehow, when they built the canal overtop they cut right into this ancient cavern."

"Fascinating," Neil said. He walked over and took a close look at the stone.

Larry smiled, "We are standing in living history."

"Is that what you call it?" Neil said, examining the brown sludge that covered the floor and much of his clothes. "There are a few different words I could think of."

Neil closed his eyes and took a deep breath through his nose. The sewage in the room and on his clothes made it incredibly difficult to pick up any other smells, but he could still detect a few out-of-place odors. "There's corn oil, masa dough and lavender, clinging to the stone."

"They couldn't have been washed here by the water?"

"They don't smell like that. They smell like they've been rubbed into the crevices. There's too much here for that to be an accident."

"By someone?"

"Isabella. She knows that I can pick up anything that smells out of the ordinary, and she knows that I'll be looking for her. She's making sure there's a trail for me to follow."

"All this while being held prisoner?"

"Isabella is no dummy."

"And yet she hangs around with you."

"She's trying to send us messages." Neil ignored the insult. "She rubbed food in her hair so we could follow that lead. Then she rubbed food into this stone."

"Well, at least we know they're treating her okay— letting her eat good food, surrounding her with flowers."

"We should head back upstairs and see if we can find anything else."

"The ground looked pretty baked. I don't think we'll see any footsteps."

Larry was right. The sunlight was bright and hot as they emerged from the archway, and the ground was as hard as stone. Neil was able to follow a trail of sludgy smells for a few feet, but it disappeared by the side of a dirt service road.

"They must have gotten into a car or truck or something . . . but it couldn't have been too heavy a vehicle. There are no tracks."

"Well," Larry said, "I guess there's only one thing to do."

"Let me guess," Neil said. "Get a coffee."

Larry nodded. The boy chef was definitely getting quicker.

CHAPTER TWENTY-ONE

PAST AND PRESENTS

Angel Jícama sat down on one side of the enormous Zócalo square and looked up at the blazing hot sun. He smiled. This was a beautiful place to be. A marketplace had sprung up, and dozens of vendors packed the square, selling all kinds of fruits, vegetables, finger food and clothes. Angel revelled in the smells, sights, sounds and tastes of a culture that mixed the extremely old with the very modern. A man in traditional Aztec clothes, all feathers and leather, walked up to him.

"Would you like a cleansing?" the man asked.

"Why not," Angel said. He stood up as the man lit a bowl of herbs and walked in a slow circle around Angel, waving clouds of aromatic smoke. It was an ancient tradition, but the man had lit the herbs with a butane lighter. Angel smiled. Ancient and modern.

As Angel let the smoke envelop him, he watched the incredible bulk of humanity that passed through the square. It has always been like this, he thought. The Aztecs had built a civilization here that

rivalled the greatest in Europe. They'd had street markets, too. Then Cortez and the Spanish had come, and it had all crumbled within a few years. But it hadn't disappeared. Traditions from that world ran through modern Mexican culture like veins through a well-aged blue cheese.

The man finished the cleansing and held out his hand.

"*Gracias*," Angel said, handing him a few pesos. The man bowed and walked away. Angel watched as he joined up with other Aztec dancers and they began a loud drumming ceremony under the Mexican flag.

Angel's reverie was shaken by Sean Nakamura, who sidled up next to him with a laboured sigh. "Breathing the air here is like sucking on a bus's tailpipe."

"Sometimes," Angel said. "Especially when you've been standing next to a burning restaurant for an hour."

"Luckily there was no one inside the ruins."

"That is very good news."

"But it doesn't make the investigation any easier. 'Bodies are great clues' the chief always says."

"That's a wonderful sentiment. She should put it on a greeting card."

"She probably has." Nakamura didn't laugh. "And it was nice of Neil and Larry to let me know they were going on a hike. By the time I reached them on the phone, they were on the subway heading back to the hotel."

"Why didn't they come back to the restaurant?"

"Larry said something about sewage and needing to change their clothes. I was just as glad not to see them."

"Those poor people on the subway."

"Speaking of smells, I've been running tests on some of the clues we do have, and there's something I want to ask you about."

"Of course."

"Remember how Neil smelled crushed bugs, or something like that?"

"Yes."

"Well, I didn't find bugs in Isabella's hair, but I did find two fibers that aren't hair." Nakamura held up a plastic vial with two thin red fibers inside.

"What are they?" Angel asked, peering at the threads.

"I'm not sure. Fabric of some kind, but they seem to be dyed a deep red color."

"It's not blood?"

"No. Blood turns brown quickly when it's exposed to the air. These are still bright red. Any ideas?"

Angel stroked his beard. Red cloth and bugs. Angel's memory snapped back to his grandmother's kitchen. She was using a stone to grind a red paste.

"Is that dinner?" the young Angel had asked.

"No, my little Angel," she had said, laughing boisterously. "You would not want to eat this. It is for the wool I will use to make you a lovely red sweater."

"What is it?"

"Boiled bugs."

Angel now said the same thing to Nakamura. "The Aztecs would capture these tiny red bugs, boil them then mash them up to get the color red."

"So Neil smelled the bugs that are in the dye?"

"It makes sense," Angel agreed.

"Does red cloth mean anything?"

"For the Aztecs, red was important for all sorts of ceremonies. They even dyed cocoa drinks red for big events. Sometimes it represented blood. Sometimes it just made things look interesting."

"Like red velvet cake?"

"Exactly like red velvet cake. And red shoes or clothes grab our attention. Some Aztec women dyed their teeth red to attract men. Red is a powerful color, but there's no simple meaning, then or now."

Nakamura got up. "Well, let's see if the dim-witted duo has returned from the trip down the eerie canal. We should regroup and compare notes."

Neil and Larry were sitting in the hotel restaurant, Larry with a look of intense satisfaction on his face, Neil with one of intense confusion. Larry had three empty cups in front of him, and a third steaming hot one was on the way. Neil had his notebook in front of him, and was busily scribbling away on the last few blank pages.

"XT," he said over and over again. "Xipe Totec. Xochipilli Taberna. Xochipilli Tallo . . . and on and on. XT must be the national acronym of Mexico!"

He was drawing arrows

from one to the other, desperately searching for some link or pattern. He couldn't see one anywhere. On the next page he had drawn a map of where Isabella had been over the past three days.

1. The Bella Artes subway station platform.
2. The Nezhazatcóyotl dump, with corn oil.
3. Maybe the Xochipilli Tallo . . . with corn oil. Burned to ground. No evidence.
4. An Aztec bathhouse. With food from Margarita . . . and with corn oil. *Taberna* burned to ground. No evidence.

The comatose Rodrigo was a prime suspect. He smelled of corn oil. He had threatened Neil, sort of. He was the only one with access to the secret ingredient chests. Too bad there was no way to question him. But if the latest note was sent after Rodrigo's accident, then someone else had taken over. Or Rodrigo was just Rodrigo, and someone else was XT.

"Who's behind all this?" Neil muttered. "Giselle works for a maniacal dictator, so she has the backing. She'd love to humiliate me. Margarita and her sister are missing. Maybe they're behind this, but want it to look like they're innocent. Maybe it's a corrupt police officer?"

"Are you asking, or just thinking out loud?" Larry asked.

"Who would want me to lose so badly?"

"Neil, I know this may be difficult for you to believe, but not everything is always about you."

Neil looked wounded. "I'm worried, that's all. And I am involved. Someone wants me to lose."

"What I mean is that maybe this whole kidnapping thing is about Isabella, and only about her. Maybe you and I got caught in the middle of something. She's not as annoying as you, but she might have enemies as well."

Neil considered this. "You may have something . . . a brain injury! They sent me a note before we even left to come here. Me."

"Isabella was here a few days before us, remember," Larry said. "And if you hadn't come they might still have nabbed Isabella. Didn't the note say they wanted the Flower Bringer?"

Neil nodded unhappily.

"Maybe they wanted Isabella as alone as they could get her," Larry continued. "And with you concentrating on the *Cocina*, they knew no one would be looking out for her full-time."

Neil thought about this for a long while, silently repeating the words from the notes and staring at the unrelated scribbles in his notebook. Finally, he spoke. "Let's assume that your brain has suddenly started working, and your theory is right."

"Oh, thank you, my fearless leader," Larry said with a mock bow of his head.

"Then that means the kidnappers want Isabella for something . . . but what? Money? I'm sure she has offered them plenty to let her go."

"That's a good question. So far, they want to feed her and give her a bunch of haircuts. Not a pattern I can make out."

"And why take her to a dump?"

"Dunno."

"Why take her to an ancient bathhouse underneath a canal?"

"She smelled like a dump?"

"But she doesn't have any soap in her hair. I would have smelled it."

"Maybe someone wants to steal her perfume formulas?" Larry said.

Neil considered this. "Could be, but the note called her the Flower Bringer, not the Perfume Bringer."

"Flowers, perfumes . . . could be the same thing." Larry said.

"What do you know about flowers and perfumes in Mexican history?" Neil asked.

"Whew, that's a tall order. I know the Aztecs loved flowers. They even had this thing called a Flower War."

"They fought over flowers?"

"Well, not exactly. I'd need to do a little more research."

Neil stared at Larry.

"What?" Larry said.

"You're waiting for what, exactly?"

Larry slid off his chair. "Okay, I can take a hint. I've got a couple of books in the room. Just make sure the waiter brings me another coffee and maybe some more of those chips."

Neil signaled to the waiter.

"And no tap water!" Larry added as he walked into the lobby.

Neil placed Larry's order and then went back to staring at his notes and scribbles. A few minutes later Angel and Nakamura walked up to the table, just as Larry returned, out of breath, carrying another envelope.

CHAPTER TWENTY-TWO

CLEAN SWEEP

"She's had a bath," Neil said with certainty. "They used some kind of a fruit-based soap on her hair."

"The Aztecs used to make soap from fruit trees," Larry said, looking up briefly from his copy of the codex. A stack of other books sat next to him on the table. He was thumbing through, marking pages with sticky notes and strips of napkin.

"Soap wood," Angel said. "It's pretty good at lathering up in water and it gets you nice and clean."

"But why not use regular soap? Why go to the trouble?" Nakamura asked.

"These kidnappers seem to like going old school," Larry said.

Neil nodded. "Angel, you said the bugs I smelled were from the red dye."

Angel nodded.

"And the paper they've been using is made from thin pieces of some kind of plant," Neil continued. "Nakamura, the fibers you found in Isabella's hair?"

"Plant fiber." Nakamura handed the sample to Neil, who opened the lid and took a sniff. Now that they were separate from Isabella's hair he could smell them more clearly.

"Some kind of cactus," Neil said. "Agave most likely. Those big spiky plants are everywhere. There has to be some reason they're using Aztec symbols, papers, clothes and dyes and doing it so . . . religiously."

"Talk about authentic," Larry said.

"It's not unheard of," Angel said. "There was a real Aztec revival back at the turn of the last century. Artists such as Diego Rivera and Frida Kahlo and many intellectuals looked at the time before the Spanish arrived as a kind of golden era. They rediscovered ancient techniques for making clothes and art. There had been so much corruption, violence and religious persecution under the Spanish that they felt there was perhaps a simpler time in the past that could lead to a better future."

"Not that it was paradise," Nakamura said. "The Aztecs were a pretty violent bunch as well."

Angel nodded. "Have you seen the Rivera murals in the presidential palace? They tell this history in beautiful detail."

"We have a battle there tomorrow," Neil said.

"You will be impressed."

"So will the judges," Neil said.

"I was talking about the murals."

"Ah, here it is," Larry interrupted, pointing to a page in his illustrated book. "The Aztec Flower Wars. They weren't really about flowers. They were 'flowery' wars."

"Meaning?"

"I'm not entirely sure how to describe it. Flowery means they were decorative. Not real wars, the way we think of them, but highly ritualized. Kind of like theater."

"Theater? Like a play? So no one was really hurt?"

"It's more complicated than that," Larry said, reading on. "The Aztecs and another empire agreed to go to war. Instead of fighting until one side was destroyed, they would agree in advance as to when the war would end."

"How?"

"The codex says that they would usually set a limit or goal on the number of prisoners. First one to capture that number was the winner." Larry looked up from the book. "Hey, that's one heck of a floral arrangement," he smiled.

"And you call my jokes lame?" Nakamura said dryly.

"So who were the Aztecs fighting?" Neil asked, trying to reset the conversation.

Larry looked back at his book. "XT," he said.

"XT? Again?"

"Yup. Tlaxcala was the kingdom they made the deal with."

"What's the X?"

"*Xochiyaoyotl*. The Aztec name for a flower war," Larry said.

"Hmmm," Angel said. "Tlaxcala is where the flower farm was located."

"So maybe someone is waging war with the flower farm people, and Isabella is a prisoner?" Nakamura offered.

Neil shook his head. "But, why send me a note warning me that there would be a war if we came? Why involve us at all?"

Larry continued to read. "There were formal arrangements to end the war, and also to start the war. Oh, this is interesting! The Aztecs would send envoys to the other side. They would warn them that they were doomed. Basically, the envoys said they would attack unless the other side swore to disarm and swear loyalty to the Aztecs."

Neil leaned forward. "Okay, now we may be onto something. Maybe that was the warning in the note they left inside the new fridge."

"If the enemy refused, they would come back with another warning. This time they would actually arm the enemy, to show that they wanted a fair and even fight."

"Hmm. Anyone give you any free knives lately?" Nakamura asked.

"No, but they have given me ingredients to cook with—if this is all tied in to the *Cocina* somehow."

Nakamura snapped his fingers. "Let's work out some of the details later and go with this theory a little longer.

What happens if you ignore the second warning?"

"They come back and warn you again. Then, boom, war," Larry said.

Angel had a thought. "Maybe Rodrigo was the real target. He invited you to the Cocina, so you are really one of his troops . . . so to speak. Have you asked any other chefs if they were warned off from the competition?"

"Why would they be?" Neil asked. "I'm the only real contender."

"Nevertheless," Angel said with a sigh, "Nakamura and I will track some of them down tomorrow and ask. Maybe you should go watch tonight's broadcast to see whom you're facing tomorrow."

"Not a bad idea," Neil said, "but I need some food first." He was used to late suppers. It was common for chefs to eat only after the last customer left the restaurant.

"I'm getting a little peckish as well," Larry said. "How's about we go look for some grub. Not grubs, though. I'm abstaining from bugs."

"Fine," Neil said, "but bring the books. We need to keep researching."

Neil and Larry walked to the doorway. Something was nagging him about Larry's story. Actually, plenty was nagging him about the whole jumbled mess, but one question in particular needed answering now. He turned to Larry, who was somehow walking and reading at the same time. "What happened to the prisoners who were captured in this flowery war scenario?" he asked.

Larry flipped through the book, and a look of shock crossed his face. His eyes were wide as he turned back to face Neil.

"They were sacrificed to the gods."

CHAPTER TWENTY-THREE

FEVER BEANS

Giant flames flew from the grill as the fat from the marinated pork tenderloin hit the red hot coals. The fire licked the meat, searing the outside and sealing the juices inside. The spicy wonders would be finished just in time to plate and serve to the ravenous judges.

Neil's face was illuminated by the inferno, like some diabolical blacksmith. He needed to cook to keep down his growing sense of worry and apprehension.

"Two minutes, sorry, three minutes, um, are left, I mean, remain," fumbled Jose Aciete, not quite comfortable in his role as the new emcee of the *Azteca Cocina*.

Neil quickly flipped the kebabs off the grill and onto a

waiting platter, already garnished with a fried squash blossom, stuffed with goat cheese and corn.

Neil's dread had nothing to do with today's competition. His opponent, Sam Smythe, wasn't much of a chef. He had lucked out in the last round when the assistant to his opponent, the far more talented Tony Coco, used salt instead of sugar in the turkey drumstick ice cream. The result had been a clump of disgusting goo that had left Coco in tears, his assistant looking for work, and the judges searching for extra-strength throat lozenges.

No, Neil wasn't too concerned about his inevitable victory.

"One minute!"

Neil drizzled a dark smoky mole sauce over the lot, wiped an errant drip off the edge of the plate with his towel, and stood back to admire his work—a rich pork-based soup to start; a selection of mini pulled-pork sandwiches followed by the pork tenderloin and squash blossom; and the grand finale—a selection of Mexican cheeses and a pork pâté that would melt in the judges' mouths.

Neil wasn't worried about winning. He was worried about the images running through his brain—images Larry had shown him from the *Codex Mendoza*.

"And stop cooking, the cooking is now over, so stop, please . . . um, now," Jose cried. The crowd applauded.

Neil put down his knife and shuddered. According to the codex the Aztecs didn't just sacrifice the prisoners of the Flower Wars, they sometimes ate them. The most bizarre part, as far as Neil was concerned, was that the prisoners went along with this willingly. They felt that they were giving their lives to placate the gods, to keep them happy. They felt honored to be killed and eaten. Was this the fate XT had in mind for Isabella? It was crazy!

Jose was spewing some overblown gobbledygook about the importance of using the proper corn oil in any good kitchen.

"And the best corn oil? Cortez Cooking Oil!" he said, lifting a giant tank of the stuff over his head. A little trickled out of the spout and landed on his hair.

Neil gave an exasperated moan. At least Rodrigo had been more concerned with the cooking than the product placement.

As Jose continued to address the crowd, Neil took in his surroundings. They were inside the foyer of the presidential palace. The walls were covered with a sprawling mural by Diego Rivera, depicting everything that had happened in Mexico from the dawn of time to the day he'd made the paintings.

Angel had said the murals were spectacular and they were. Aztec farmers hoed the ground, coaxing luscious fruits and vegetables from the red earth. Spanish conquistadors, looking diseased and cruel, prepared to attack the great Aztec capital Tenochtitlán.

Angel had told him that the mural he was looking at was called *The Grand Tenochtitlán*—Rivera's depiction of a typical market day in the old capital. Angel and Nakamura weren't at today's duel. They were out searching for any trace of Isabella. Neil sighed and looked back at the mural. His eyes passed over a strange image of a woman in the lower right of the scene. His heart leaped. She looked like Isabella, but older. The woman was dressed in a red and white dress, with a turquoise neck-lace, and was carrying flowers. Her face and hair were decorated with red paint.

"Larry, come here," Neil called. His hands shook.

Larry walked over. "That is gross," he said.

"What's gross?" Neil asked. He was so absorbed with the woman's face that he hadn't taken in the surrounding scene.

"Well, I don't think that's a side of beef that guy is offering her," Larry said.

Neil looked at the vendors around the woman and realized with a jolt that one of them was offering her a severed human arm. Rivera had painted it blue and dripping.

More human sacrifice, Neil thought angrily. Was it everywhere? Why add such a bizarre detail to this depiction of a typical market day? Neil looked more closely at the painting as a whole. The woman wasn't looking at the arm. She was looking up toward the sky. No, Neil saw, she was actually looking toward some dignitary who was being carried down the street in high procession.

"That could be the emperor," Larry said, following Neil's gaze. "Maybe they're in love?"

"Maybe," Neil said. But there was something behind the emperor that caught Neil's eye. There was a pyramid, hidden in the top left of the picture. Neil gasped. The steps of the pyramid were drenched with blood.

Neil felt a hand on his shoulder and he jumped. He smelled corn oil. It was Jose Aciete.

"Chef Flambé," he said. "I see you like the great Rivera."

Neil was too shocked to answer.

"But the time for art appreciation is over. Now we must appreciate your food. The judges would like you to explain your dishes." He walked away.

Neil composed himself. He needed to present the dishes confidently. He'd have to worry about everything else later. Neil walked to the judges' platform and bowed.

"The dishes are all based on my experience with foods I have encountered here in Mexico City," Neil said. "I've taken those wonderful sauces and combined them with the flame-braised meat and cheeses. The result, I'm sure you'll agree, is a sublime mixture of hard and soft, spicy and sweet."

It was a handy victory. Neil received top marks. Smythe had reverted to form, serving the bland pasta that had condemned him to life as a line-cook back home in Los Angeles. The judges promptly ordered him to return on the earliest possible flight.

As Smythe stormed off indignantly, Neil waited for the camera crew to interview him. The codex images of the willing human sacrifices came rushing back. He had received another lock of Isabella's hair that morning, and had hesitated before examining the delicate curls. What if he smelled blood?

But he hadn't. Instead, he'd smelled more soap, more squashed bugs and a lot of corn. Nakamura had even discovered microscopic bits of masa flour. That was another sign, Neil felt, that Isabella was purposefully sending a message, but what was she trying to say?

The camera crew turned on their lights and the

reporter walked up to Neil. "Chef Flambé, do you have anything you'd like to say to the viewers about your meal?"

Neil's mind wasn't on food anymore, it was back on Aztec sacrifice.

"The best is yet to come," he mumbled. "I'm only warming up."

The reporter kept the microphone ready in case more pearls of wisdom were forthcoming. Neil was about to wave her away when something occurred to him. Larry had said that the Flower Wars were formalized, that there were set rules of engagement and a kind of etiquette to the battles. He grabbed the microphone from the surprised reporter and looked straight into the camera.

"I do have something to say. I need to speak to XT. XT, if you're watching, and I know you are, you must call me immediately. You win. Now let us work out the terms of surrender."

Neil handed the microphone back, continuing to glare at the camera. He heard the cameraman say "*Jefe de cocina es loco*," but Neil noticed the camera never strayed from his face. Neil had spent enough time in front of cameras to know this outburst was going to be a highlight of that night's broadcast. Now he just had to turn on his cell phone and wait for XT to call.

Neil sat on the edge of his bed, the TV tuned to the *Azteca Cocina*. He had it on mute. There was no need to relive the details of the battle, but Neil was waiting for the moment that he made his plea to XT. Larry sat on the couch, scouring a pile of books, occasionally calling out tidbits of information that Neil might find helpful.

Some tidbits he did.

"Hey, Neil, did you know that the Aztecs had a caviar made from insect eggs? Gross!"

Some he didn't.

"Did you know that they used to play a kind of basketball where they shot the ball through a hoop with their butts? How cool is that?"

Larry spent the next five minutes unsuccessfully trying to use his rear end to bounce one of his slippers into the garbage can. "Good thing I'm no good," he said at last. "They used to sacrifice the winning team."

"The winning team?"

"Yup. They were grateful to do it. The Aztecs believed if they didn't satisfy the gods with sacrifice and blood then the world would come to an end. The so-called victims were given the honor of saving the world and keeping the earth moving through the sky. I'm glad they don't have the same rule in our restaurant soccer league."

"It just seems so stupid, inhumane, bizarre! All I can think is that XT has a plan in place to kill all those poor people who just wanted to cook food, make perfume and grow flowers."

"Maybe they're volunteers, going along willingly to save the universe. Cutting flowers and cooking and then offering their lives with a grin."

"I know Isabella isn't," Neil said angrily. He looked up at the TV. "Okay, here we go!" The screen was filled with a close-up of Neil's face, staring at the camera and grabbing the microphone from the surprised reporter. Neil turned off the TV and stared at his cell phone.

"XT didn't phone before the show went to air, so I assume he's not part of the TV crew or the production team," Larry offered, resuming his attempts to butt-kick his slipper.

"Or is shrewd enough to not tip us off," Neil said. He stared at the phone for a good ten minutes. Nothing. Larry had gone back to reading. Neil stood up and paced.

"Why won't he call?" Neil shouted, waving his arms.

"Hey, now this is interesting—" Larry was cut off by the loud ring of Neil's phone.

Neil flipped the phone open, "XT, I presume."

"Neil Flambé, I presume." A chill ran down Neil's spine. The voice that answered was the strangest Neil had ever heard. It was very low, but it was also distorted, as if the speaker were talking through some mechanical system. "You asked me to contact you. What do you wish to say?"

Neil wished to say that he was going to grab XT by whatever throat he was speaking through and strangle him. But this was not the time to lose his cool.

"I submit," Neil said. "You win. I promise to serve you and will not oppose you and whatever else it is that you need from me to end this stupid war or whatever you want to call it. I submit."

"I see you have been studying the Flower Wars," XT said, chuckling. "But I am afraid that when you ignored my warnings you accepted a war that cannot now be stopped by mere surrender. It is like the stars. Once set in motion, they move of their own accord."

"But I didn't get the first warning until I was already here!" Neil cried.

"Would you have stayed away if you had seen it?" XT hissed.

Neil didn't answer.

"Precisely. We have watched you for some time, young man, and we know our enemy. And we have already set the rules for victory. You must lose in the final and not contact the police. Once that is done, the war will end."

"And once that happens, you will free Isabella?"

Silence.

"How can you do this to innocent people?" Neil yelled. "You can't just kill people! It's horrible. Death is horrible."

"Death is horrible? Death is part of life," the strange voice said. "Death spawns life, which spawns death, which spawns life. It is the way of all things."

"No, it's murder!"

"You dare to lecture me about death? Let me ask you a question, Neil Flambé." Neil could almost hear the sneer in XT's voice. "You are so proud to be a chef? You are an agent of death! You kill everything you touch in order to feed the living. Is there anything you serve to your guests that is not dead?"

Neil was speechless. It was true. Meat came from animals. Plants were cut and chopped and dried. Even cheese was a living culture that died after being cooked or eaten. Did XT have a point? No. It was unthinkable. Neil shook his head. "I don't kill people."

"Then that is the only line that you will not cross. We

do not kill for pleasure or for sport, unlike the infamous conquistadors. If we kill it is to serve a higher purpose."

"But Rodrigo and Lily and Margarita . . ." Neil began.

XT cut him off. "People die all the time. How lucky are those who get to choose to die in order to please the gods."

"And Isabella?"

"The Flower Bringer is no prisoner. She is to be honored above all. Farewell."

"You're insane!"

XT didn't respond. Neil held the phone to his ear. A few seconds later, a series of electronic beeps signaled that XT had ended the call.

"NOOOO!" Neil yelled shaking with fury. "NOOOOOO NO NO!" He snapped the phone shut and put his head in his hands. Tears welled in his eyes, as much from frustration as from anger or worry.

"Neil, you okay?"

Neil kept his head in his hands and gave a deep sigh, "Yeah, fine."

"You wanna talk about the call?"

"There's not much to tell. Later, over a coffee."

Neil was going to have a coffee? He *was* feeling loopy, Larry thought.

Neil spoke softly, breathing unevenly. "Now, what was that bit of info you had about winning the wars?"

"Well, there is apparently another way to end a war, other than giving in."

Neil lifted his head slowly. His eyes were red. "And that is?"

"Well, you could defeat the enemy by taking more

prisoners OR by attacking their temple and destroying the statues or paintings of their particular god. That told the enemy that the gods had spoken and chosen a winner. 'My god is bigger than your god,' that sort of thing."

"Seriously?"

"Yeah, look," Larry said, holding up his book. "See this symbol of a temple with a burning arrow sticking in it?"

"Yes."

"That's the Aztec symbol for victory."

Neil walked over and peered closely at the image. Was this a way around the rules XT had set out? "It sounds more like some kind of a chess match."

"In a way," Larry nodded.

"Larry, you might be onto something."

"I am? What?" Larry said, standing up and looking at the chair where he'd been sitting. "Does it smell?"

Neil waved his hand at Larry. "Don't be an idiot, for once. I mean, you might be onto another way to solve this mess."

"Oh. Well, good for me," Larry said, patting himself on the head.

Neil lay down on his bed and yawned. He felt deflated and absolutely exhausted. "Now all we have to do is find their temple," he said.

CHAPTER TWENTY-FOUR

MUSEUM MADNESS

Neil and Larry were awake long before the bells. Neil had had nonstop nightmares of bloody arms and horrid-looking stews. Waking early was actually a relief.

"Good morning, sleepyhead," Larry said with a smile as Neil lifted himself off his bed.

Larry was sitting on the edge of his couch carefully marking pages in his many reference books with sticky notes. There were lots of sticky notes.

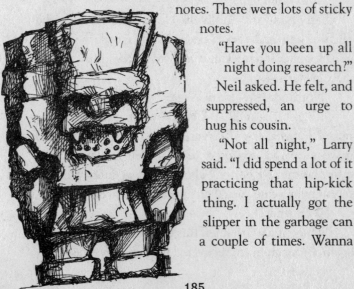

"Have you been up all night doing research?" Neil asked. He felt, and suppressed, an urge to hug his cousin.

"Not all night," Larry said. "I did spend a lot of it practicing that hip-kick thing. I actually got the slipper in the garbage can a couple of times. Wanna see?" He stood up excitedly, wiggling his rear end. "Just let me warm up the old tooshie first."

The urge to hug Larry disappeared. "No, thanks. We should maybe get together with Nakamura and Angel for breakfast and compare notes." Neil wasn't confident this would get them any closer to finding Isabella, but he had to do something. "If this Shippy jerk is some Aztec-obsessed maniac, then there might be a pattern to this stuff."

"Nakamura left us a note under the door. He and Angel were going to head out early to ride the subway, looking for clues. He said to meet them at some museum when we got up."

"Fine. I'm going to shower, and then we'll head out."

"Wait, Neil. Someone slipped another envelope under the door as well."

"Let me guess," Neil said wearily.

"Yup. More hair."

Larry handed Neil the envelope. Neil carefully slid out the hair and took a deep smell. Isabella had been gone for almost a week now and yet he could still see her face. He sighed.

"Nothing new?" Larry asked.

"It's just that, well . . ." Neil was going to say that he missed Isabella. It was certainly true, but saying it would make it seem too serious, or too real. Neil and Larry talked a lot, but almost entirely about work, or money, or the research for a case. Neil didn't want to talk about Isabella.

"Well what?"

"There is a weird smell this time around." He sniffed again. "Your stomach recovered from the revenge?"

"Yes, why?"

"More bugs. Grasshoppers."

"Ugh," Larry said. "How do you even know what that smells like?"

"I've eaten them at Angel's. As a snack."

"What, potato chips are too dull for the big guy?"

"He cooked them with garlic and lemon juice. They were quite good. These seem to be prepared the same way."

"And you think Isabella rubbed that in her hair?"

"Yes."

Larry shuddered. "Weird shampoo. Is this some Aztec cure for dandruff?"

"Again, there's too much rubbed in for it to be an accident. I think she's being careful to only rub in food that's important for some reason."

"You think she's trying to tell us she's being fed bugs? Does that count as torture?"

"Let's just find Angel and see what he can tell us."

Angel stood under the giant water fountain in the middle of the Museum of Anthropology's stone court-yard. The fountain was an impressive structure, immense yet graceful. The thin base rose from the center of the courtyard like the trunk of a tree. Three stories in the air it spread out into a giant canopy. This enormous metal disk provided shade against the sun. Water was carried up inside the trunk and spilled out over the disk. It was so high that the falling water turned to a gentle mist by the time it hit the ground.

Neil and Nakamura walked up to the fountain, passing quickly through the veil of droplets.

"Where's Larry?"

"Cafeteria," Neil said. "Getting a coffee."

"Where else?" Nakamura said.

"Angel, I have a weird question," Neil said, shuffling his feet. "Do you remember those lemon grasshoppers you cooked last year?"

"Of course."

"Did you say cooked grasshoppers?" Nakamura said.

Neil nodded. "They were delicious."

"I'll take your word for it. Actually, that's ringing a bell, so to speak." Nakamura's ears were still ringing from his 5 a.m. wake-up. "Give me a second to think." Nakamura walked off rubbing his mustached upper lip and muttering "grasshopper" over and over again.

Neil turned back to Angel. "I picked up the exact same smells on Isabella's hair."

"It's a pretty common food here."

"But I think Isabella is trying to tell me something. Did the Aztecs cook grasshopper for special occasions? Or do they have any particular meaning that you know of?"

"Not as far as I know," Angel said. "It's just something my grandmother used to make for me when I was a boy."

Neil let out a big sigh. He looked up at the fountain. "Did you see that gigantic statue by the entrance, as we walked in? Kind of a scary looking statue with those fangs and big googly eyes. It's as big as this tree fountain thingy."

"Yes," Angel said. "That was a statue of one of the oldest and most important gods, Tlaloc."

"Tallick?"

"Tuh-lah-luck," Angel said, more slowly. "He was the god of rain, fertility, caves, mountains . . . many things. There's a holy Mount Tlaloc just east of the city."

Larry joined them under the canopy. "I was just reading about Tlaloc last night. He would help the Aztecs, unless they ticked him off by not providing proper sacrifice—and we all know what kind of sacrifice that was supposed to be."

"What if they didn't give him what he wanted?"

"Then it was all floods and lightning and death and drowning," Larry said, sipping his coffee. "Not a guy you wanted to tick off, for sure. Like the guy who kidnapped his first wife."

"What are you talking about?" Neil said.

"Tlaloc was married to a goddess—Xochiquetzal. Then another god came along and kidnapped her. Tlaloc wasn't happy. He rained down fire, curses, thunderstorms . . ."

"Wait, wait, wait," Neil said, closing his eyes and concentrating. "More XT?"

Larry nodded. "Xochiquetzal and Tlaloc; Tlaloc and Xochiquetzal."

Neil looked up at the fountain. "Angel, did you say that Tlaloc was the god of rain?"

"Water in general."

Neil was thinking. Solving mysteries, he found, was sometimes like dissecting a complicated recipe. A great chef could tell each ingredient apart, and explain how they worked together. Right now, he had lots of the ingredients, but he couldn't yet put them together into an edible dish. "Maybe the bathhouse was some sort of shrine to Tlaloc, to water. Maybe Isabella was being held there to be close to this Tlaloc."

"It's possible," Angel said. "But why?"

"Larry, what can you tell me about Xochiquetzal?" Neil asked.

"She was known as the goddess of flowers. But before you get excited, she wasn't the only one."

Neil sat down on the ground and pulled out his notebook. The notes had called Isabella the "Flower Bringer." Was that a reference to this Shoochi-whatever-she-was-called goddess? Tlaloc's wife? Neil thought about the water and the cave. He strummed his fingers as he worked out possible connections.

"Oh no," Neil said. A horrible thought had occurred to him. "What if she's been kidnapped to be Tlaloc's wife?"

Just then, Nakamura came running up. "I've got it! Grasshoppers! Do you have that subway map?"

Neil pulled the map from his pocket. His fingers were shaking.

Nakamura scanned the map closely. "Aha! I was right. I knew I'd seen a grasshopper to-day. Look."

He held the map up to Neil, pointing at the symbol for the Chapultepec subway station— right next to the museum. It was a small green grasshopper.

* * *

Isabella was not surprised to find herself waking up in yet another underground cave. There had been at least two since the flood and the meeting with the man whom everyone called Tlaloc. She had only seen him for a very short time, long enough for him to creep her out, blindfold her, bind her and throw her into the back of a truck. He'd also said, "She is the one." Then he'd passed some kind of liquid over her gag, and she had passed out.

Since then, Isabella had been washed, cleaned, washed again, and fed plenty of glorious food. She felt like a prized turkey just a few days before Thanksgiving. It was not an impression she liked.

Finally, there was a glimmer of hope. The day before, the servants had given her an unintentional gift. The women had never spoken in her presence before. But yesterday, she'd pretended to be asleep, and they had chatted while laying out her clothes and breakfast. She'd only made out a few words, but it was enough. The women were talking about a cave, a castle and the important word that made it all fit: Chapultepec.

She must be somewhere in, or near, Chapultepec castle. She and Jones had visited the enormous castle on their first day in the city as part of a double-decker bus tour. It sat on top of a hill in a giant park. She'd even made a song out of the musical name "Chah-pool-ta-peck! How Aztec!" Then she added, "I think I'll name one of the fragrances Chapultepec No. 5."

Jones had not been impressed and had added the line "Chapultepec . . . what the heck does that even mean? Be careful, it could be Mexican for dead fish."

"Fine. I'll find out, you spoilsport," she said, and hailed the bus driver.

"What does this beautiful word 'Chapultepec' mean?" she asked as he pulled over to let them out in the parking lot.

"Señorita, it is an ancient word that means 'grasshopper hill.'"

"Hah!" Isabella said, turning on Jones. "That is a beautiful name for a perfume."

On their tour of the castle, they learned that the site had once been sacred to the Aztecs. The Spanish had built the castle, and at different points in history it had been home to a military academy, a French emperor, and numerous presidents. And now Isabella was "visiting" again—at least she thought she was. But how to tell Neil?

The women had eventually awoken her and the bricklayer came in with some hot cocoa and a plate of corn tamales. Isabella looked up at him with a sweet smile.

"I have a question."

"*Sí?*"

"You said I could order anything I wanted?"

"Yes, of course. You are not a prisoner but an honored guest." Isabella stared at the metal rings that held her to another slab of rock.

"That is for your own protection," the bricklayer said.

"You have an odd sense of hospitality," she said.

"Would you like more corn? It seems to have been your favorite these past few days."

Isabella was sick of corn. She had asked for it repeatedly for lack of a better "here's a culinary clue that I've been kidnapped by crazy Aztecs who called themselves names like Tlaloc" option to rub in her hair. If Neil was, in fact, receiving the locks of her hair, she hoped he'd make the connection as well.

Now it was time to take a chance on something else. And this was just the sort of bizarre info that Larry might know.

"I'd like cooked grasshoppers." Isabella held her breath. She hoped this request wasn't so weird that it was a tipoff. "Please?" she smiled.

The man looked surprised, and for a second Isabella was certain she'd lost her chance. But then his mouth broke into a wide smile. "Grasshopper! You know about this delicacy? It was one of my favorite foods when I was a little *chico*."

The gamble had paid off.

A short time later the man had happily returned with a steaming bag of freshly cooked grasshoppers. They ate a few before Isabella yawned and said she needed a nap. As soon as the man left, she rubbed as much of the crispy bug bits into her hair as possible.

Later that day, the man had snipped a good length of her hair.

Now she just hoped that Neil—and Larry—would pick up on the hint.

It hadn't taken long to examine the Chapultepec subway stop. There was no trail there. But Chapultepec wasn't just the name of the station; it was the name of the enormous Chapultepec Park. The park housed a zoo, a giant castle, an amusement park and a number of museums. There were plenty of hills and fields and lakes and public spaces in between.

Angel and Nakamura had agreed to search the green spaces. Neil and Larry would go from building to building as quickly and thoroughly as they could.

"She couldn't have rubbed something more specific in her hair?" Larry said, surveying the seemingly endless expanse, "like pine needles or maybe bamboo?"

"Bamboo?"

"The zoo here has three pandas, very cute and very popular."

"I think I'd have noticed if Isabella had been hanging out with animals."

Larry reluctantly let that one pass. He needed to keep Neil's spirits up, but that straight line had been too easy, even for him.

They had started by scouring the rest of the anthropology museum. Larry looked wistfully at all the information on the walls and the displays while Neil did his best to sniff for traces of Isabella. There was nothing there, just huge displays of sacrificial altars and frightening stone knives—with handles carved in the shapes of skulls.

"I think we can guess what those were for," Larry shuddered.

"Let's keep moving," was all Neil could say. He could feel a lump forming in his throat. Neil often felt stressed with his life back home—running a restaurant, helping the police, trying not to fail grade ten—but he usually felt in control. If he screwed up he would hurt only himself. Of course, he never screwed up, so it hadn't really been a concern. But here, he felt like the ground was shaking beneath him. He could lose everything—Isabella and Chez Flambé. His life was balanced on a knife edge as sharp as any Aztec blade.

"Let's head up the hill," Neil said.

"Okay," Larry said. "But can we at least stop and get a cold drink and a snack that's not some fried dog or baked insect?"

"Fine. There's a plaza with food stands on the map, near the castle."

Neil marched down the pebbled pathway, with Larry dragging behind, and soon emerged into a giant stone plaza, adorned with dozens of statues of ancient and modern warriors. It was yet another interesting Mexico City surprise. Halfway across the square, Neil stopped and stood as still as a statue. He sniffed the air. "Corn oil," he said, sniffing again, "and soap wood." His eyes darted around, looking for the source. He spied a group of scantily clad dancers, wearing leather boots and enormous feathered headdresses. He had seen the Aztec dancers all over town, but there was one dancer in this particular group who caught his attention. He was enormous. Their eyes met and Neil gasped—it was the man who had picked up the food at Margarita's restaurant. "Larry!" Neil called. "I smell the oil and soap. It's coming from him!"

The man grimaced as Neil started to run toward him. He turned and bolted in the exact opposite direction, right toward Larry.

"Get him!" Neil yelled.

Larry looked at the enormous feathered fury barreling toward him. "Are you nuts?" He tried to get out of the way, but the man slammed into him at full speed. The collision knocked Larry out cold, but the momentum kept his limp body clinging to the man, like a moth on the front grill of a moving car. The man didn't even slow down.

Neil stopped in his tracks, frozen in shock. What had just happened? "Larry!" he croaked.

Then he was yelling, "LARRY!"

Neil found his feet. "LARRY!" Neil sprinted to catch the man, but he had a huge head start and an athlete's legs. Neil had to rely on his nose. He followed the giant man's aroma through a maze of trees and bushes. The trail led up a steep hill and ended at the edge of an oddly colored pool of water. They had vanished.

Neil sniffed the air and the ground. Nothing. The trail definitely ended here. He looked at the pool more closely. It was actually a huge mosaic fountain, rimmed by a stone wall about three feet tall. What seemed to be a huge rolling mound of colored tile broke the surface of a green pool of water. Rising from the far end of the mound was one of the most hideous things Neil had ever seen—a giant scowling face with bulging eyes made of thousands of multicolored tiles, and a nose formed by a coiled serpent. The mouth was a twisted frown, dominated by bejeweled fangs. He'd seen the same hideous face just an hour before.

"Tlaloc," Neil said angrily. He ran around the entire rim of the fountain, searching for a hidden entrance in the head or body of the ancient deity. There was nothing. They could have jumped over the wall and onto the mound, but where could they have gone? Frustrated, he kicked at the stones as the fountain continued to splash and trickle.

Neil was completely lost. He needed Larry, or Angel, or Nakamura. Angel and Nakamura! Neil flipped open his cell and dialed. It seemed to take forever for the phone to connect.

"What is it, Nose?" Nakamura's voice crackled.

"Larry. He's taken Larry," Neil said, his voice shaking.

"Where are you? Who's taken Larry?"

"I have no idea! I'm next to some fountain of that Tlaloc god. The trail ends here but it's like they vanished into thin air. Look, I need you right away," Neil fought back tears.

"We're coming, Neil. You stay on the line."

"No, I don't want to waste any battery power. I'll be fine. I won't do a thing until you get here." Neil flipped his phone shut.

Calmer now, Neil searched the entire fountain again. There were no doors or telltale aromas. He sat down on the stone edging, completely drained. He looked back at the scowling face of the rain god. Why was such an elaborate sculpture here, in the middle of nowhere? He stared at the fountain. Even the layout didn't make any sense. From ground level even a tall person like Neil could barely make out the face. You'd need to be twenty feet up to see the patterns in the mosaic tiles underneath the water.

Neil looked up. There were no trees or steps or ladders nearby. He stood on the edge of the pool. That helped a little. The mound turned out to be the body of the water god, and Tlaloc seemed to be running. Neil jumped up as high as he could—and could see that the green water was in fact an underwater mosaic depicting giant serpents. He landed back on the stone embankment with a loud crack, and fell backward onto the path. The stone had split in two.

"I've broken it!" Neil thought. But as soon as the thought entered his mind, the loose piece of stone slid back into place, leaving no trace of a crack. Neil looked up, amazed. He was even more amazed to see Tlaloc's mouth opening wide, revealing the curved stone walls of a tunnel inside. Just as quickly the mouth began to close.

Neil had told Nakamura he would wait for him, but he had no idea if he could recreate whatever combination of jumps and weight had triggered the mechanism. He leaped over the wall and onto the body and ran straight for the mouth. He jumped in just as the fanged mouth snapped shut behind him and threw him into darkness.

When Angel and Nakamura arrived they didn't see Neil. They did see the cell phone he'd left behind. It was still sitting there, its tiny camera directed at Tlaloc's mouth, filming the toothy grimace of the water god.

Nakamura picked up the phone and hit "stop."

"Now, how the heck do you rewind this thing?"

CHAPTER TWENTY-FIVE

WHEN THE RAIN GOD POURS

Larry came to just as a set of enormous fangs snapped shut behind him. His head and jaw ached like crazy. It felt like his ribs were being squeezed in a vise, and his arms were pinned down in the same grip. He groggily recalled the giant Aztec dancer slamming into him.

"Hey, mountain man, what gives?" Larry said in his best Nahuatl. The man didn't stop running.

"You know the ancient language?"

"Um, a little," Larry said. He wondered if this was going to make his situation better or worse.

"The *tlatoani* will be pleased."

Tlatoani? Larry thought. That was the Aztec word for leader or king. "You mean you're not the *tlatoani?*" Larry asked.

"I control the waters and the food," the man said, not stopping. Larry hoped there was nothing to trip over in the pathway ahead. The guy was as big as a side of beef and Larry didn't relish the thought of being trapped between his bulk and hard stone.

"Maybe you could slow down a little," Larry suggested. "It's kind of dark in here."

"This is my home," the man said. "I know the way. And we must hurry."

"We've been running for a long time, gorilla," Larry said. "How big is your home? The air-conditioning bills must be murder."

Again, no answer. As they continued to run the tunnel gradually grew lighter. Burning straw torches rested in iron sconces on the walls, which were carved right out of the solid stone.

"You really do go retro, don't you?"

They turned a corner, and Larry caught the unmistakable smell of food and flowers.

Finally, the giant man stopped. He deftly slung Larry down off his shoulder, bound his hands with some kind of rope, and pushed him ahead into a huge, well-lit cave. A much smaller man in a tidy suit looked at them with surprise and alarm. "Tlaloc! What are you doing bringing him here?" he asked, clearly not happy.

Tlaloc! Larry's eyes grew wide. These people were nuts.

"They must have discovered us," Tlaloc said quickly. "The young one saw me. I had to take this one prisoner or I might have been caught."

"What? Discovered us? How?" the man said.

"We must leave now. I will go back and ensure that I was not followed."

Tlaloc disappeared back down the tunnel.

The man in the tidy suit walked behind Larry and shoved him. "Move or I will kill you."

"Not a very fair choice," Larry said. The man ushered him into the middle of the room, parted a cloth curtain and shoved Larry behind it. Immediately, Larry saw two things that made his heart jump: a giant sacrificial altar stone surrounded by flowers and, attached to it, Isabella. She was wearing a white robe with red trim. Larry thought it looked familiar, but he couldn't quite place it.

"Hey, babe," Larry said with a smile. Humor was always the best policy in his universe. Isabella stared at him with wide eyes, too shocked to reply.

"Shut up and sit down," the man ordered, pulling out a long knife of his own and pointing it at Larry's chest. Larry sat on the floor. The man unlocked the chain from the stone, and then Isabella's leg. In an instant, he'd linked Larry and Isabella together at the ankles. Then he stormed off.

"Don't rush back on my account, Weasel Boy!" Larry called after him. He examined the heavy metal chain that bound him to Isabella.

"I guess there's no way we're getting out of here with this thing on our legs."

"What are you doing here?" Isabella whispered.

"Glad to see me?" He smiled.

"No! Not here, anyway," she said.

"Time to compare notes. You go first. Where is here?"

"Under Chapultepec Castle, I think," Isabella replied. "That's why I ordered the grasshoppers."

"Neat trick. Neil knew you were rubbing the food in your hair on purpose."

"So, they have been sending my hair to you?"

"Yes. Nice haircut by the way," Larry said with a grimace. The front of Isabella's hair had been left almost completely untouched, but the back was quite short. Larry noticed that it left her neck exposed—a fact that tweaked something unpleasant in his subconscious. "What was up with the corn tamales and stuff? Did you order those as well?" he asked.

"It was the only food I knew that connected to the Aztecs."

"Hairless dog didn't occur to you?"

Isabella frowned. "Is everything a joke to you?"

Larry just rolled his eyes. Sometimes, Isabella could be a lot like Neil. "Not everything. There's nothing funny about coffee, for example."

Isabella pursed her lips.

"Focus," she said.

Great! Now she even sounded like Neil. "Fine, I'll be serious. We've also smelled lots of flowers in your hair."

"As you can see," she said, looking around the cave, "they always make sure my prisons are well perfumed. But the flowers are beginning to wilt."

"Well, if they grabbed them all from that farm then they're starting to get a little old. The good news is that they probably keep Lily around to take care of them."

"Lily?"

"Yeah, they burned down her farm—after taking all the flowers."

Isabella was silent. "I thought the flowers were hers, but I have not seen Lily here. The man you call Weasel-Boy— I call him the bricklayer—keeps referring to prisoners."

"He calls them prisoners?"

"Yes."

"That's not such a good sign. All right, my turn . . ."

Larry told Isabella about the notes, the threats and warnings, and their theory that the mysterious XT was waging a flower war on them. "If we only knew who the real mastermind is, we could maybe figure out the motive. I had assumed Mount Tlaloc back there was the leader, but he's led me to believe otherwise."

"I've not been told why I am here, only that I am to be made royalty of some kind and that is why they treat me so well."

"We have a working theory," Larry said, leaning in closer. "We think that they think you are a reincarnation of the flower goddess Xochiquetzal, and that you're supposed to marry Tlaloc."

Isabella gasped. "What? But I'm only sixteen!"

"Yeah, but everything fits. In Aztec weddings they ritually fed and washed the bride to be, then clothed her with red feathers."

Isabella thought about this. "No one has ever decorated me with feathers. There have been plenty of flowers and much corn, but no feathers."

"We smelled red dye in your hair," Larry said. "We assumed you'd rubbed it in, but then Nakamura said it was from some fabric."

"It must be from these clothes—the dress and the slippers."

Isabella and Larry sat thinking. "How is Neil?" she asked softly. "They never mention him to me."

"Neil's doing his best to keep winning in the tournament and he's spending all of his free time looking for you. I think he's doing both to make sure you're safe."

Isabella smiled. "Let's hope he succeeds."

"He's probably right above us now, if I know his talent for following a trail. Old Tlaloc was pretty stinky."

Their conversation was cut short by the return of the bricklayer, who now pointed a gun at them and ordered them to move.

"Not a very Aztec-looking weapon, Weasel Boy," Larry said sarcastically.

"It will kill you just the same," the man replied.

Neil ran down the tunnel as quickly as he dared. The gloom was overwhelming, and the heavy air made it feel like the walls were closing in. He had no idea of where the tunnel turned, curved or went up or down; it was an odd feeling to be dashing into the complete unknown. Suddenly, a sound like metal sliding along stone stopped him in his tracks. He'd kicked something. Neil got down on his hands and knees and felt around. His fingers touched the cool metal of a set of keys. Could it be? Larry's keys! They must have fallen out when he was being carried. Neil picked them up and felt for the compact flashlight. He pushed the button and the tunnel was suddenly flooded with light. It was so bright it hurt his eyes. "Thank you, Larry," he murmured. His eyes adjusted quickly and he moved along at a faster pace.

It was the smell of the giant man that gave Neil the split-second advantage he needed to avoid being squashed like a bug. He recognized the smell of oil and soap coming toward him. For a moment, he stood completely still. What was he going to do? The tunnel was carved out of solid rock. There was nowhere to hide.

Then Neil had an idea. He flicked off the light, held the keychain tightly and stood in the middle of the tunnel. As soon as he heard footsteps he got down on his hands and knees, turning his side toward the oncoming man. This is going to hurt, he thought, and it did. The man smashed right into Neil's rib cage and fell over with a thud so loud that Neil worried it would bring down the tunnel around them.

Neil also heard the sound he was hoping for—the sound of a weapon sliding across the floor, away from the man's hand. Neil remembered the obsidian knives he'd seen in the museum. He ignored the pain in his side and walked quickly to where the man lay on the tunnel floor. Neil pointed the flashlight right in his eyes and turned it on.

"Too bright!" he growled. "¡Mis ojos! My eyes!"

Neil had to act fast, before the man was able to recover. He ran over quickly and scooped up the knife. Then he stood as tall as he could manage and pointed the knife at the man.

"Stay there," Neil yelled. "Don't move or I'll kill you."

The man scoffed. "You? Kill me? I am a warrior! I

will crush you!" He struggled to get to his feet, still rubbing his eyes.

If there was one weapon Neil Flambé knew how to wield as well as any warrior, it was a knife. "I don't need to overpower you," Neil said. "I just need to hit a vital organ. Have you seen me in the kitchen? I'm very coordinated and very fast."

The man hesitated.

"Good," Neil said. "So you know who I am. And bear in mind that you still have red dots swimming in front of your eyes and I don't." Neil hoped he sounded more confident than he felt.

"Now, I want some answers," Neil said. "Why did you take Isabella?"

The man said nothing.

"I know she's supposed to marry Tlaloc," Neil said. He was sure the man's eyes had widened, but that was the only suggestion of a response.

"Where is this Tlaloc?" Neil said, his voice getting more high-pitched. "Who is he? Why does he want to marry her?"

Now the man definitely sneered. "You know nothing." Neil didn't see that the giant had slipped something out of the satchel at his waist, or that he'd now hidden the object in his enormous hand. The man started to move toward Neil.

"Put your arms above your head," Neil said, thrusting the knife forward. The man obliged. He also smiled— a smile Neil didn't like in the least.

As he raised his arms in the air, the man also released his grip on a small, hard rubber ball. As the ball fell, he swiveled his hips with such force that they struck the ball like a bat, sending it flying through the air. The ball smashed Neil right on the nose.

"OUCH!" Neil yelled as blood began to spurt from his nostrils. The knife fell to the ground as Neil held his hands to his face, trying to stop the pain and the bleeding. The man leaped over and picked up the weapon.

"You puny fool!" the man said, towering over Neil. "I am Tlaloc." He lifted the knife in the air.

Neil was too scared and hurt to move. He closed his eyes and cringed, preparing for the moment of his own death. But the moment didn't come. Instead, a shot rang out in the tunnel, echoing off the walls like thunder.

Neil's eyes snapped open, and he watched in horror as Tlaloc's eyes glazed over and began to roll back in his head. The knife fell to the floor, and Tlaloc swayed like a tree that has been cut at the roots.

"I am coming, Xochiquetzal," he said with a smile, blood rising to his lips. He gave a final gasp and collapsed.

Neil heard footsteps, coming from the tunnel behind him. He reached around for the flashlight, and turned it off. He crouched against the wall as a very faint blue light reflected off the stones.

"Neil, are you okay?" came a voice. It was Sean Nakamura.

He was holding Neil's cell phone in front of them, using its pale light to guide his and Angel's steps.

"It was a good thing you kept yelling 'jump on the rock' into the camera as you ran into the fountain," Angel said.

"Angel practically cracked the stone in half on his

first try," Nakamura said. He noticed the blood. "Holy mackerel, Nose, look at your nose!"

"I'm fine," Neil said. "But I need a handkerchief."

Angel helped Neil as Nakamura walked over to the enormous body. With an effort, he turned the dead man over, the blue light illuminating his face.

Nakamura's eyes opened wide with shock. "Enrique?"

"You know him?" Neil said.

"He's my contact on the Mexico City Police Force."

"Why did you shoot him, then?"

"I didn't!" Nakamura said.

"Then who did?" Angel asked.

All three looked at Enrique, but he was unable to answer.

CHAPTER TWENTY-SIX

ON THE MOVE, AGAIN

Larry and Isabella stood in a wide passageway, where the bricklayer had forced them to go. They watched as he turned back and dumped a giant vat of corn oil and gasoline across the floor of the cave. The stone wouldn't burn, but there was enough cloth, wood and other material there to cover their tracks. He threw a match and the room erupted in flames with a loud *whoosh*. There was no going back that way. The entrance to the tunnel Larry had come through was on the far side of the room. He hoped Neil wasn't anywhere near the fire. He was certain his cousin had followed him, and he was pretty sure Tlaloc had been certain too, judging by how quickly he'd bolted back up the tunnel. Of course, if Tlaloc had reached Neil with that knife, the fire might be the least of Neil's worries.

The bricklayer slammed a huge iron door shut behind them.

"Move," he said. Larry and Isabella shuffled as quickly as they could.

Isabella looked around. There were now about a dozen other people in the passageway with them. Larry had been right: Lily, whom she'd met only once, was there. Their eyes met briefly, but Lily quickly turned away. Another woman, who looked much like Lily, was there as well, along with a few more women and young men. Their hands were bound and a number of people dressed as Aztec dancers or as workers kept them all moving.

"Where's that big baboon, Tlaloc?" Larry asked.

"He is now with the great burning sun," the man said.

"Oh," Larry said with a shudder. "Well, um, good for him then." He hoped that meant Neil was okay.

Isabella waited until the bricklayer moved farther up the line of prisoners before she spoke again. "What does that mean?" she asked.

"It means Tlaloc died in battle," Larry said. "In the Aztec world, if you died in battle you went straight to the sun."

"I am sorry. I do not wish death for anybody, but if I was supposed to be marrying him, then why not let me go now? There's no reason to keep me here."

Larry was thinking about this latest development. "There are two weird things about this whole scene: One is that in the Aztec religion, dying was not a bad thing. Sacrificial victims were often willing, even more so with the victims who were to become gods."

"I don't understand—become gods?"

"Some victims got special treatment. They were dressed up like specific gods, then killed on specific days and, in a weird way, became the god—joined him or her in the sky."

"So this man who called himself Tlaloc became Tlaloc when he died?"

"But Weasel Boy didn't say that. He said he was with the sun. So maybe they're going to pick another Tlaloc to marry you."

"Stop talking!" yelled the man.

Isabella looked like she was going to cry.

"The second thing that's bugging me: how the heck does Weasel Boy know that Tlaloc is dead?"

Isabella shrugged a listless shrug. Larry looked at her. She was so beautiful in her fresh clean clothes and that turquoise necklace with the shiny golden disk that hung around her neck. Turquoise necklace! A horrible light bulb flashed on in Larry's head.

"Wait," Larry said, stopping. "Isabella, listen to me."

"What?"

"Shut up!" the bricklayer said, running toward them. "I said shut up and move."

Larry spoke quickly. "From now on you've got to order raw corn, and wear nothing but lilies in your hair. And order lots of coffee. Lots. Let's hope Neil can read," Larry said, just before the man knocked him on the head with the butt of his gun.

Neil smelled the smoke first. He, Angel and Nakamura were walking down the tunnel when he picked up the unmistakable odor of burning wood, flowers and oil. "We've got to get out of here, fast."

"What is it, Nose?" Nakamura said.

"Fire," Neil said. "There's a huge fire down there and

the smoke is heading our way." Neil had been forced to take numerous fire-safety courses in order to keep his restaurant license, and he knew the smoke was often more dangerous than the flames.

He turned and ran, with Angel and Nakamura right behind. Neil prayed he'd caught the scent in time. "My stupid nose," he said, feeling it throb. "I should have smelled the smoke way earlier. The swelling is dulling my senses."

"It already looked like a toucan beak," Nakamura said as they sprinted away from the fumes.

"You'll look like a charcoal briquette if we don't move faster," Neil called over his shoulder. Nakamura, who still hadn't adjusted to the thin mountain air, was huffing and puffing. Angel, on the other hand, was surprisingly quick for such a large man. He grabbed Nakamura by the arm. "Tending goats is a good workout."

"If those stupid goats help get us out of here, I'll personally donate a truckload of hay for the pests."

The light on Larry's keychain started to flicker. Neil shook it and swore under his breath. Larry had said it ate up batteries like crazy. "Throw me the cell phone," Neil yelled. Nakamura tossed it forward, coughing as the combination of musty air and smoke began to sear his lungs. Neil held it open as he ran, trying to shine its pale blue light into the darkness ahead.

"Almost there," Neil yelled as he felt a slight breeze. He turned a corner and found himself at the back of the fountain's fangs. "We made it!" he said with a rush of relief.

"Great," Nakamura said, doubling over in an effort

to catch his breath. "Now how do we open this from inside?"

Neil had no idea. He felt around, searching for anything resembling a lever or loose stone. Smoke was pouring up the tunnel now, making it harder to see, and even harder to breathe.

"Over here!" Angel yelled between coughs. "There's a draft coming from this stone."

Small rivulets of smoke were twirling in front of a large stone about halfway up the wall. Angel pushed, but it didn't move. Neil and Nakamura joined him and together they shoved with all their might. At last, the stone sank into the wall and the fangs began to open. Neil scrambled out first. He reached back and helped pull Angel through. As quickly as the mouth had opened, it began to close.

"Pull!" Neil yelled as he took one of Nakamura's arms. Angel grabbed the other, and together, they helped a nearly lifeless police inspector back through the tunnel entrance. The jaws snapped shut just as his feet passed over the lips.

Neil and Angel fell back onto the great god's tiled chest. Nakamura gasped for air next to them, coughing and clearing his lungs. A moment later, the earth shook with an enormous thundering crash, like an earthquake or explosion. Giant cracks formed in the water god's head, and the force created waves in the water. It lapped up against and over the giant's body, soaking them.

"What the heck was that?" Neil said. Plumes of acrid smoke began to rise from somewhere in the middle of the park. The ground rumbled again, and a few feet away, underground pipes began to snap, spewing water and steam into the air. The fountain was starting to sink.

"Please don't say—" Nakamura panted.

"RUN!" Neil yelled.

"—run." Nakamura got to his feet weakly and ran.

They sloshed through the water and over the stone walls as dust, smoke and jets of water filled the air. They stopped about a short way off, and Neil looked back over the devastation. The fountain was cracked beyond repair, and as they watched, Tlaloc's head sank into the steaming mess that had, only minutes before, been the sparkling pool.

"I'm glad we didn't get caught in that," Nakamura said, between heavy breaths.

Neil had a horrible vision of Larry and Isabella under a pile of rubble. He struggled to push it out of his mind as police sirens wailed in the distance.

"We'd better get out of here," Angel said.

"A very sensible suggestion," Nakamura said, wobbling a bit as he stood. "The cops will be here soon and the one I thought I could trust turned out to be a traitor. I don't know whether that makes the rest of the force more or less trustworthy, and I don't want to find out while standing next to a piece of ruined modern sculpture."

Neil knew Angel and Nakamura were right, but he couldn't shake the image of Larry and Isabella. "You go. I've got to get a closer look."

Before Angel and Nakamura could stop him, Neil bolted back toward the tunnel.

Neil ran past the ruined fountain just seconds before the first police car arrived. The fountain was at a high point in the park and the ground behind it sloped down. Neil could see that there was a long gash in the green of the park, like a huge smoldering scar—the tunnel had collapsed. At the far end there was a giant hole. What looked to be a large cave had collapsed in on itself like an enormous pothole. Was that where Tlaloc had dumped Larry? Was that where Isabella was being held? Had they both escaped?

Neil sprinted. He arrived at the hole just as more police cars screeched to a halt a short distance away. He'd have to be fast.

Neil searched the ground. It was soft and almost muddy. He could hear doors slamming. The police couldn't drive here—they'd have to park and then proceed on foot—but they would arrive soon enough. He couldn't be caught.

He ran around the hole, looking for any sign. Grass, sticks, corn. . . . Then he saw them—footprints! There were dozens of them. Some had been made by bare feet, some by boots, and one by sneakers with the initials L and F carved into the soles. Larry! Neil's heart leaped.

The footprints led away from the hole, toward a small stand of trees. Luckily, the trees were in the opposite direction from where the police had parked their cars. Neil smashed through branches and tripped over rocks, as the ground got drier and the footprints fainter. Finally, he emerged from the trees at the edge of a paved road.

Neil's eyes darted both ways. He heard the rumble of an engine coming from his left and sprinted down the road. He turned a corner just in time to see a large tour bus pulling away.

On the side of the bus was an image of a giant pyramid. As the driver zoomed away, Neil caught a glimpse of the sign in the window—T ... T ... something. The bus was moving too fast for him to make out the word.

Out of breath, Neil stood in the middle of the road, panting. His nose throbbed with pain, but he was sure he could make out the smells of smoke, oil and flowers lingering in the air with the diesel exhaust. He knew Isabella was on that bus. Was it possible that Larry was with her? He hoped so.

Neil's cell phone rang. He picked it up and flipped it open. "What?"

The eerie mechanical voice answered. "You have destroyed the temple of Tlaloc. That was very impressive."

Neil remembered what Larry had said about ending the flower wars by capturing the enemy temple. "That means I won. Now give me my friends back!"

"That was not my temple," the voice said angrily. "I repeat my warning: Lose in the final. If you do not, two deaths will be on your head." XT hung up.

"AHHHHHHHHHHHHHHHHHHH," Neil yelled at the silent phone. He walked over and collapsed on the side of the road. XT had confirmed that Isabella and Larry were still alive, but he'd also confirmed that their fate depended on him.

His phone rang again. The theme from *Batman*. "Nose, where are you? Are you okay?"

Neil wasn't sure how to answer. "I'm fine," he said, as he got up and walked down the road. "I'll meet you at the subway."

CHAPTER TWENTY-SEVEN

RISING ABOVE IT ALL

Neil stabbed his maple chopping block forcefully and repeatedly. He was doing his best to concentrate. Today's venue was a giant hotel lobby decorated with more Diego Rivera murals. These didn't depict ancient history, but instead a strange wedding feast with grinning skeletons as the bride and groom.

"It's the *Día de los Muertos* celebration, the Day of the Dead," Angel said. "The message is that death is not something to be feared. It is just a part of life."

This was not a message Neil was particularly interested in right now. Instead he turned his attention to the day's secret ingredient—corn. Thankfully, Neil's nose had bounced back from the knock the late Enrique "Tlaloc" Juarez had delivered. Neil had smelled the corn before the crew had even wheeled it in from backstage and had already planned an ideal menu. His mind was now on other things.

The image of the pyramid on the side of the bus was

219

still in his head, and it rattled him. It was almost exactly like the pyramid in the Rivera painting—the pyramid with the steps that had been covered in blood.

"T . . . something," he said, over and over again.

Angel had suggested the bus was heading for Teotihuacán, a huge tourist attraction located a two-hour drive outside of town. There was no way they could have all gotten there last night. And today, Neil had to compete. Two more wins and he'd be in the final. Time was running out.

Neil had tried calling his parents again. He'd had to leave a message for his dad. He reached his mum, but before he could explain that he needed some help she'd said, "I have to run to court dear. It's a big lawsuit, very important. I expect you're doing well?"

"Well, I, actually Mum—"

"That's great son, love you. I'll call later," and she'd hung up.

Neil resumed stabbing the cutting board.

Nakamura was heading to Teotihuacán on his own while Neil cooked. He said he was going to "dig around" the archaeological site (ha ha) as quietly as he could, to see if the tour bus had actually been heading there. Angel had stayed behind to help Neil. Neil looked over at his sous-chef. Working with Angel was an unexpected joy, there was no doubt. But Neil was confused as well. He hated to admit it, but he missed Larry. Larry the bonehead, the nonstop goofball, was a companion Neil would never have chosen in a million years, but his absence made the kitchen a little less . . . fun.

"Angel," Neil whispered, leaning over while still

stabbing his chopping block. "It's corn. I want to make chowder, a seafood and citrus fruit salad—"

"Ceviche." Angel nodded his approval. "That will be very, very good. I can smell that the fish on the back table is very fresh."

"So are the limes and avocados. And we'll close with a roasted corn and poultry pie. A kind of chili-infused tourtière."

"A little bit of Canada mixed with a little bit of Mexico. I heartily agree."

An hour later, it was another victory for Neil Flambé. His opponent, Paul Klöss, had tried making tamales and corn cakes, but the judges had seen Neil prepare the same dishes two days before, and they knocked Klöss for a lack of originality. His dumplings were a hit, but not enough to knock the young chef off his pedestal.

Neil was one step closer to his goal of winning the *Cocina*, but he felt less and less motivated. Making the food was still wonderful, and watching the judges' eyes well up with tears of joy? Okay, that was pretty good, too. Imagining the guests who would soon be paying even more for his food in a renovated Chez Flambé? That was the part he was having trouble with. He still wanted to see that vision realized, desperately. But now that he was getting closer to the prize money, he knew he couldn't risk winning if he didn't reach his other—and, he had to admit now—bigger goal: finding Isabella . . . and Larry.

"You don't think they'll kill Larry right away, do you?" Neil asked nervously. He and Angel were sitting in the hotel dining room, under the smiling skulls, waiting for word from Nakamura. Neil had proposed looking for the tour bus themselves, but Angel had pointed out the futility of that wild goose chase.

"I don't know," Angel said. "Enrique could have killed him in the park, and didn't."

"Look how well that turned out for Enrique." Neil stared at the mural, and a felt a chill. "I'm sick of this place."

Angel placed a hand on Neil's shoulder. Neil loved to present a tough face to the world, but Angel knew there was a fourteen-year-old boy inside.

"XT has been plotting this for a while," Neil said, still staring at the gruesome bride and groom. "He wants to humiliate me and hurt all the people that I, that I—" Neil wasn't sure what word he wanted to say next.

"Love?" Angel suggested.

Neil quickly went on. "But who could hate me that much?" Neil didn't really need Angel to answer. It was a long list. "This flower-war thing is stupid."

"You prefer the Spanish way . . . all-out destruction?"

"I'd prefer peace."

"Finally, a glimmer of hope," Angel said softly. "How are these duels you enjoy so much different from this war?"

"No one dies in a cooking duel," Neil said, and immediately wanted to kick himself. He turned and saw the look of heartache in Angel's eyes. He changed the subject. "I hope Nakamura has good news."

"So do I."

Just then a very hot and sunburned Sean Nakamura walked up to their table and sat down. "I need a cold drink. That Teotihuacán is one exposed site, and huge!"

"Were they there?" Neil asked.

"No. I saw lots of tour buses, but no sign of Isabella, Larry or any crazy Aztecs. Turns out the Aztecs didn't even build the place."

"What?" Neil asked.

"I hired a guide. Teotihuacán was a pre-Aztec city. Kind of a creepy place, too. The main street was called the Avenue of the Dead." Nakamura shuddered. "There were two pyramids, huge ones—the pyramids of the sun and moon. The guide I hired said there were sacrifices there as well—they used to push people down the steps—but that the Aztecs stayed away. They thought it was built by the gods—and they didn't want to tamper with the place."

Neil slumped back in his chair. "So not much of a lead. Great."

"But this is where it gets interesting. The pyramids you saw on the bus looked exactly like the pyramids in the murals because the Aztecs copied that style when they built their own city."

"Where?"

"Here."

"Here?"

"Yes."

Just then the waiter arrived, not with a cold drink, but with another envelope for Neil.

"This was left for you at the front desk," the man said.

The envelope was made from agave paper. It contained a lock of Isabella's hair, and one of Larry's.

"That's a good sign," Angel said hopefully. "And at least Larry is finally getting a haircut."

Neil actually gave a small chuckle. Then he let out a great sigh.

"There's a note. 'The calendar is in our favor. The sacred ceremonies are underway. XT.' That's it?" Neil turned the note over, his anger rising. "What kind of stupid message is that?"

Neil crumpled the paper and threw the note onto the table. He fingered the hair, and then carefully sniffed. He shook his head. "That's weird," he said, sniffing more closely to be sure. "Larry's hair smells like coffee, fresh coffee."

"More than you'd expect?" Angel asked.

Neil nodded. "But Isabella's hair smells like raw corn."

"Raw corn?" Nakamura asked.

"Yes."

Neil looked at Isabella's hair for a long while, rubbing it gently between his fingers.

"You miss her, don't you?" Angel said.

"Yes." It felt nice to admit it. He looked more closely at the hair, thinking of Isabella. Then he lifted the hairs right up to his eye and squinted. "Now that's really weird."

"What is it? What do you see?"

"There's corn silk braided in with her hair."

224

CHAPTER TWENTY-EIGHT

CALENDAR CONUNDRUM

Neil sat on the edge of his bed, racking his brain. "Raw corn. Raw corn. Corn silk and coffee. What the heck kind of message is he trying to send me?" Neil knew Larry was going to be as specific as possible. He could even imagine a tiny Larry sitting on his shoulder smacking his head. "C'mon cousin, think."

Larry knew that Isabella had been sending Neil hints. So Larry knew that Neil would be smelling his hair and hers. There had to be some code behind this choice of food.

"Angel, what the heck does raw corn silk have to do with the Aztecs?"

Angel was sitting across the room on Larry's couch, looking incredulously at the collection of empty

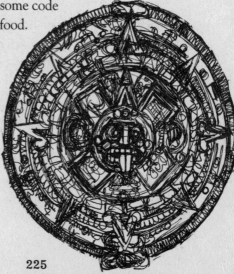

225

coffee cups Larry had stacked in the shape of the nearby cathedral.

"The first corn of the season was very important," Angel said, turning his attention back to Neil, "but that's not an Aztec thing. Every culture celebrates the first crop of the year. In North America it's Thanksgiving. The ancient Greeks held feasts for Demeter—the goddess of the harvest."

"But were there any special corn-related festivals? Was it a wedding symbol?" Neil couldn't shake the idea that Isabella was supposed to marry somebody.

Angel nodded. "Yes, but it was a symbol for many other things as well—life, death, sustenance, the favor of the gods."

"Wait a minute," Neil snapped his fingers. "Isabella only started the raw corn after Larry was taken. She'd rubbed corn in her hair before, but not raw corn. This has to be Larry's idea—at least, let's go with that theory for a second."

"Okay."

"And she made sure to include strands of corn silk in her hair as well. That's no accident either." Neil's mind was racing. Maybe Larry had seen something in his research that he wanted Neil to find. Larry had been extremely active with his books and sticky notes, and he'd told Neil he wanted to go over some ideas after the visit to the museum. Neil realized with a chill that if he didn't guess what Larry's clues meant, they might never have the chance to chat again.

"Angel, throw me that book Larry has under his pillow."

Angel pulled out a dog-eared copy of *Aztec Cosmology for Idiots*. "For idiots?"

"I gave it to him as a joke for the flight here," Neil said, catching the book. He began flipping through the pages. "Larry actually found it pretty useful. He's been researching all the X and T combinations he could find. Some were geographical, in case XT referred to a place where they might be hiding Isabella, but he had started looking at all the XT gods and goddesses, too." A number of the pages were marked with pink and yellow sticky notes decorated with Larry's exclamation-point system. One was interesting. Five was something really interesting. Neil opened the book to the first "!!!!!" he could find.

"This is about the importance of dating in Aztec culture," Neil said, disappointed. "I'm sure Larry found that fascinating, but I think it's a bit off-topic for us." He flipped to another "!!!!!".

"This one is about Tlaloc, but we know that stuff already." He flipped again.

"There are a lot of gods in the Aztec religion," Angel said. "This could take a while."

"True enough," said Neil. "Almost every page has a sticky. Wait, here's one he also marked with a used coffee stir stick." Neil grabbed the sliver of wood and put it on the bed sheet. "Xilonen," he read.

"I don't know anything about her," Angel said. "Was she a major deity?"

"It says she was a harvest goddess.

Larry circled some bits here. Her name comes from the word for—I don't believe it—corn silk!"

"Does it say anything else?"

Neil's finger followed the words on the page. "She's often portrayed as a young woman holding corn. Sometimes, she's also shown carrying flowers. . . . Holy cow! The Flower Bringer! This all fits."

Angel walked over and looked at the book. "Larry wrote something next to her name," he said, peering at the page.

Neil looked closely. Larry's chicken scratch was barely legible at the best of times, and he'd clearly written this note in a hurry, perhaps before they'd left for the museum.

"It says Codex Maggala-something."

Neil put down the book and ran to Larry's couch. One by one he began lifting books from the stack. Halfway through, he found it: the *Codex Magliabechiano*. It was a thin book, and it seemed to contain a number of symbols for food and various deities, along with graphic illustrations of human sacrifices on pyramids. Neil did his best to ignore those as he thumbed through the pages.

Neil brought the book over to Angel. "I need some help. The notes are in Spanish."

Angel looked carefully at the pages. "It's a calendar, a kind of list of religious ceremonies and rituals and when and how they happen."

"Does it mention anything to do with Xilonen?"

Angel turned a few pages and then nodded. "There's a picture of her here." The picture showed a young woman with a feathered headdress, carrying young corn and flowers. She wore a red and white dress and a turquoise necklace.

"It's the same outfit that woman in the Rivera painting is wearing!" Neil said.

"The one you said looks like Isabella."

Neil nodded.

Angel read on. As he did, a look of profound sadness crossed his face.

"Angel, what's wrong?"

Angel closed the book. "The feast of Xilonen is a harvest festival. It celebrates the importance of the earth and the new corn in the lives of the Aztecs."

"But aren't harvest festivals usually happy occasions? You don't look happy at all."

Angel nodded. "The feast of Xilonen is a happy occasion . . . in an Aztec kind of way. One young woman was chosen to be the goddess. She was fed and cleaned and treated like royalty for a period of ten days. Then she would 'become' the goddess Xilonen."

"What do you mean 'become'?" Neil felt a menacing tingle run up his spine.

"The Aztecs believed the goddess would assume the young woman's body for a last few hours of wild celebration. Then the girl was led to the temple, and her head was cut off."

Neil shook from head to toe.

"Wh . . . wh . . . why? Why kill her? These people are insane!"

"For the Aztecs, this final act of sacrifice kept the world in motion, the stars in motion, the corn growing and the gods happy."

Neil sat in shock. Isabella was the key, but she wasn't being saved for something romantic like a wedding. She was a lamb being led to a slaughter. "The codex said the victim was held for ten days of special celebration?"

Angel nodded.

Neil did some quick math, suppressing his rising horror. "Let's assume that XT is a stickler for ritual. He wouldn't count the day in the dump toward the preparation. By my count, ten days will be up the day after the semifinal."

"You are going to continue with the *Cocina*?" Angel said calmly.

Neil thought about this. Did it really matter what his plans were now? If they were right about Larry's hints, these people were going to kill Isabella whether he won or lost. If that was true, there was no point competing, was there? But if he lost the *Cocina*, he would lose Chez Flambé. That was a sacrifice he'd be willing to make, if it truly meant saving Isabella, but he needed to be darned sure. The best idea of all, though, would be to avoid the decision altogether.

"We have to try to find them before the semifinal," Neil said.

"Because you need to win?"

"Because of the timing," Neil said, struggling to piece it all together. "If I forfeit, they might kill her immediately, and we don't know what they've got planned for Larry."

The look on Neil's face hinted at the conflict that was taking place in his young heart and mind. Angel decided not to argue.

"So," Neil continued, "Larry is sending us a pretty specific message. Isabella is Xilonen. But does that give us any leads on finding them?"

"We should get some sleep," Angel said. "And get up early."

Neil ignored him and kept talking. "But this still doesn't make sense. Why do they care about me at all? If Isabella is fulfilling some bizarre ritual, what on earth do I have to do with it?"

"Maybe Nakamura is right: maybe there's also some big gambling scam."

"If only I knew where they were, or were going to be," Neil said. He punched his mattress, sending Larry's stir stick bookmarker flying into the air. Neil grabbed it and examined it closely. He smiled at Angel. "I think I know where we can look. Let's hope Larry and I are both thinking the same thing."

"A very scary thought, indeed," Angel said.

CHAPTER TWENTY-NINE

HAPPY TRAILS?

Neil was not very good at disguises; his large nose was a dead giveaway. But today, he really needed to sink into the background. Nakamura, who had been on a number of stakeouts, had a few tips. "A good disguise doesn't have to be perfect, just good enough so you don't attract attention. Remember, you won't be in contact with the suspect. You just need to observe him without being observed by him."

He handed Neil a baseball hat, which Neil placed over his head.

Nakamura nodded his approval. "That's a good start. Now try on my trench coat." Neil was both taller and skinnier than Nakamura, but it fit him pretty well. "The red hair and freakish nose are still dead giveaways—"

Neil frowned.

"—so I'm suggesting a wig, a fake mustache, and a beard."

"That won't look weird?"

"If someone tries to kiss you or give you a shave, yes.

But if you're just some hipster student sitting at a table with a laptop you'll look right at home."

"Won't the sales staff get suspicious?"

"At what? A university student who wants to grab a seat at a place with Wi-Fi, but who's too cheap to pay for more than one cup of coffee an hour? Dime a dozen. Don't tip. That would look suspicious."

"I'm as ready as I'll ever be," Neil said, adjusting the scratchy beard and whiskers.

"Off you go then, my fine lad," Nakamura said. "Just remember to lay low and speak as little as possible. And if someone serves you a pastry that's below your standards, eat it and shut up."

Neil took a last look at the swizzle stick Larry had used as a bookmark. It was from—where else?—the Guada-Latte Café. The name was embossed into the thin wood. Neil was certain that Larry remembered he'd used the stick to mark the Xilonen passage. That was why he'd dipped his hair in coffee. He wanted Neil to make the connection between coffee, Xilonen and the café. It was, Neil hoped, just the sort of nutso connection Larry would make.

He walked out of the hotel and headed for the café. The plan was to sit there and wait. Isabella had been able to smudge very specific food in her hair. The codex suggested she was being treated like royalty. Neil had a hunch that she was being given the special right to choose her food—and Larry had added coffee to that menu. If Neil's hunch was right, someone would either have to come to the café a number of times to satisfy Larry's coffee consumption, or would come once with a humongous thermos. Either way, Neil was sure he'd be able to pick the person out. That's why he was under-cover and not Nakamura. Neil was the only one who could smell if the delivery man or woman had been using Aztec soap and corn oil.

But the whole plan was also a big risk. What if he were wrong? He'd waste hours sitting in one spot instead of do-ing his best to help Angel and Nakamura. They were going out to scour the city as best as they could, but there were few real leads to go on. He hoped his hunch was right.

Neil took a seat near the back of the café and fired up his laptop. At least he could work on some recipes. Tomorrow he was taking on a chef he actually respected, Mario Bucati, a true wizard with seafood, pizza, and pasta. This was a duel Neil would have to work a lot harder at to win—well, okay, a little harder.

The waitress ambled over.

"*Solamente una café, por favor*," Neil blurted out before she could ask him something that would expose his lack of Spanish. Then he concentrated on his blank computer screen as if it were the most fascinating thing in the world.

The waitress frowned and walked away, mumbling.

Neil could make out a few of the words, including *barato* and *estupido*—"cheap" and "stupid."

So far, so good.

Neil was well into his third page of recipes for mole sauces when the unmistakable smell of corn oil, soap, burned ceremonial herbs and flowers broke through his concentration. He pulled his baseball hat over his eyes, and peered cautiously over the laptop.

A well-tanned man with a mustache was standing at

the counter. Neil watched as he handed the server a big thermos. The man was also carrying a large cloth bag stuffed to overflowing with raw corn. As accurately as Neil could tell, in a café filled with coffee aromas, it was new corn, very fresh—Palomero, the same variety he'd smelled in Isabella's hair. The man looked around as he waited for the woman to fill the thermos to the brim. Neil ducked his head back down quickly and began typing furiously.

XT XT XT XT XT XT XT XT XT XT XT XT XT
XT XT XT XT XT XT XT XT XT XT XT XT XT XT
XT XT XT XT XT XT XT XT XT XT XT XT XT XT
XT XT XT XT XT XT XT XT XT XT XT XT XT XT
XT XT XT XT XT XT XT XT!

When he looked back up, just a moment later, the man had gone. "Oh no!" Neil said. He threw a few pesos on the table and scrambled to shove his laptop into his backpack before the trail was completely lost. He rushed out of the front door and sniffed the air. The breeze was coming from his right, but the coffee and corn smell wasn't there. If the man had gone that way, Neil would be able to smell him. Neil turned left.

The narrow street was crammed with stalls and shoppers grabbing their breakfast before heading off to work. Neil bobbed and weaved, crashing into more than a few angry people, and knocking his false beard hopelessly loose. He pulled it off and sped up. Finally, he spied the man up ahead, but a crush of people stood between them. Neil did his best to stay both inconspicuous and close.

He ducked into doorways and hid behind stalls. He fiddled with his baseball hat. He was sure he looked exactly like a stupid kid who was following someone. He was just as sure that Nakamura would be shaking his head in disgust. "Jeepers kid, why don't you just ask the guy if you can dance with him!"—that sort of thing.

Luckily for Neil, the man didn't seem to notice that he was being followed. After a few minutes he turned a corner and walked into the Zócalo. It was still morning, but the entire place was packed. Tourists milled about, clutching maps, guidebooks and digital cameras. Anti-government protestors stood in front of the presidential palace, yelling slogans through bullhorns. Aztec dancers shook and swayed and sent plumes of aromatic smoke into the air in front of the cathedral. Neil avoided them all.

Souvenir stands dotted the landscape. Neil hurried over to one and pretended to study the selection of hand-stitched shirts and pants as he watched the man approach a group of laborers. The man seemed to know them and they nodded as he spoke.

"So that's one group of spies," Neil thought, frowning. He'd passed groups of laborers like this almost every day on his way to and from the hotel. They must have been keeping an eye on him, maybe even dropping off the notes. One of the men in the group looked in Neil's direction. He hoped his beard was still fitting okay. He felt his face and was startled to feel the smoothness of his own skin. He'd forgotten that he'd yanked the beard off!

He turned around quickly to replace it and found himself face-to-back with a circle of energetic Aztec dancers. Neil had no idea if they were the same ones Tlaloc had been performing with in the park, and he didn't want to find out. Neil turned around and spied the man a short distance away, heading for the cathedral. Neil followed, doing his best to hide his partially bearded face from the laborers who were milling around the entrance to the nearby subway station. He hurried through the iron front gates and into the enormous stone edifice.

Neil was no stranger to church—he had once been kicked out of his first communion class for suggesting a better recipe for the Eucharistic wafer—but this church was unlike any he'd ever seen before.

The columns that supported the ceiling rose seemingly forever, forming graceful arches way up in the sky. Gilded statues, paintings and leaded glass adorned every niche. Neil thought of Larry. He would love this place. He made a vow to himself: when this was all over, they would come back and explore. But right now, he had to find the man with the corn and coffee.

Mass was well underway. The priest chanted something in Spanish and the congregation sat down. Over their bowed heads, Neil saw the man. He was walking slowly down a side aisle, rubbing something small between his fingers. It looked like he was saying a rosary.

Neil hid behind a pillar to watch. The priest said something else and the congregation stood up, momentarily cutting off Neil's view. By the time the worshipers sat back down, the man was gone.

Neil hustled as quickly as he could up the outside aisle, where he'd last seen the man walking. He glanced into each pew as he passed. Nothing. Where had he gone?

The lingering scent of corn and coffee hung in the air. Neil looked closely at the wall. Nearly hidden from view was a tiny chapel, built back from the aisle and sandwiched between two pillars. You had to look straight at it to see it. There was an altar, a few chairs and a mournful looking statue. The figure was sitting down, with a basket between his feet. Neil looked at the basket. It was filled with cocoa beans.

"I looked everywhere," Neil said. He, Angel and Naka-mura were sitting in a small restaurant on the roof of an old house with a view of the back of the cathedral. "I know the layout of that cathedral better than the guy who built it!"

The sun had set hours before, and Neil was feeling completely drained. "I looked for loose stones, secret levers, pulleys, anything. I even tried moving the cocoa beans in the basket before some lady in a black shawl started smacking me with her cane."

Nakamura chuckled as the image of this encounter played out in his imagination. Neil looked at Angel, who was trying to suppress a smile of his own.

"They were real beans, by the way. I'm telling you, the guy walked into that church and vanished."

"Maybe the lady with the cane was him in disguise," Nakamura said, still chuckling.

"And what great leads did you two find?"

Nakamura stopped smiling. Angel let out a sigh. "We went to Mount Tlaloc. It was one of the main Aztec sites for sacrifices."

Neil sat up in his seat. "And?"

"Nothing," Nakamura said, shaking his head. "There are still the remains of an ancient temple there, impressive really, but there was no evidence that our modern Aztecs either are or were anywhere near. By the time we got there, looked around and came back, the day was pretty much shot. Sorry, Nose."

"One day left," Neil said as his chicken mole and beans arrived. The meal smelled wonderful, but he had lost his appetite.

CHAPTER THIRTY

MURALS AND MORALS

Neil actually went up to shake the hand of his opponent before they began their match. Mario Bucati was clearly taken aback. "Neil Flambé giving a warm greeting to another chef?"

"I'm only rude to chefs I don't respect," Neil said. "I'm still going to beat you, but I respect you."

"Well, um, thank you, Neil . . . I guess. Too bad you will lose today."

"I can't lose, and I mean that in every way imaginable," Neil said cryptically.

There had been yet another envelope awaiting Neil as he made his way downstairs that morning. No note, just two more locks of hair. One was black, curly and had bits of corn silk mixed in. The other was dirty, light brown, and coffee-saturated— and definitely with the coffee that Neil had smelled in the Guade-Latte. The little man had somehow gotten the food to Larry and Isabella.

The bottom line? Once he'd dealt with Bucati, he was going to have to make some extremely difficult decisions. He'd have just a few hours left to find Isabella and Larry, or he'd lose everything.

Jose Aciete stepped up to the microphone, made his usual spiel for Cortez Corn oil, and prepared to open the boxes with the secret ingredients. Neil already knew it was all vegetables: local staples such as tomatoes, yams, and potatoes.

Jose waved his hand and the waiters lifted the tops of the boxes.

Bucati had a crestfallen look on his face. He was an unapologetic carnivore, whereas Neil, ever since his conversation about death with XT, had been working on more vegetarian meals for his menu. It was almost as if someone had hand-picked the perfect ingredients for Neil to mop the floor with Bucati.

Neil looked at Angel. "I'm thinking a curried roti."

"I will try to honor my mother's memory," Angel said.

"Fine. Let's just win and get back to looking for Isabella and Larry."

The final result was surprisingly close. As soon as Bucati had gotten over his initial panic, he'd prepared a four-course meal of increasing perplexity. It had started with a vegetarian ceviche and ended with an incredible vegetable pie with a puff-pastry crust. It was exactly the sort of thing Neil would have ordered, if his own dishes hadn't been offered at the same time.

In the end, Neil won the panel over with his more "cohesive journey," as the judges described it. He'd started with a tangy sesame vinaigrette and cucumber salad, then followed with a mix of lightly braised root vegetables cooked *en papillote*—sealed and then baked in carefully folded parchment paper, retaining every morsel of flavor. That led into Angel's fabulous curry, and the whole meal ended with deep-fried vanilla ice cream in a sweet mole sauce and a side of strong coffee.

"The coffee was a nod to someone who could not be with me today, but will be soon," Neil added, turning and sneering at the camera.

"Perhaps another veiled message to the mysterious 'XT' you berated earlier this week?" Jose asked. Now that the *Cocina* was at the semifinal stage, Jose seemed to be taking a more direct role in the broadcasts.

"You got that right," Neil said. As Jose slapped him on the back and then walked away, Neil's nose detected an unmistakable odor: antiseptic soap.

"Mr. Aciete," Neil called after him. "Did you hurt yourself recently?"

Jose looked surprised. "Yes, a gash on my hand." He held up his hand, revealing a large while bandage. "It's very embarrassing. It happened the other day when I spilled that corn oil on myself. It dripped all over the place. I slipped backstage and cut my arm on something." He shrugged. "I'm a bit, I think clumsy is what you say in English?"

Neil nodded, but his mind was somewhere else. Jose waited for more conversation, then shrugged and walked away.

Neil tapped his chin for a few seconds before speaking. The smell of the antiseptic soap had ignited an idea in Neil's mind. "Angel, let's get Nakamura. Something just occurred to me."

"Are we heading back to the cathedral?"

"No. We're heading to the hospital."

CHAPTER THIRTY-ONE

COMAS AND
CARDS

Isabella had spent an extremely strange and disconcerting few days. She had been kidnapped, cleaned, fed, almost drowned, almost crushed, blindfolded, then cleaned and fed again. And now she was in yet another cave, this one richly decorated with all sorts of painted statues of various gods and serpents, skulls carved from everything from dark obsidian to clear crystal and huge stone slabs. It was like being held prisoner in a museum, except everything looked freshly cleaned and repainted.

But even all that weirdness hadn't prepared her for what was happening now.

The bricklayer and his henchmen had ushered in all the prisoners. Lily, her sister, the poor tour-bus driver the bricklayer had held up at gunpoint at the park, and about twenty others. They were all dressed in white robes, with their faces painted a sickly blood red. The men held tall staffs made from corn stalks tied together with a kind of rough twine. The women wore bright feathers in their hair and around their necks and were dancing around the cave in a kind of slow, strange ballet. Isabella watched. They looked miserable, and, she thought, drugged. They moved mechanically, almost like robots. What the heck was going on?

She was sure Larry would be able to tell her, but she hadn't been able to speak to him since they'd been forced to run from the Chapultepec cave-in. At least, they hadn't spoken in words.

The bricklayer had gagged Larry after he'd woken up on the bus. He'd been chained to her again, though, and their eyes had met. Larry had looked quickly from her face down to his jacket pocket. Somehow, he had extracted a napkin from somewhere in his outfit and had maneuvered it so that she could read the print. She had a vague memory of him once dating a circus performer. She looked quickly at the napkin. It read Guade-Latte Café.

Once they'd arrived at this new cave, they had immediately been separated and she hadn't seen him since.

The bricklayer walked up to her now, offering her a drink of warm sweet cocoa and a small round cake. "The stars are in our favor!" he smiled.

"That's not raw corn. I asked for raw corn," Isabella said, frowning. "And coffee from the Guade-Latte."

"You had those this morning. It is no longer time for requests. The celebration has begun. This food is cooked from the new corn. It is a sacrament, a custom that is ordained from the heavens."

"You're awfully informative all of a sudden," Isabella said, grabbing the cake and devouring it greedily. The raw corn she'd been ordering had not been very filling. In fact, it had made her feel rather sick.

"That's because the time is at hand to usher in a new era. It is so exciting! Our leader has only to make an offering to please the gods and then Mexico will be ours again." The bricklayer pulled a conch shell from the wall. He began to blow, creating a ghostlike sound.

In Italy, Isabella had seen paintings of ancient rites known as Bacchanalia, in which the god Bacchus incited young women and men to enact bizarre rituals in the woods. Some danced with such a frenzy they turned into animals. Others became so crazed that they killed themselves or their companions. Isabella had always been afraid of the devilish dioramas. Now she felt as if she had been dropped into the middle of one, albeit with a Mexican twist.

"I wish to leave," she said for the hundredth time.

"You will leave, very soon." The bricklayer stopped his blowing to answer her. "You are no longer merely the Flower Bringer. You are the corn goddess!" He resumed his awful playing with a crazed look in his eyes.

Isabella felt tears welling up—tears of fear, frustration and confusion.

"I need to speak to my husband."

The bricklayer dropped his conch shell. He looked at Isabella as if he had been shaken from a trance. "Your . . . your husband?"

"The man you brought in here the other day? The coffee drinker? He is my husband."

246

* * *

Neil marched up the stairs of the Xoco Hospital. "Of course they'd choose a hospital with an X in the name," Neil said.

Angel and Nakamura were trying to keep up with him. "So run this by me again. You think Rodrigo is XT?" Nakamura said.

Neil nodded. "Who told you he was in a coma?" he asked.

"Enrique."

"The corrupt cop."

"Yes, you know that already." Nakamura was still miffed that his trust had been so badly placed.

"I'm just saying that we've been taking his word for it that Rodrigo was actually in an accident. You said the Cortez Corn Oil company had been buying lots of other companies."

"So?"

"So Rodrigo needed cash. He bets on me to lose, at incredibly long odds, given my abilities—"

Nakamura rolled his eyes.

"—and then he covers the costs of his expansion by making millions. He had access to the chests with the ingredients. He smelled like corn oil, and the envelopes smell like corn oil."

"So why do the whole Xilonen sacrifice thing," Nakamura wondered, "if this is all about business?"

"Maybe he's a businessman with some crazed love for Aztec culture."

Angel nodded. "Maybe to him, the continued existence of the world rests on the sacrifices ordained by the Aztec calendar. Business is better if the world doesn't end."

"Killing Isabella represents a return to the old way of life," Neil added. "Then they get money from me and run the food industry."

"So it's religion and business mixed together?"

"Yes," Neil said firmly. It was the only explanation. "Now you'll see. Rodrigo is faking his own coma and is running his business from his hospital room."

They reached the patients' wing. Neil opened the door and marched down the hallway. As Neil expected, burly bodyguards stood in front of the door. He pretended he was walking past the room then made a sudden swerve and bolted inside.

There, lying on a bed surrounded with what seemed like a hundred blinking lights and humming machines, was Rodrigo Hernandez. A tube in his nose fed him oxygen. He had IV tubes in both arms. He wasn't moving.

Neil felt his heart fall into his shoes. He had been so sure that Rodrigo was the mastermind—that the coma had been a ruse. But something else was bugging Neil. Why hadn't the security guards stormed in after him? Reluctantly he turned around. He could see Angel having an animated conversation with them in Spanish. He caught Angel's eye. Angel smiled and nodded at Neil. Somehow, Angel was buying him time.

Neil walked to the side of the bed. Goose bumps rose on his arms. If Rodrigo wasn't the mastermind, who was?

Rodrigo's chest rose and fell weakly. Neil felt a twinge of guilt. He'd been so ready to think the worst of him. But really, Rodrigo Hernandez had thought up the whole idea of the *Cocina*, and had taken a chance on inviting a teenage chef from Canada to take part. Neil wished he could say sorry, and thanks, and to wish Rodrigo well.

Many others had had the same feeling. The room was filled with beautiful flowers and dozens of "get well" cards. Most had images of Our Lady of Guadalupe. A few were nice scenes of fields and puffy clouds.

At the foot of the bed there was an enormous bouquet of lilies and dahlias, supported by corn-stalk stakes in a terra-cotta pot. The lilies smelled . . . familiar. Neil looked at the bouquet more closely. There was a card attached. The paper was odd—translucent. On the front, executed in red ink, was a hand-drawn picture of a pyramid and the words "Templo Mayor."

Neil sidled over to get a closer look, and sniff. There were more words inside. "*Pronto, el Templo se levantra . . .*" Neil reached over to fully open the card.

"I'm afraid I cannot allow you any closer," said a voice behind him. He turned to see a security guard with a sympathetic look on his face. "Your friend has explained to us that you wanted to pay your respects to this great man, but as you can see, he could die from a simple cold, and the machines are very delicate, you understand."

Neil took a deep nasal breath. He also arched his neck for one last peek at the card. His eyes grew wide.

"Thank you," he said to the guard as he backed out the door quickly. As soon as he, Nakamura and Angel were outside, Neil turned to Angel. "What does '*Pronto el Templo se levantra*' mean?"

"The temple will soon rise again."

"I know who the mastermind is now, and I know where to find him."

"Who?"

"Where?"

"Let me answer that with another question. Angel, where would we find the temple from the Rivera painting?"

CHAPTER THIRTY-TWO

TEMPLO MAYOR

Isabella and Larry were chained together again. The dancers had been unceremoniously ushered out of the room and the bricklayer had gone to confer with his leader, whoever the heck that was.

"You said I was your what?" Larry said, spewing his coffee all over the floor. He watched sadly as his Guade-Latte special leaked away between the stones.

"*Mio marido*, 'my husband,'" Isabella said as quietly as she could. She was completely embarrassed.

Larry couldn't suppress a loud guffaw. "Did we invite Neil to the wedding?"

Now she was just ticked. "I didn't know what else to say. I needed to ask you what was going on, and I took a chance that it was the only way they were going to let us meet again."

"Well, you were right. It sure took them by surprise, and it might have mucked things up for them a bit, and not necessarily in a good way for us."

"What do you mean?"

Larry moved closer to her and spoke quickly. "Look, here's the deal, as close as I can figure. These guys are modern-day Aztecs, right?"

"I figured that out on my own, thanks." Isabella frowned.

"But they're taking the Aztec thing to the extreme." Larry made a circling gesture around his ear and mouthed the words "cuckoo, cuckoo." "They want to recreate the old ways, the old festivals and rituals. I speak a little bit of their language so I've picked up some stuff."

Isabella was about say "you're kidding," but then remembered she was talking to Larry, the walking Wikipedia. She nodded for him to continue.

"They think the gods have been angry since the Spanish squashed the Aztec religions back in the 1500s. The Spanish burned all the old books, smashed statues, that sort of stuff. They think if they make the gods happy again, then the gods will help them with their bigger plan."

"Which is?"

"That bit I don't know yet."

"So what does any of this have to do with me being married? Why is it such a problem?"

"Because you are their pick for Xilonen—the flower bringer and goddess of new corn. You have to be young and unattached, new. This is one of those big festivals they want to bring back to make the gods happy. They have to do it right or the whole plan will fall apart."

"And what happens to her, I mean to me?"

"She gets treated like a queen for about ten days and then—" Larry stopped.

Isabella frowned. "I'm not three. You can't shock me."

"And then they take her to the temple and chop her head off."

Isabella gasped.

"You look shocked," Larry said.

"But if I'm married to you, then I can't be Xilonen, right?"

Larry opened his palms. "Voila! And if you can't be Xilonen then there's no reason for them not to just kill us both right now."

Isabella pondered this as she heard the bricklayer enter the room and walk quickly toward them. "I guess I should tell him that we are not really married."

"Not married . . . yet," Larry said with a wink.

The Zócalo subway station is just in front of the cathedral. If you turn right at the bottom of the stairs you hit the ticket kiosk and the trains. If you turn left, there's a hallway with doors for the cleaning closets, electrical rooms and so on. Right in the middle is a series of historical dioramas of Mexico City from pre-Aztec times to modern times. Neil, Angel and Nakamura were flitting between two of the displays: Tenochtitlán, 1521, and Mexico City, 1824. "Tenochtitlán was the name the Aztecs gave to this area," Angel read.

"So the Zócalo was always a kind of big open square?" Neil asked. "Even back before the Spanish showed up?"

Angel nodded. "And if the two dioramas are laid out accurately, then the Aztec temples were built along the sides of the square, much like the modern buildings." Angel pointed at the 1521 diorama. All four sides of the square were boxed in by enormous temples and pyramids.

"But none of that is left," Neil said.

"The Spanish plowed it under and built a new city on top," Angel said, reading from the plaque.

Neil held a map of the center of town, and was looking from it to the diorama, trying to match the modern layout with the ancient city. "So the presidential palace sits on the remains of Montezuma's palace."

"The palace looks huge," Nakamura said, gazing at the diorama. "Too bad it's gone."

"So is the Templo Mayor, the main temple—that's the one we're looking for."

Neil flipped to another section of the guidebook. "It was the spiritual center of the Aztec nation. The book says there is some dispute about exactly where the temple sat."

"It must have been amazing to see," Angel said, also looking at the panorama. "What year is that guidebook?"

Neil flipped to the front. "About a year old."

"Look at this," Angel pointed to a very shiny plaque inside the glass case. Neil looked at it. He saw the words Templo Mayor, but the rest was in Spanish.

"It says recent excavations, as in the past few months, have uncovered ruins, right next to the cathedral, that they believe are the remains of the temple," Angel translated.

"Next to the cathedral?" Neil said. "You mean that pile of rubble we walked by the other day? That's actually the Templo?"

"The plaque says that's the foundation and a few steps. They believe further excavations will reveal even more, including tombs and temples underneath."

Neil read some more. "The Spanish destroyed the temple during their siege of the city. Then they used the stones to build their own cathedral." Neil closed the book with a clap. "So, the temple we've been looking for is right next to the cathedral, just a stone's throw from our stupid hotel."

"The temple, as you pointed out, doesn't exist anymore. There are just ruins," Nakamura said.

Neil scratched his head. "The Spanish used the stones from the temple to build the cathedral. Could these crazy nut jobs think the cathedral is the temple?"

"Like the stones themselves are still sacred?" Nakamura nodded. "You did see the guy with the coffee go in there."

"And disappear." Neil opened the guidebook again, to the section on the cathedral. "It says the ancient Aztecs would build their temples over sacred streams and underground caves. The cathedral is sinking, and one reason is that it's built over a stream."

Neil snapped the book shut. "Let's go get some cocoa beans," Neil said. "I need to make an offering."

The statue Neil had seen in the chapel turned out to be a fairly famous work of Spanish art—*Nostro Señor del Cacao, Our Lord of Cacao.* Cortez himself had placed the statue in front of the ruined Aztec temple to solicit donations. "He asked people to drop in money to help pay for the new church," Neil read from the book as he stood in front of the chapel.

"And they dropped in cocoa beans instead?" Nakamura asked.

Angel nodded. "Cocoa was valuable. It was a kind of currency."

"But I'll bet the statue is still a pretty awful symbol for these modern Aztecs," Nakamura said. "They would see it as a reminder of the fact that their people paid for their own temple to be replaced."

"Who cares what they think?" Neil seethed. "Do you know what the Aztecs had in front of their temple? They stacked the heads of all their sacrificial victims on top of each other, like a giant wall. It was twenty storeys high by the time the Spanish knocked it down. I'll take a statue of a man with cocoa beans anytime."

Neil examined the beans in the statue's basket. "The

man I followed wasn't saying a rosary. He was counting out cocoa beans to put in the middle of the bowl!"

"Why?" Nakamura asked.

"It would look like he was making an offering, but the bowl must trigger some hidden doorway. Once we figure out the right number of cocoa beans, we should be able to trigger the entrance."

"I'll keep a watch out for old ladies with canes," Nakamura chuckled. The church was actually pretty empty, with just a few people saying their prayers.

Neil knelt down by the bowl. He began adding beans one handful at a time. He'd put in about fifty, but nothing moved. He needed to think. Did he need to add more? Had he added too many?

"Neil, have you thought about what to do if you do find some secret passage?" Angel asked as Neil tried adding more beans, then a combination of smaller beans and larger beans.

"No."

"There are only three of us. XT may have an army down there," Angel said.

"And they can spare a guy every day to do the grocery shopping," Nakamura added. "We should maybe figure out a plan of attack first."

"We don't have time," Neil said. "Isabella and Larry could be dead by the time we come up with a plan." Neil threw in all his beans, but nothing happened. "RATS!" he yelled. He was tempted to put all the beans back in the bag and throw the entire thing at the altar.

What was the key? A thought occurred to him. Maybe the man had been saying a kind of rosary after all. Maybe it was the number of beans that was important. There were fifty-nine or sixty beads on a standard rosary. Neil counted out fifty-nine beans, and threw them on the pile. Nothing happened. He scooped them out.

"Maybe *saying* a rosary would be more helpful," Nakamura joked.

Neil ignored him. Instead, he began to drop the beans in one at a time. By the time he counted fifty he could hear the faint whirl of gears coming from the altar behind the statue. He kept the same rhythm and dropped in the final nine beans, then stopped. He heard a small click like the sound of a key in a lock. On the altar, a wooden panel had opened a crack.

"I'll go alone," Neil said, "and I'll try to be quiet. You two stay here and wait for me."

"No." Angel said. Then he looked at the tiny opening. There was no way he was going to fit. "There must be another entrance somewhere."

"Stay here and don't worry," Neil said, touching his nose. "I can smell trouble coming a mile away."

CHAPTER THIRTY-THREE

TROUBLE STINKS

The wood panel opened onto a tunnel so small that Neil had to slide down the first part on his stomach. Within a few feet it opened into a larger passageway. He stood up and flicked on Larry's keychain flashlight. After his last experience in a dark cave, he'd been sure to stock up on batteries.

He was surprised to find that he was standing on an iron walkway. There was no railing—just rope strung between iron posts. The tops of the posts were forged serpent heads, and the rope passed between their fangs. Neil gulped. "Nice decor," he thought grimly. He looked down at his shoes. Through the grate of the walkway, he could see a stream of running water about three feet below. The tunnel walls seemed to be made of smoothed dirt and stone carved by centuries of moving water. The tunnel sloped downward, away from the church, and followed the course of the stream. Neil wasn't completely certain, but it seemed to be heading in the direction of the ruins of the Templo Mayor. Neil started walking.

After a few minutes the gentle flow of the water turned into a loud *whoosh*. Neil lifted the flashlight. Just ahead was a gap in the rope, on both sides, of about three or four feet. He inched his way forward, looked down, and found himself staring into a deep well, at least ten feet below. The stream ended in a violent, cascading water-fall. Neil pointed his light into the middle of the hole.

Jagged rocks stuck up through the foam and the stream bubbled like a boiling pot of pasta as it swirled around before resuming its flow, Neil presumed, through some hidden gap in the rock. To Neil, the well or hole or whatever it was looked a little like the open mouth of some big serpent. This was a dangerous spot, probably a trap for anyone foolish enough to sneak in without knowing the way. He pointed the flashlight to the other side of the gap, where the rope picked up again. The ground underneath began to slope up and the walkway ended, like a bridge, at a large opening in the opposite wall. The rock around the hole was carved with suns and stars and weird animal symbols.

Neil walked carefully past the gap, over the rest of the walkway and through this opening, silently thanking Larry for his flashlight keychain. He stopped. There were voices ahead. He pressed himself tightly against the stone, trying to blend into the wall, but the voices weren't moving toward him. Somewhere up ahead, two

people were having a conversation, and not a friendly one. He heard a loud bang, like a sledgehammer on a wooden surface. He shuffled forward carefully, an inch at a time. Just ahead, the tunnel took an abrupt right turn.

Neil crept to the corner and peered around. A few feet past the bend, he could make out a recessed doorway carved into the wall. The tunnel, which was lit just outside the room by a single, burning torch, continued past. There wasn't another person in sight. Neil slipped silently into the doorway and held his breath. Now, only the wooden door stood between him and the argument. Wrought-iron bars, in the shape of coiled snakes, covered a window about three-quarters of the way up.

Inside the room, two men were arguing. Neil could make out only a few words. *Azteca*, *Mexica* and Xilonen were mentioned a few times. And the word Flambé was followed by more pounding. He stood on his toes and peeked in the window.

Neil's eyes grew wide. Pillars in the shape of Aztec gods held up the roof. The walls were decorated with all sorts of artifacts—crystal and gold skulls, elaborate feathered headdresses, woven tapestries showing Aztec sacrificial rites. This was a room fit for a king.

There, standing in the middle of the room, was the tanned and mustached man he'd followed into the church. The man was arguing with someone Neil couldn't see, but he must have been sitting behind the giant wooden table that Neil could just make out behind one of the massive pillars. Señor Mustache wasn't at all happy with what the other man was saying, and he paced the room in a huff. Neil's eyes followed him as he stalked from one side of the room to the other. As the man approached the far corner, he drew Neil's gaze to a sight that nearly made Neil gasp out loud. There, tied to chair, gagged and clearly roughed up, was Larry.

Every muscle in Neil's body tensed. He felt a tremendous urge to rush right in but he could hear Nakamura's voice in his head: "barging in gets you killed." He clenched his fists. He needed to think. Larry was just a few feet away from him. He could still see Señor Mustache pacing, and knew there was at least one more person in the room. Were they armed? Were there others in the room as well? He peered in again.

This time, he did gasp. Neil hadn't noticed before, but the entire far wall of the room was stacked with sticks of dynamite, tied together in bundles with wires and tape. Neil was no explosives expert, but there seemed to be enough to blow the place sky-high. Neil watched as the man untied Larry and forced him to stand. Larry looked a little wobbly, but he stayed upright. A large hand pushed an Aztec knife across the top of the table toward the man. The hand was bandaged!

Señor Mustache picked up the knife and held it against Larry's throat. Just as Neil put his hand on the door and started to push, the hidden man yelled something else, and Señor Mustache nodded, lowering the knife. Neil exhaled and relaxed his grip in the door handle. What on earth was going on in there? There was no time to find out. The man grabbed Larry and together they turned toward the door. In an instant, Neil turned and bolted back up the tunnel toward the waterfall. He stopped just around the corner and hugged the wall. He needed a plan and he needed it fast.

He peered around the corner. The man pushed Larry out of the doorway first, then turned back to close the door. They went a short way down the tunnel, away from Neil, and grabbed the torch. Then, to Neil's surprise, they turned back around and began heading straight for him. Luckily, Larry was blocking the shorter man's view. Neil began to back up.

Neil had a sinking feeling in the pit of his stomach: he knew where the man was taking Larry—the well. What better place to dispose of an unwanted prisoner. He needed to get there first. He ran as quietly and quickly as he could. Luckily Larry didn't look like somebody who was ready to run a hundred-yard dash any time soon.

Neil passed the well and crouched down on the walkway a few feet away. He turned off his light and waited. A minute later the man and Larry arrived. He shoved Larry to his knees on the edge of the path and began to chant.

Neil watched as the man put down his torch, then drew the knife back. It was time.

"AHHHHHHHH," Neil leaped at the man, catching him completely off guard. Neil grabbed his arms in a bear hug and together they flew back onto the metal walkway and landed in a heap. The knife came loose and skidded away.

"You!" the man yelled, staring up into Neil's eyes with rage. "I save your life, and this is how you repay me?"

Neil stared at the man in shock. What was he talking about? When had he saved his life? In a flash, Neil made the connection. "Tlaloc!" he said. "You shot Tlaloc—I mean, Enrique!"

"As soon as Tlaloc brought this fool back with him, I knew he had lost his senses. I followed him. If he had killed you, our entire plan would have failed. We needed you to keep winning! So I killed him instead. And if you leave me no choice, I will kill you." The man gritted his teeth and struggled to loosen Neil's grasp.

"You are not going to kill me or my cousin!" Neil snuck a look at Larry. He was still kneeling on the edge of the path, his eyes barely open. This would have to be a one-Flambé battle, and Neil needed to win it. He struggled to his knees, lifted the man by the wrists and slammed him back against the iron walkway. The vibration sent the torch over the edge. It hit the water and went out with a sizzle.

At that moment Neil made a mistake—a big one. He let go of one of the man's hands, not on purpose, but because the man's knee had come up and hit him in the ribs, which were still bruised from his encounter with Enrique. The man now punched at Neil, grazing his face just enough to knock Neil off balance, and free his other hand. Neil flailed away in the darkness, but the man must have retreated. Neil felt one leg slip over the edge of the walkway, and he righted himself quickly.

"Where are you?" Neil yelled. He didn't hear footsteps running off in the darkness, so he knew the man was still nearby. "Why don't you run back and tell your precious leader that I'm onto him?"

Neil heard the man chuckle. He also heard the sound of a stone being scraped against metal. The knife!

"Why waste my breath," the man said. "I said if you left me no choice I would kill you. Your threats have decided your fate."

Neil thought quickly. The man could only come at him from one direction, which was good, but Neil would be completely unable to defend himself in the dark, which was bad. He got down on his knees and felt frantically for Larry. Somehow, he had to pull him away and make a run for it.

"Into the burning water!" the man yelled, and Neil heard him run across the metal floor. Where was Larry?

The man yelled again, and Neil winced, waiting to feel the sharp blade of the knife. But this time the man was yelling in panic, and his voice was fading—fast. A moment later, Neil heard the sickening thud of bone on rock and then a splash. Then there was nothing but the sound of the rushing water.

Neil stood up carefully, his relief mixed with shock. The man was surely dead.

"Neil? Zat you?" said a groggy voice in the darkness.

"Yes! Larry, it's me."

"I stood up and then some guy bumped into me. Are we in the subway?"

Stood up? Oh no. Neil tried to make his voice sound as calm as possible.

"Larry, listen carefully. Don't move. Stay perfectly still. I've got your light here somewhere. Give me a second. Just DO NOT MOVE, okay?"

"I'm feeling groggy, Neil. I just gotta sit for a moment. I'm a little dizzy."

"Stop! Larry, stop!" Neil hurriedly felt around in his pocket for the keys. Somehow he pulled them from his jeans without dropping them and pushed the button.

The light shone on Larry, who was teetering on the edge of the precipice. Neil jumped and grabbed him, just in time. The flashlight clanged off the walls, shattering into pieces.

Neil and Larry stood face to face in the total darkness.

"Larry," Neil whispered. The last thing he wanted was to startle his cousin into any sudden movement. "Hold onto me as tightly as you can."

"Okay, Neil," Larry said, swaying. "You know something? I like you, Neil. I really do."

"Thanks, Larry," Neil said struggling to stay balanced. The light had gone out before he'd gotten a good look, but Neil thought they were still dangerously close to the edge. "Now just listen to what I tell you. We are going to back up two steps together. I'm going backward. You are going to step forward." Neil tightened his hold on Larry and felt for the walkway with the toe of his shoe. Together they took two steps.

"Now we are going to turn left just a bit."

"Your left or my left?"

"My left."

"Cool."

Neil was certain they were now facing the right direction. "Now, let go of me slowly. I'll hold you, but you've got to turn around and face away from me, okay?"

"This is a nice dance you've come up with, Neil. Did I mention I like you?"

"Yes, and I like you too, Larry."

"I mean, you can be a real one-hundred percent jerk sometimes, but I like you."

"You do realize that I'm trying to save your life," Neil said.

"Sorry. How about ninety percent jerk? Is that better?"

Neil gave a nervous chuckle as they began to shuffle forward. They were joking. Joking felt nice.

After a few steps, Neil reached out with one hand. He was delighted when he could feel the rope. He let out a deep breath and his muscles relaxed. It hit him just how close they had been to dying.

"Okay, Larry, let's get out of here. Move it."

"*Sí, sí, mi capitán.*"

They hurried up the tunnel as quickly as Larry could manage. Every few minutes, Neil made them stop and listen. No one, it seemed, was following them.

Finally, they reached the door. Neil crawled past Larry and felt around for a latch. On this side, thank goodness, it was a simple switch, not some massive stone or complicated device. Neil flicked it and a sliver of light crept into the tunnel as the door slowly swung open. Neil stuck his head through the narrow crack and blinked as his eyes adjusted to the light. Angel was standing in the chapel.

"We were worried," Angel said. "Hurry up! Nakamura is keeping people away, but you were gone so long there's a mass starting soon."

Larry crept out after Neil and they slid the door shut. Larry shook his head a few times and took a deep breath. After a minute, he was able to stand and walk on his own.

"They had this weird smoke they used to knock me out . . . after they found out I wasn't married to Isabella."

"Whoa, wait, wasn't what to Isabella?" Neil said.

"Not a biggie, I'll explain later. Man, did that stuff knock me for a wallop."

"A cleansing before sacrifice," Angel said. "They wanted you as docile and dopey as possible."

"A normal Larry wasn't dopey enough?" Nakamura joked as they joined him and made their way back out into the Zócalo. The square was even more packed than it had been in the morning. Neil watched as the TV crew gathered around the giant flagpole, setting up the kitchens for the final. It was now less than twenty-four hours away. Another crew of workers was setting up loudspeakers on the balcony of the presidential palace.

Neil stopped to watch. "What are they doing that for?" he wondered. "We already competed in the palace two days ago."

"It's nothing to do with the *Cocina*," Angel said. "Tomorrow is September 15."

"Oh, yeah!" Larry said. "That's a big one down here."

Neil looked from Angel to Larry and back. "Translation please?"

"September 15," Larry said. "Tomorrow's *Grito de Dolores*, The Cry of Dolores."

"Who's Dolores?"

"Dolores is a where, not a who. It's a town a couple hundred miles from here, and it's where the Mexican revolution started," Larry said.

Angel nodded. "In 1810, a priest named Hidalgo made an inflammatory speech in Dolores. He rang the bells of the local church and when everyone arrived he told them to revolt."

"Inflammatory?"

"He said that they should, 'Recover the lands that were stolen three hundred years before by the hated Spaniards. Death to bad government! Death to the *gachupínes*!'" Larry added.

"Gachu-peenays? And they are?" Neil said, with a touch of impatience. He was used to Larry's boring history lectures, but this one was in stereo.

"The *gachupínes* were sort of the Spanish elite,"

Larry said. "Like those snobby types you're always trying to attract to the restaurant."

Neil scowled. "I liked you better groggy."

"It was not a pretty war," Larry said.

"Mexico won its independence from Spain," Angel said, "but it didn't change much. Corrupt and equally oppressive governments ruled the country until very recently. There are always moves for revolution here, and they are always bloody. That is why September 15 is also a sad day."

"Okay," Neil said. "But that was two hundred miles away, and two hundred years ago, so why are they setting up the loudspeakers? What happens here tomorrow?"

"Just before midnight, the president gets up on the balcony, waves the flag and repeats the speech for the crowd," Angel said. Larry looked up at the enormous speakers. "Man, that speech is going to boom out of those babies. It's like the stage at a thrash metal rock concert."

"Been to a few of those?" Nakamura asked.

Larry gave a wistful sigh. "Not enough."

Neil's ears perked up. "Booming! That's it—the dynamite. They're like the priest in Dolores. They want to revolt and they're going to use the dynamite to do it!"

He grabbed Larry by the shoulders and shook him. "We've got to go back down there right now, before they realize the mustache man isn't coming back and that you're gone."

"Not a good idea," Larry said.

"But you know where they are holding Isabella. And we've got to stop them."

"Yes, and I know you're not going to get anywhere near her or the dynamite by rushing in like a chicken with your head cut off."

"So we just let them kill her?"

"No," Larry said. "I have a plan. I'll tell you all about it . . . over a nice cup of coffee."

CHAPTER THIRTY-FOUR

AZTEC AMBUSH

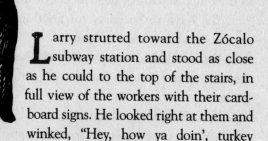

Larry strutted toward the Zócalo subway station and stood as close as he could to the top of the stairs, in full view of the workers with their cardboard signs. He looked right at them and winked, "Hey, how ya doin', turkey necks?" Then he bounded down the stairs and turned left. He began to stroll down the hallway.

Within seconds, the wannabe plumbers and carpenters had rushed down the stairs after him. They crowded around, shielding him from sight, then grabbed his arms. "Hey, this is my best suit," he grumbled. "Careful with the stitching!"

The circle of men pulled him to the very back of the hallway, toward a metal door with *peligro eléctrico*, "danger electricity," painted on the front. There was a ripping sound as they opened the door and shoved him through. "Now you've gone and ripped a pocket," Larry said, as the door began to swing closed behind them. "Are any of you idiots looking for a job as a tailor?" Larry flailed around and spilled his cup of coffee on the electrical panel, which hissed and spat and sputtered. Lights flickered and went out down the length of the hallway.

Nakamura and Neil slipped down the stairs and followed. Neil felt partly stupid and partly like a two-bit actor in a thriller movie. They were wearing the darkest clothes they could find, and Nakamura had smudged their faces with black greasepaint.

"What don't you have in your luggage?" Neil asked as they slipped past the dead security cameras.

"You have to be ready for anything," Nakamura replied. They reached the door.

"You should become a spy," Neil joked as he looked around to make sure no one was watching them in the gloom.

"How do you know I'm not?"

Larry's pocket had conveniently ripped right over the latch of the door, preventing it from clicking shut. Just inside the first door, according to Larry, was another door, almost completely indistinguishable from the wall. Neil and Nakamura never would have found it, except for the fact that it was still open. As he'd been dragged away, Larry had carefully slid his travel mug into the perfect spot to create a jam. "Dating that Olympic curler finally paid off," Neil said as he and Nakamura slipped inside XT's lair.

"So far so good," Nakamura said.

"Now it gets weird," Neil said. He'd once been forced by a babysitter to watch a TV show where the hero was always saying, "This plan is so crazy it just might work." Neil thought of that line now. Larry had devised this plan, so it was certainly crazy. Then again, coming from Larry, there was no guarantee it would work.

Larry had quickly laid out the details just a short time before, over a tray of coffee at the most secluded café they could find.

"I'll make sure that they're all concentrating on me," Larry had said as he began drawing a map on the back of a paper placemat. "You'll have just a few seconds to sneak in before they send someone back to double-check the doors. Make sure the doors are closed behind you so they don't suspect anything, then get out of the way."

Larry finished the map. He'd been carried through most of the lair during the past couple of days. "They don't have cameras, as far as I know. It's more 'rustic Aztec,' shall we say. The mustache man, as you call him, always used the church entrance. It's easier to come and go through that one without being seen."

"In a church?"

"People are looking forward, not sideways." Larry explained. "They used the bigger door in the metro for the prisoners—but not during normal business hours. After the cave-in, they hijacked a tour bus and kept driving around the city until the metro closed. They have a key to the place, probably thanks to someone on the inside. They brought us all in through here."

So far Larry's plan was working well. Larry was inside and he'd distracted the laborers and jammed the doors.

Neil quietly closed the second door behind him and pulled out the map. Torches lined the walls and lit the tunnel with a soft glow. Just inside the doors, the tunnel divided into two paths. One went left, toward what Larry had labeled the main prison cell. The other went right, toward the main hall, which was where Isabella was being held. The two rooms were connected by a door. There was then a door at the back of the main hall. It led to what Larry called the back tunnel. That ran for about a hundred feet before it came to XT's room and then the well and, finally, the cathedral.

The key, they'd decided, was to get to the prisoners quickly. Larry said he'd seen at least a dozen, mostly cooks and servants. They would need their help to have any chance of overwhelming the guards.

"You need to head down that tunnel," Neil said to Nakamura, pointing toward the left. "The prison is a big room at the very end. There's a doorway that connects it

to the main room. That's where I'm headed. We need to attack at exactly the same time for this to work."

Nakamura took two large paper coffee cups out of his backpack and handed them to Neil. Each had a wick sticking out of the lid. He handed Neil a lighter. Then he pulled out two more cups and held them tightly. "I hope these work," he said.

"They will, trust me," Neil said. This was the one part of the plan Neil trusted completely—the one part he'd come up with himself. His expert knowledge of food was the key to surprising the guards.

"Explain your big idea again," Nakamura said. "I'm about to throw these at guys who are the size of gorillas and I'd like to know they aren't going to make them a whole lot angrier."

"Pepper spray. Very common in crowd control, right?"

Nakamura nodded. "And very effective."

"And it's made from?"

"Pepper?"

"Chili powder." Neil had been drying chilies in his room ever since they'd arrived. It was the only way he could bring them back home in his luggage. It had taken him just a few minutes to grind them all into a very fine dust. "Get a few good teaspoons of this powder in their eyes and mouths and they'll be wishing they'd never been born. So we create these smoke bombs to get the powder into their eyes."

"This cup will actually work like a tear gas bomb?"

"Amber and Zoë assure me it will." Neil had called them earlier. They'd recommended a combination of

cornstarch, flour, and the worst coffee Neil could lay his
hands on. It would smolder like tear gas, the twins had
said, not blow up like a bomb. They'd also told Neil
that they'd had to spend more money on new fire extin-
guishers. He hoped the two bits of information weren't
related.

Nakamura looked at his watch. "Now, in exactly
fifteen minutes we light these, throw them at the guards
and burst in, right?"

"Right. Any last advice?"

Nakamura handed Neil a bandana. "Light the wick
and then put this over your mouth. Remember to take a
deep breath. Close your eyes. Wait for the yelps of pain.
Then it's safe to run in." He patted Neil on the back
and then headed toward the cells. He turned around
and added, "And let's hope Angel was able to get clear
up top."

Neil nodded as he started down the tunnel on the
right. Up ahead, he could hear Larry and the guards
struggling. He made sure to stay far enough behind not
to be noticed. He didn't want to be captured—not yet.
Neil turned a corner and found himself staring down a
long, straight and dark hallway. The doorway at the very
end made him shudder. It was carved in the shape of an
enormous serpent's head. You actually had to pass
through the gaping jaws to enter.

The guards pulled Larry through the door, slamming
it shut behind them. That sent a burst of air rolling back
toward Neil. He closed his eyes and sniffed. "Isabella,"
he said. Larry had been right: she was in there. He
checked his watch. Ten minutes to go. Neil took a deep

breath. It was time. He walked under the fangs, opened the door, and marched into the belly of the beast.

Sean Nakamura had conducted more sting operations than anyone he knew, and they always made him nervous. There were so many variables. Plans were based on the idea that criminals would act consistently, but the only thing criminals consistently do is act inconsistently.

As he walked on he could hear a strange noise up ahead. He hugged the wall and peeked around the corner. Two guards were bouncing a rubber ball back and forth with their rear ends. *What the—?* he thought. That was the most bizarre thing he had ever seen. He bit his lip to stop from chuckling. Two guards wouldn't be too much of a problem, especially these two oddballs.

Nakamura looked at his watch. Ten minutes to go.

Angel Jícama couldn't believe what he was about to do. He was an admirer, not a lover, of the ancient Aztec culture, but he was certainly not someone who relished the idea of breaking into an Aztec archaeological site with a backpack of homemade smoke bombs. He liked reading about history, seeing history, not destroying it.

"I'm too old for this," he said, feeling a bit like an ancient artifact himself. "I hope there are no dogs patrolling the place."

He checked his watch. "Ten minutes to go." Angel walked up to the ruins of the Templo Mayor and took out his bolt cutters. They cut through the chain link fence like a hot knife through butter.

"Neil!" Isabella yelled. Neil's heart leaped as he caught sight of her. Her hair was shorter, which somehow made her look even more beautiful. You could see more of her face, Neil thought. She was dressed in brilliant white clothes, with red shoes and a turquoise necklace.

"Hey, cuz!" Larry yelled with a huge smile. "Nice to see ya!" The surprised guards stopped their task of chaining him to a large stone slab.

The biggest guard ran toward Neil, who raised his arms in a sign of surrender. "I am here to submit to the *tlatoani*," he said in Nahuatl—at least that's what he hoped he'd said. Larry had taught him the phrase phonetically. His words shocked the guard, who froze on the spot. Neil walked slowly forward, keeping his arms in the air.

"It's a trap, Neil," Isabella said. "Whatever you are doing here, it's a trap."

"It's okay, Isabella," Neil said. "I'm ready to die as a sacrifice for the gods." He repeated his words in Nahuatl. *Phew*, Neil thought. There was only one more phrase he needed to remember. But then the guard grabbed Neil's arms and asked him something else. Now what? Neil looked over at Larry, who was quickly bobbing his eyes up and down.

Neil nodded his head "yes" and the guard lowered his

arms, tying Neil's hands together behind his back. In a moment, he was chained to the same stone as Isabella. The guard quickly ran off through a door at the back of the room.

"Are you crazy?" Isabella said, as quietly as she could. "They are going to kill you."

"Not if I can help it," Neil said. He wanted to say more, to talk to Isabella about everything that had been happening, but he needed to concentrate.

Isabella just shook her head, too shocked to say anything else.

Neil turned his wrist to see his watch. Seven minutes, he thought. Seven minutes until this was over, one way or another. The door at the back of the room opened, and in walked a large man in an expensive business suit.

"Neil Flambé. It is not good to see you."

"Jose Aciete," Neil said. "My name is not Neil Flambé anymore." He took a deep breath and spoke his final Nahuatl phrase. "Now I am Tezcatlipoca."

Jose's face twisted into a menacing scowl. He walked up to Neil, unlocked his leg, grabbed him roughly by the arm and dragged him across the floor.

"Ouch!" Neil said, in English. Jose had grabbed him so tightly he could feel his bones cracking.

"NOOOOOO," Isabella yelled as the door slammed behind them.

Neil could feel his butt bruising as he bounced over the tunnel floor. Jose opened a door and lifted Neil into an old carved stone chair, the same chair he'd seen Larry sitting in earlier.

"Tezcatlipoca," Jose said, sneering. "The Aztec god of food. Seriously?"

"Yes," Neil said. "And Xilonen's real husband. I know what you want to do with Isabella. I am offering myself in her stead."

"I don't care about all that Aztec mumbo-jumbo," Jose said with a scoff. "I just needed you to lose in the final, you idiot."

Neil was taken aback. He'd figured out that Jose was the leader; he'd just assumed he was the mastermind behind all the Aztec business as well. Jose had signed the Templo Mayor card in Rodrigo's hospital room. He'd taken over the company. He smelled of corn oil. His bandaged hand had pushed the knife to the mustached man.

"Aren't you the leader? The *tlatoani*?"

"Listen to me, you little worm," Jose said, gripping Neil's arm like a vise. "For five hundred years there have been people trying to bring back the old Aztec world. They have always had the numbers. You see them every day on the streets of this city—selling ancient crafts, performing ancient rituals."

"I've seen them, trust me. Smelled them, too."

Jose released his arm. "So, if they have the numbers, why haven't they succeeded, you ask?"

"Actually, I was going to ask why you're such a jerk."

Jose slapped him across the cheek. Neil's head bobbed to the side. But he also caught sight of Jose's watch. Five minutes. He needed to keep Jose distracted a little longer.

"Okay, so why haven't they succeeded, I ask."

"They have always lacked a leader with vision; someone who could unite them under a common cause."

"Like the leaders who thought it was a great idea to build a city on a swampy tectonic fault line. Geniuses. You fit right in."

Jose slapped Neil again. That was okay. As long as Jose was concentrating on his face, he wouldn't notice that Neil had very carefully slipped a paring knife out of sleeve and into his hand. Not that Neil was enjoying the pain in his jaw.

"I get ambition, Jose. I've got plenty myself. You want to be number one. I get that, too. So you buy up all the food companies, creating one big monopoly. As rich as Cortez Oil is, there's no way you had enough money to do that without assuming a lot of debt. You bet on me to lose—an incredible long shot, I might add—and then collect millions."

"To add to the smaller fortune I've been amassing along the way with hundreds of bets my followers have been making in your favor. It's made me much more than I could ever have expected from a ransom. I gambled that the young woman was special enough to make you play along. I was right about that. So far you are, how do you say, 'right on the money.'"

"Why go for all the Aztec stuff then?" Neil began carefully slicing through the rope that bound his hands. "If this is about getting rich."

"Is that all your puny mind thinks this is about?" Jose said.

Neil maneuvered one of his free hands into his back

pocket. "If it's not all about money either, then what are you after?"

"Everything! I am a leader with vision, one who can rally the sleeping Aztec army by proving how far I'm willing to go to bring them the world they want."

"How far?"

"Thanks to your girlfriend, I'll show them. As soon as I chop off her head, thousands will swear their loyalty to me."

Neil struggled to keep his hands steady.

"I care only about how useful their Aztec religion is . . . to me. To them I will become the new *tlatoani*," Jose said, his eyes flashing. "The new supreme and holy ruler who acts in accordance with the ancient rules, who pleases the gods with sacrifice." He laughed. "They'll do anything I ask."

"Why XT? Are you Xipe Totec? Tlaloc, *tlatoani*, Xochipilli?"

Jose laughed again. "The ancients loved mazes. XT is a maze. It stands for everything you have mentioned and so much more. It is a circle within a circle within a circle of meaning. . . . My minions go crazy for stuff like that."

Neil was tempted to simply lunge at Jose with the knife, but he had to stick to Larry's plan.

"Even now my army is gathering in the city," Jose waved his with a flourish, and Neil glanced at his watch. One minute.

Jose now seemed to be speaking to an imaginary crowd of millions. "There will be chaos at first, of course. My people will need a stable food supply to begin this new age. That was the key to ancient Aztec empire, you know. The leaders always made sure the people had food."

Chaos? New Age? A horrible idea was beginning to dawn on Neil, and Jose confirmed it with a wave of his hand toward the stockpile of explosives.

"You think the only thing I want to rule is Cortez Corn Oil?" Jose laughed incredulously. "Tomorrow at midnight I will become an emperor."

Neil gasped. "You are going to blow up the president!"

Jose gave him a look like a schoolteacher gives a D-plus student who has finally figured out that two plus two equals four. "'Death to the *gachupínes*,' that was Hidalgo's cry. 'Take back the land that was stolen.' For generations those have been empty words. Tomorrow, they will become real. The prisoners will walk under the Zócalo, under the palace, under the cathedral—each bringing death to this world."

"Under?"

"The Aztecs were forced to build this new Spanish city over the remains of the old. But they hid as much of the old world as they could—in tunnels, secret caves, sacred spaces. They have all waited in silence for the day the Aztecs would rise again."

"But I thought sacrificial victims were supposed to be willing," Neil said, his anger rising. "You kidnapped Lily, Margarita . . ."

"They are willing. As soon as they used the name of the flower goddess for their businesses, they declared their willingness."

"And Isabella?"

"I had gone to the farm to take Lily for my sacrifice. But as soon as I saw your friend I knew that she was the perfect Xilonen. She looks so much like the woman in that Rivera painting, don't you think?"

"No, I don't," Neil lied.

"She certainly looked close enough to convince my followers that the time had come for our revolution. It was a divine sign to them. See? I have vision."

"I think you're a loony."

Jose turned around and walked toward the table. "It is as I told you on the phone. Death and life are one and the same. Life comes from death. My new life will rise out of the death of the idiots who are running this country now."

"I was wrong. Calling you a loony is an insult to loonies. You're a psychopath," Neil said.

Jose slammed his fist on the table. "But now you are here, and the final is tomorrow."

"And if I'm not there I lose by default, and you lose everything." A faint smell of burning corn starch and chili powder wafted into the room. Neil smirked.

Jose suddenly stood up straight and glared at Neil suspiciously. "You are a fourteen-year-old boy," he said, "and here you are, close to death, about to watch your friends die and yet you smirk? You are too young to be this bold. What are you up to?" At that moment, Neil's watch began to beep repeatedly. He took a deep breath and closed his eyes, just as plumes of smoke filled the room.

Sean Nakamura threw the coffee cup right at the feet of the surprised guards. The cloud of smoke rose quickly, stinging their eyes and lungs. They fell to their knees, screaming in pain. Nakamura sprinted straight at them and knocked them on the backs of their heads. Then he bound and gagged them, hoping there were no guards on the other side of the door. He grabbed the keys and unlocked it. Then he slipped in and shut it behind him before any of the gas could follow. He took a deep breath.

Inside, nearly twenty prisoners sat crouched along the wall. They seemed either incredibly exhausted or incredibly drugged. "No wonder there were only two guards," Nakamura thought. A makeshift kitchen had been set up in the middle of the room, with an exhaust fan over the stove, and piping that led straight to the roof. "Perfect," Nakamura said. "Just like Larry described."

He walked up to the two women who seemed to best fit Larry's description of Lily and Margarita. He tapped them on the cheek as lightly as he could. "Wake up, wake up."

Margarita slowly opened her eyes. She shuddered as she stared into the painted face of the inspector. "Don't be afraid," Nakamura said. "I need you to do something right away."

She nodded, and stood up slowly. "I need you to wake up everyone and get them ready. We need to overpower the guards. I'll knock them down with some gas, but that will only give us a very brief advantage."

Margarita nodded again, and began to do her best to rouse the rest of the prisoners.

Nakamura walked over to the exhaust pipe. The ceiling was very high, but he only needed to loosen the grill at the bottom and hope. He leaned over the stove and pulled the grill off. Out dropped a pair of bolt cutters and a handful of fresh coffee cups. "Thank you, Angel," he murmured. Nakamura had suggested this part of the plan: If he'd been caught and taken prisoner, at least there'd be a fresh supply of chili-powder smoke bombs hidden in the prison for Neil or Larry to use.

Nakamura looked back at the prisoners. Most were now standing up, though many were still wobbly and glassy-eyed. It wasn't the best backup team Nakamura had ever had, but it was all he was going to get. He handed the keys to Margarita.

"As soon as we get into the next room, go straight through the back door. Follow the tunnel until you see a door in the wall. Neil will be inside that room. You must get these keys to him." Nakamura looked straight in her eyes. She was a little groggy but seemed more alert than any of the others.

"*Sí*, I understand," Margarita said.

Nakamura spoke to the others. "The rest of you stay here until I come back. If anybody else comes in, through either the front door or this side door, knock them out with whatever you can." Nakamura pointed to the large frying pans.

He walked over to the door that led to the main hall, where Isabella and Larry were being held. He opened it and threw in four lit coffee cups. He saw Larry and Isabella shut their eyes and take deep breaths, just as the surprised guards began gagging and choking.

"Now!" Nakamura yelled. Margarita went in and immediately turned left. Nakamura sprinted across the floor to Larry, and in a split second cut through the metal chain around his ankle. He slid across to Isabella and did the same. He looked over, and as expected, the guards who weren't choking were trying to escape into the kitchen. He heard the sound of crashing pots, and took that as a good sign. Nakamura tied up the guards and nodded at Larry.

"Things seem to be going well here," he said. "Nice plan, Larry."

"Thanks," Larry said.

"We need to find Neil," Isabella said.

Neil thought about what Jose had said, about him being a kid. He was scared all right, but he was also furious and confused. He'd cooked twenty-page-long recipes that were less convoluted than Jose's crazy Aztec plot. But the great thing about complex plans was that there are thousands of tiny details that have to go right. Any one of them could go wrong and mess up the whole thing. Like not keeping a closer eye on a fourteen-year-old chef who's walked right into your inner sanctum with a paring knife hidden in his sleeve and smoke bombs in his jacket.

It hadn't been too difficult to cut the ropes. Heck, he'd deboned and filleted chickens with less room to move. Slipping the coffee cups from around his waist had been a little trickier. He hoped they hadn't been damaged. He'd snuck the lighter out of his pocket, waited for his watch alarm to go off, and lit them. The chili-infused smoke had quickly filled the room. Neil's eyes were shut, but they still stung like crazy. He had pulled the bandana over his mouth but he was running out of breath, and out of time.

Jose was somewhere in the room, and Neil was sure he was armed. But Neil was also pretty sure he didn't have a gas mask. He heard the door open, then shut. He opened his eyes, rushed over and felt for the handle. It was locked. Neil leaned against the doorframe as the room started to spin. If he didn't take a breath soon he was going to pass out. He heard a jingle of keys and the lock turned. The door opened and Neil fell out into the tunnel. He gasped and breathed in as much fresh air as his lungs would hold. Then he looked up.

Margarita was standing over him, holding a set of keys.

Jose was standing behind her, with a knife at her throat.

"Move," he said to Neil in a raspy voice. Neil pulled off the bandana, coughed and stood up slowly. This was not part of Larry's plan. Jose was supposed to be back in his office, overcome by spicy smoke. Instead, he was pressing his knife against Margarita's throat so hard that a small line of blood was forming on her skin. "I said move."

Jose nodded up the tunnel toward the cathedral. Neil moved forward, slowly. Was Jose going to kill them and drop them in the well? Was he leading an escape of some kind? Were the others also being held prisoner? Were they dead? Neil shuddered.

"Now you look more like a scared fourteen-year-old kid should look," Jose spat.

As they walked, Neil's brain kept working.

"Was trying to kill Rodrigo part of the plan?" he called back.

"When I saw him talking to you I knew he was trying to warn you. He'd put the envelope into the first ingredient chest for me, and given me your phone number. But he had been growing nervous about the scale of the plan. Like you, he thought it was just about business. When I saw he suspected more, I cut his break cables, and cut my hand as well."

"He wasn't warning me about the plan! He was just mad that I had ditched an interview."

"He had to go eventually, so that I could take over the company."

As they continued to walk forward, Neil heard the sound of the waterfall. He tried to think of a way to slow things down, to buy himself some time to figure out a new plan. But nothing came to mind.

When they reached the well, Jose told him to stop and turn around. Neil obeyed. He had no other choice. The water swirled and foamed below.

Neil saw the look of panic in Margarita's eyes and wondered if it matched his own. This is it, he thought. He's going to kill us. He entertained a split-second hope that he could take a run at Jose and knock him into the well, but Jose had different plans and he moved quickly.

"Now Flambé, it is time for you and me to proceed, alone." Jose grabbed Margarita by the wrists and dangled her over the edge of the walkway.

She screamed. He lowered her down so that her fingers were grazing the side of the walkway. Then he let go.

Margarita screamed again, but she reached out with her fingers just soon enough to hold onto the slick metal. Her grip was not good, Neil could see that. If she tried to pull herself up she would certainly slip and fall onto the jagged rocks.

Jose leaned over the edge and smiled at her. "If any of this boy's friends are following us, they will not let you die. If my warriors are coming, they will. Let us hope you can hang on long enough to see who comes first."

Jose pointed the knife at Neil and raised his foot over top of Margarita's fingers. "Move or I step on her right now."

Neil moved. He glanced back. Margarita was still holding on. He thought he saw a dim light in the tunnel beyond, but he couldn't be sure.

He turned and walked toward the cathedral. Soon they reached the tiny passageway behind the altar. Neil could hear singing and chanting coming from the other side of the door.

There was a mass going on. Jose shoved the knife point into Neil's leg, causing a sharp stab of pain. "Don't do anything stupid," Jose hissed. "You are going to cook tomorrow, and you are going to lose."

Neil could smell incense as the door opened a crack. All eyes would be directed at the front of the church for the central part of the mass. No one would be looking at the side chapels. Neil took another deep breath. Almost no one, he thought with a sudden smile. He slipped out of the door. Jose followed quickly.

Smash!

Neil heard a sickening thud behind him.

He swung around. Jose was lying on the ground, his head surrounded with the shattered remains of a sculpted bowl of cocoa beans.

Neil looked up. A beaming Angel Jícama was perched on the stone altar, straining to balance on the thin table of marble.

"I have never been so happy to smell two-day-old curry in my life," Neil said. A breeze wafted up from the tunnel. "Or Guade-Latte coffee."

CHAPTER THIRTY-FIVE

GRAND FINALE

Neil Flambé couldn't believe the size of the crowd. More than 100,000 people had packed the Zócalo for the final of the *Azteca Cocina*. Not one of them knew how close they had come to being the victims of a crazy Aztec plot to take over the country.

Everything had happened quickly once Neil emerged from the tunnel. The presidential guard had been alerted by the clouds of eye-burning smoke that had billowed into the air conditioning system of the palace, and had rushed out into the square with their weapons at the ready. They'd found Jose bound and gagged at the foot of the Templo Mayor, with

Angel calmly pointing an obsidian knife at his chest, just in case he had tried to escape. Neil had sped back down the tunnel in time to see Larry and Isabella pulling Margarita up onto the walkway.

Nakamura had made his way over to the subway station to explain everything to the troops who had followed the trail of smoke that had begun pouring from the electrical room.

President Felipe Lobo had agreed that it was best to keep the story quiet, for now. He would hold an investigation in the following days to see just how far reaching Jose's Aztec network actually was. There would be stories for weeks of government raids on police stations, subway offices and subsidiaries of the Cortez Corn Oil Company. Whole troops of Aztec dancers traded in feathers for prison uniforms.

Neil was perfectly happy to keep the story quiet. It meant he could focus on winning the competition.

"There are a lot of bets on you to lose today," Nakamura said, as he did a last-second sweep of the kitchen area.

"Well, I hate to disappoint them," Neil said. "On second thought, I love to disappoint them. Jose is about to lose a lot of money." He examined his knives one more time. The television lights flooded on and the waiters wheeled up the chests with the final secret ingredient. Neil sniffed. He almost laughed out loud. Potatoes!

President Lobo himself walked up to the microphone. "Señors and señoras, I am sad to say that your usual emcee Jose Aciete has been taken ill with a case of . . . gas. But how can a mere politician explain the significance of such a stupendous day. Let me humbly try." He pulled out a five-page speech. Lobo was going to take a while to set up how important it was to have the final competition happen on the same day as the Grito de Dolores.

Neil looked over at his sous-chef, the only assistant he wanted by his side today. He frowned.

"What are you wearing?" Neil said with contempt.

Larry stared back at him from underneath the brim of an enormous red and silver sombrero. "It's for good luck," he said. "It was a gift from that mariachi band I was jamming with last night."

"It's not going to bring you any luck if you lean over a hot stove. It'll bring you third-degrees burns on your eyebrows and me a lot of grief."

"I'm touched. You care about my safety," Larry said, wiping away an imaginary tear.

"You are touched—touched in the head," Neil replied. "I'm worried about the food. I don't need any goofy hats getting in the way of my new kitchen."

"All right, all right, I'll take it off." Larry threw it into the crowd like a giant Frisbee. Neil watched it sail over the outstretched hands of the crowd before landing somewhere near the enormous flagpole.

Lobo was on page three

when Neil's eyes met Isabella's. She was taking her seat in the front row, her hair cut into a tight curly bob. Angel was hovering over her like a mother hen over a chick. Jones had finally checked his messages and had threatened to kill Neil and Larry the first chance he got. The fact he was recovering from frostbite on all of his toes was the only thing that had kept him from flying down right away. Signora Tortellini had returned from her mountain retreat refreshed and casually unconcerned about her daughter's recent brush with death.

"She is okay now?" she had asked Nakamura over the phone, "Good. Isabella is a smart girl. I'm sure she can handle any old Aztec bully. Tell her I love her." Nakamura sometimes wondered how any of these kids ended up as well-adjusted as they had.

In a bit of a surprise, Neil's parents had even called that morning. Neil felt a lump in his throat as his father told him they had recorded the TV shows and had watched them all, although much, he admitted, had been on fast-forward. "Good luck, son," he'd said, interrupted by beeps that told Neil there was another call on the line. "Gotta go."

"*Buona fortuna*," Isabella called to Neil. She had said the same thing a little more than a week before and had then disappeared. Neil didn't think that was a possibility now, but he kept his eyes on her even as more TV lights began to flicker on.

"Keep it simple," Angel yelled as Lobo reached the end of his speech.

"I'll keep it simply amazing, how about that?"

In the end, the final was a bit of an anticlimax. There

was no way Neil was going to let anyone beat him today. He took his revenge out on his opponent, Rick Laurel, an expert in Mexican cuisine, but no match for Neil when it came to *papas*, "potatoes."

Neil channeled his anger into a fiery baked potato with bits of ham and chili. His relief went into a fluffy potato and meat pie, made with poblano chilis prepared in the same way he'd seen Margarita prepare them in her kitchen. And dessert was an improbable ice cream made from fifty-nine fresh cocoa beans, the silky flesh of a baked potato and grilled corn. Neil wouldn't necessarily have used the word love to describe what went into that impromptu recipe, but the judges certainly loved the result.

Neil was crowned on a stage set right in the center of the Zócalo. President Lobo handed him a giant check as he waved and smiled. Neil had already decided to give a third of the prize to Margarita to help build a new and improved Xochipilli Taberna.

"Isn't that going to leave you with more debt than you'd planned?" Angel had asked.

"I guess I'll just have to work a little harder and have a little patience," Neil had replied. "Scrimp a little."

"Scrimp on shrimp!" Larry had said. "Budget on burgers!"

"Cut costs on caffeine," Neil had suggested.

"Now you're talking crazy!"

Neil held out his hand, and pulled Larry up onto the podium with him. Someone threw the red sombrero back and Larry proudly placed it on Neil's head.

"You look like an idiot," Larry yelled into his ear

over the crowd. Neil spied Isabella and Angel, who were nearly bent over laughing.

Neil raised his trophy in the air and yelled, "Viva Zapata! Viva Team Flambé!"

EPILOGUE

W ould you like a paper?" the flight attendant asked
as she made her way down the aisle of the plane.

"Of course!" Larry said as he settled into his seat.
"The local papers, please."

On the front of *La Reforma* was a picture of President Lobo, waving the Mexican flag over a Zócalo that
was packed to overflowing. The article said more than
a few people wondered who the mysterious bearded
man with the baseball hat was on the balcony during
the Grito ceremony. "No mention of the gorgeous
young woman or the handsome dishwasher!" Larry said
with disgust.

"You were in the background, I guess," Neil
said, leaning as far back into his pillow as he
could.

"In your gigantic shadow, you mean?" Larry
said. "Or the shadow of your gigantic nose?"

Isabella had ended her trip on a
much happier note as well. She and
Lily had agreed on a deal with an

advance payment that would see the farm rebuilt. The first shipment of flower-based oils would be ready in less than a year. Tortellini's Aroma Azteca line would be on the shelves soon after that.

"I won't need to scrimp," Isabella said patting Neil on the hand. "I'm better at business than you." She chuckled as she sat back in her chair and closed her eyes. Neil looked at her face and let his eyes linger there for more than a few moments. Her hair had been chopped and burned, and it still smelled of tear gas, raw corn and garbage, but the fact that he could sit so close to her again, and feel safe, made that aroma smell wonderful.

"Corporate cop!"

"Free-range moron!"

Neil jerked his head around. Nakamura and Angel had taken their seats just a few rows back and were apparently resuming their long-standing argument about goat cheese.

Suddenly Larry sat straight up. "Hey, Neil," he said, as the engines fired. "I just remembered something."

"What? The number for the waitress at the Guade-Latte?"

"No, I got that. Next week is your fifteenth birthday!"

"I know," Neil smiled. The restaurant would be completely renovated. Isabella was safe from harm. Angel was willing to work with him again, when Larry couldn't. And he was about to turn fifteen.

"My fifteenth birthday party is going to be the grand reopening of Chez Flambé," he said. "We'll invite all the celebrities and critics. We'll work out a new menu. It's going to be great."

"Yeah," Larry said with a big smile as he prepared to ignore the safety video. "Great idea. A birthday party. I love birthday parties. What could possibly go wrong at a birthday party?"

ACKNOWLEDGMENTS

This one has to have a special gracias to everyone at Massey College. I spent a wonderful year at Massey—a wonderful place. Thanks to Anna Luengo and John Fraser who keep the place running.

Marcus Gee, Nazim Baksh, Emmanuel Akli, and Rob "The Monster" Warner all made our trip to the mind-blowing Mexico City amazing. Shanti, our guide with the wonderful singing voice, told us all the interesting history you don't get in guidebooks.

There are countless amazing people in Mexico doing their best to help lift the poor to the level of the "haves." The women at Una Semilla para el Futuro—"A Seed for the Future"—welcomed us to their kitchen and workshop and showed that there can be hope even next to a giant garbage dump.

And amazing food.

See what Neil is cooking up next!

"Good fun."
—GORDON RAMSAY,
celebrity chef

Neil Flambé
and the
CRUSADER'S CURSE

KEVIN SYLVESTER

FOUR AND TWENTY THOUSAND BLACK BIRDS

Every night, around dinnertime, all the crows in Vancouver fly east, abandoning downtown for the surrounding suburbs and their hills. It's an amazing sight, a sky filled with cawing black birds, moving over the houses and parks like an enormous living storm cloud. No one knows for sure why they do this. Some believe they sense night is coming on, and bad things happen in the city at night.

Neil Flambé, on his fifteenth birthday, burst out of the back door of his kitchen and into the alleyway behind his restaurant, Chez Flambé. He was hyperventilating. His eyes were wide with panic. A crow gave a loud caw and Neil glanced toward the sky. As he gulped desperately for air he watched the birds pass over his head, momentarily blocking out the setting sun. He felt a chill run down his spine, but it wasn't the cool evening air. The dark murder of crows seemed to match his mood perfectly.

Neil took a deep breath and tried to calm down. He could hear the Soba twins back in the kitchen calling in more dinner orders. Neil shook as his sense of rising panic returned. He prided himself on running the kitchen like a finely tuned clock, but it didn't take long for orders to back up—one more disaster he couldn't deal with right now. The crows continued to stream overhead. His foot tingled. Maybe he could just run away? No. Yes. What was going on? "Calm down!" he yelled at himself.

His birthday had not gone well. He'd gotten into fights with his girlfriend, Isabella; his cousin, Larry; and his mentor, Angel. Of course, that wasn't so different from an ordinary day. But what had *just* happened was so shocking he could scarcely believe it.

The first group of customers had arrived early for their dinners at the grand reopening of the newly (and expensively) renovated Chez Flambé. They'd arrived to new tables, new engraved silverware, new linen, new dishes, and wonderful food.

Neil had cooked and served them a dozen of his latest creations, perfectly balanced and chosen for the occasion: mouthwatering mushroom risottos, succulent zucchini flowers stuffed with ricotta cheese and fried in olive oil, perfect pesto and Manchego cheese pizzas. He'd even allowed himself a smile at the thought of the compliments that would soon come flooding back through his gleaming stainless steel kitchen doors.

Instead, what had come back to the kitchen were at least half of the plates.

The customers had sent their dinners back.

Neil had to say it out loud to himself again now to actually believe it. "They sent their dinners back. They sent *my* dinners *back*."

Amber and Zoe, his twin waitresses, had barely whispered the complaints.

"Too salty."

"Too sweet."

"Something tastes off."

"Tastes like a can."

"Over-seasoned."

What? These dishes were prepared by Neil Flambé, not some hack with a hot plate! Neil had sniffed each dish closely. His incredible sense of smell—his secret weapon in the kitchen—had told him that his dishes were exactly as he had intended them. He even stuck his wooden spoon into the risotto and scooped out a huge mouthful.

It was, as he expected, sublime. "Those idiots must be drunk," Neil said.

"I thought the customer was always right," Neil's cousin, Larry, called back from the sink where he was busy washing some carrots and zucchini.

"I thought the sous-chef was always quiet," Neil shot back.

"Yes, chef." Larry sighed and turned his attention back to the vegetables.

Still, Neil had to admit Larry had a point. Customers paid his bills, and those bills were huge. Neil gritted his teeth. "Tell them I'll send a fresh order out ASAP," he hissed to the twins.

Neil prepared the dishes exactly as he had the time

before, sniffing at each tiny step to be certain that the dish was up to his exacting standard. The twins carried out the dishes with Neil's assurance that they were perfect.

But within minutes the dishes had returned again with the same complaints. Neil shook with rage. He grabbed the plates and threw the dishes through his back window, without bothering to open it, sending shards of glass and gourmet food to the cats waiting outside.

Neil cursed. "Calm down, Neil," Larry said.

"Maybe the vegetables are off?" Zoe suggested.

"Or the spices?" Amber said.

Neil shook his head. "Not in a million years. I'm going to go give these idiots a piece of my mind to chew on," Neil spat. He stormed out of the kitchen, sending the double doors swinging violently behind him. He marched toward the seated customers, and stopped dead in his tracks. Neil's nose started twitching. Something was wrong. He sniffed closely. His super-sensitive nose was picking up was the unmistakable odor of . . . glue? The customers turned to see what was going on, then quickly turned their attention back toward their plates.

The men all had beards. The women wore wigs. Larry came up beside Neil. "You okay, chef-boy? I was waiting for the sound of you alienating our clientele. . . ."

Neil started to back away. "They're all in disguise."

"What are they, spies?" Larry asked.

"Worse," Neil whispered. "Food critics." He turned toward the kitchen and quickened his pace. His chest heaved and his head spun. Of course they were critics! This was the grand reopening of the best restaurant in the city, maybe the world. They were here, in disguise, to test the new menu. Neil's throat started to constrict and his chest tightened even more.

This was serious. He didn't just *want* good reviews, he *needed* them. Neil needed these people to spread the word of his skill as thickly as one of his kalamata olive tapenades on a good crostini. But now they had already sent back not one, but two sets of dishes. This was a disaster. He sprinted past Larry, through the kitchen, and out the back door to the alley, where he sat, wondering how this could have happened.

"Neil, where are you?" came Amber's voice through the broken window. "Is everything okay?"

Neil didn't answer. He didn't know what the answer was. Had his nose failed him? His taste buds? Was he . . . losing it? It wasn't unheard of for chefs to burn out, to lose their edge, but he was at the top of his game and he was just fifteen. Was it, gulp, more puberty?

He felt the slight fuzz on his chin as he watched the cats eagerly lap up the discarded food, expertly avoiding the shards of broken window. The cats purred and chewed and purred some more. Neil stopped rubbing his chin. This was interesting. He got up slowly and walked over to where the cats were greedily eating his dinner. These were no ordinary alley cats. Raised on a steady diet of Neil's not-quite-perfect but still pretty amazing culinary rejects, they were almost as discerning as Neil when it came to food. If they were willing to risk sliced tongues to get at his risotto . . . he must be doing something right.

"Good kitty," he said, and patted the fattest cat on the head. Then he stood up straight and turned back toward the kitchen door. "But that's it. No more food tonight." The cats meowed angrily. The crows cawed overhead. Neil watched as the last of them sped off to the mountains and the last rays of sunlight glanced off the rooftops of his neighborhood.

"Time to cook," he said, his lungs now filled with air and determination.

"Um, Neil, we still running a restaurant here?" It was Larry, who held the screen door open to let Neil in.

Neil didn't answer. He marched back into the kitchen, past Larry and straight toward the stove, his face as still as stone. He had to concentrate, cook. Something weird was going on, for sure, but there was no way Neil was going to let it get the best of him. His moment of panic was just that, a moment. Okay, he'd use a little less salt, a little less seasoning, even though everything inside told him he was wrong, but he'd adjust to the critics' demands.

He'd figure out the problem later.

Larry caught the steeled expression on Neil's face.

"Good cheffy," Larry said with a smile, and he let go of the door. "Now, let's cook!"

The screen door banged shut. The noise attracted the cats, who looked lazily up at the faded green wood. One cat cocked his head. Someone had left a strange mark, like a circle and a cross, burned into the door.

There was a yell from inside the kitchen as Neil

struggled to make a slightly seasoned and barely salted order of Pommes de Terre à la Flambé. The cats, as cats do, quickly forgot the mark and licked their lips with each yell. "No more food," the tall redheaded kid in the chef hat had said, but the cats knew better. They sat gazing at the broken window, and waited.

Kevin Sylvester is an award-winning writer, illustrator, and broadcaster. *Neil Flambé and the Marco Polo Murders* won the 2011 Silver Birch Award for Fiction. Kevin was particularly pleased because kids vote! His other books include *Gold Medal for Weird* (Silver Birch winner in 2009!), *Sports Hall of Weird*, *Splinters*, and *Game Day*. He spends most of his time sitting in his attic studio, drawing and writing and listening to Neil and Larry arguing over, well, everything. He also loves to cook.

Just because you're a kid, it doesn't mean you can't solve crimes.

But it probably means you won't solve them well.

THE MISSING

"Fans of Haddix's Shadow Children books will want to jump on this time travel adventure. . . . An exciting trip through history." —*Kirkus Reviews*

← NEW YORK TIMES BESTSELLING AUTHOR →

MARGARET PETERSON HADDIX

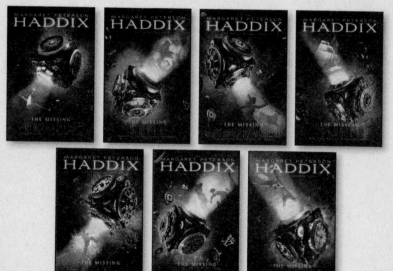